Lord Darkwood's Revenge

by

Jennifer Wenn

This is a work of fiction. Names, characters, places, and incidents are either the product of the author's imagination or are used fictitiously, and any resemblance to actual persons living or dead, business establishments, events, or locales, is entirely coincidental.

Lord Darkwood's Revenge

COPYRIGHT © 2019 by Jenny Wennergrund

Cover Art by *Abigail Owen*

The Wild Rose Press, Inc.
PO Box 708
Adams Basin, NY 14410-0708
Visit us at www.thewildrosepress.com

Publishing History
First Tea Rose Edition, 2019
Print ISBN 978-1-5092-2476-0
Digital ISBN 978-1-5092-2477-7

Published in the United States of America

"What do you want?" he asked, precariously soft.

"I-I came t-to collect the laundry," she stuttered, her heart beating wildly.

A slow smile quirked his full lips. "Did you now?" he replied with a voice as smooth as velvet, and again she forgot how to breathe as he gave her a look from the corner of his eye that had her legs turning to butter.

"Y-yes…" she whispered.

"The bed," he purred, and she looked at the large four-poster bed with a strange mix of fear and longing.

"The bed?" she repeated, dumbfounded, generating another amused chuckle from him as he left the shadows, seeming more like a predator closing in on his prey than a master moving toward his servant.

He halted just a step away from her, grabbing her chin with his strong fingers and forcing it gently upward until she could feel the heat of his breath against her face. Mesmerized, she stared into his vivid blue eyes, the sensation in her stomach growing to a crescendo. With a smug smile, he leaned even closer to her, touching her ear lightly with his hot lips.

"The laundry is by the bed," he whispered into her ear, before moving back, away from her, leaving her shaking with a need that she didn't know how to deal with. Hastily, she collected the clothes and almost ran toward the door.

Other Books by Jennifer Wenn
and available from The Wild Rose Press, Inc.

~

The Royal Family Series
A FAMILY AFFAIR
NEVER HAD A DREAM COME TRUE
THE BEAUTY OF YOU
AN HEIRESS IN DISGUISE

~

The Barnesville Collection
A FATHER FOR DAISY
ALWAYS YOU
PLEASE BE MY VALENTINE

Dedication

To my little monsters:
Mamma loves you to the moon and back.
Just don't forget to do the dishwasher…

Chapter One

Darkwood Manor, July 1805

It was an unusually warm day, even for the month of July.

Hot, unmerciful sunbeams washed over the crowd gathered on the lush, green lawn, forcing the ladies to wave their delicate fans in front of their flushing faces, while the men discreetly unbuttoned their jackets and loosened their cravats. Tray after tray filled with glasses of champagne and lemonade with just a hint of gin were brought out to the thirsty crowd, which grew merrier with every sip.

Anthony Scott hesitated behind the billowing curtains gracing the open French doors of the library. Frantically he searched the now quite tipsy crowd, looking for his cousin. He desperately needed to talk to the man. Chewing on his fingernails, his eyes flew from one dark masculine head to another, until he found the right one. There, in the middle of the almost one hundred guests, stood Douglas, the humble host of the annual summer house party at Darkwood Manor.

Leaving his hideout, Anthony slowly moved down the limestone steps which led to the lawn, making his way through the giddy crowd. Ignoring the few acquaintances who recognized him with haughty nods, he didn't stop until he had reached the small group which contained his cousin.

Arthur Basset, the Duke of Thornbury, the most prominent guest at the party, and, more importantly, Douglas's godfather, was telling something which seemed to be a hilarious tale of a one-legged man and a woman with no legs at all. Waiting for his laughing cousin to notice him, Anthony couldn't help but glance at the beautiful young woman who stood beside the Duke, a polite smile on her lovely pink lips. As always, something ugly moved inside him as he thought about his cousin's luck in life.

Douglas Scott, the Earl of Darkwood, had it all.

He was a very wealthy man, thanks to his father and the rest of his predecessors, who all very cunningly had made sure to grow the family's vast fortune even heftier. He owned two houses, this ancient country house in the south part of the Forest of Dean, and a luxurious town house at Berkeley Square in London. He had more friends than he ever could remember by name and a fiancée who outshone every other woman.

Anthony, on the other hand, had no money at all because of his and his father's extensive gambling. He lived in a small rented room in Lydney, from which he probably soon would be evicted, as he hadn't paid the rent for quite some time. The only woman he had ever wanted, the only woman who had ever made him consider he should stop fooling around and become an adult, he had lost forever when six months earlier he had proudly introduced her to his cousin.

Annabelle hadn't known about his infatuation, so he couldn't hold her responsible for her choice. She came from the same dire circumstances he did, also due to a father who couldn't stop gambling, and he could easily understand her quest for money and security. And Douglas Scott, the wealthy and well-connected Earl of Darkwood, could offer her both.

His cousin was an honest man, held in high esteem among the socialites of Gloucestershire and London—even though he was only twenty years old—not only for his noble standing but also for his handsome face, his attentive politeness, and of course his vast riches. Miss Annabelle Russell had caught herself one of England's most eligible bachelors. How could Anthony resent her for that?

Although he could resent his bloody cousin.

"Anthony!" Annabelle's smile was warm and welcoming as she noticed him standing beside them. "I didn't know you were attending today. How nice to see you again. It must have been months since we last met."

He inhaled her sweet scent as he lightly pressed his lips against the glove-clad hand she offered him in greeting. All he wanted to do was pull her closer and plaster his lips against hers until she moaned with raw pleasure, but instead he let go of her hand, nodding curtly toward the four men in the group, receiving nothing but cold bows back.

He knew they resented both him and his way of life, constantly comparing him to his perfect cousin who could do no wrong. Normally their undisguised contempt would bother him, make him feel less of a man, but for once he didn't care. His desperation was too deep, too overwhelming. All he wanted—all he needed—was his cousin's attention for a moment, and as he finally succeeded with his mission, he didn't waste any time.

"I need to speak with you," he told Douglas curtly,

his forehead and hands turning moist with sweat.

"I have guests, Tony," Douglas acknowledged, with a polite, dismissive smile. "Please feel free to join the party. As soon as all the guests have left, we can rendezvous."

"No!"

He hadn't meant to scream. Really, he hadn't. But the angst inside him was wearing him down. Ignoring the surrounding guests' baffled gazes, he took a step closer to Douglas, forcing his voice lower. "I'm desperate, Douglas. Please…"

"Tony…" Douglas looked tired, and Anthony knew he was losing this battle before it even had a chance to begin.

"For my father."

With a dejected sigh, Douglas's proud shoulders slumped, and Anthony knew he had won the first fight.

"All right, let's go to the library." Douglas turned to face Annabelle and her father. "I will be right back, my dear. Please excuse me for a moment."

"Do you want me to come with you?"

Douglas shook his head toward the Duke. "No, thank you. Please stay here with my fiancée, and I will be right back after taking care of this."

Following his cousin through the milling crowd, Anthony started to feel nauseous. What was this? What was Douglas going to take care of? If he wasn't mistaken, it had sounded as if Anthony was a problem. The Duke's offer to stand by Douglas's side scared him more than anything, because that meant his cousin had an agenda.

Shivers of fear ran down his spine, together with a waterfall of sweat, as he walked into the dark library.

Now, when he had his cousin to himself, he didn't know how to start. He was aware of them having had this conversation more times than he wanted to admit. Every time his despair for funding was too deep, and he couldn't find another way out, he had come to Darkwood Manor to beg for money. To crawl for help.

However, this time something was different, and he couldn't tell what. Usually, Douglas would look at him, patronizingly, and Anthony would have to endure a long lecture about money and gambling before he was given the amount he had come for. His cousin never failed to include some extra, which was meant to go to pay his future bills and give him a fresh start, but it always ended up on the gambling tables as soon he had paid off his debts.

This time Douglas seemed sad, silently withdrawing himself, and Anthony knew he had to move fast. This was not the time for any light conversation before getting to the core of the matter, and so he threw himself into it head first.

"I need money."

Looking at him with the same sad expression, Douglas sighed deeply. "I have come to a decision that I will not give you any more money," he replied smoothly, but Anthony could hear the determination hidden in the velvety voice.

"Why?" he asked hoarsely, his voice cracking into pieces.

"Because if I am here, constantly refilling your pockets whenever you have gambled every penny away, you will never learn how to handle money."

Anthony let out a hysterical laugh, born in the depths of his despair. "Don't you understand?" he shrieked. "I'm dead if I don't pay back the money I owe. Dead! Do you want to be the one responsible for that? What would my father think of you then, when you coldheartedly have killed his only child?"

Douglas closed his eyes for a second. "You have to find another way," he said quietly. "I know you are an intelligent man, Tony, even though your extensive gambling suggests a different story. If you just think it through, you will find a way out of your predicament. However, this time you must do it by yourself. You will never understand that you can't live life the way you do if I'm always there, picking up the pieces. I guess it is partly my fault, as I have always handed you whatever you have asked for, as did my father before me. But to save you from yourself, I have decided that enough is enough."

Anthony shook his head, searching for the right thing to say, something to make Douglas change his mind, but his cousin's words scrambled by at a speed which made him unable to come up with a convincing lie.

"I'm dead," he whispered, as he staggered toward his cousin, not able to believe this was happening. But Douglas's obvious stoic pain told him wordlessly it wasn't a bad dream; this was happening. In one last attempt to have his usual easy way out, he threw himself down on the floor, at his cousin's feet, humiliating himself. "You have to save me. Please, Cousin, you have to."

The pity in Douglas's face as he took a step back, away from Anthony, brought another wave of nausea washing over him, and he stumbled up onto his feet. Without another word, he staggered away from the library and his cousin, through the dark hallway, and continued out into the courtyard. There he grabbed his still sweaty horse and galloped away from the clearing where Darkwood Manor was situated, into the dense forest.

He could hear his cousin's voice behind him, calling out his name, but he ignored the pleading tone and instead forced the horse into an even faster pace, losing Douglas and his pathetic little perfect life behind him. Humiliation and anger roared through his mind and soul, swirling around with the fear and desperation he had lived with for too long.

It wasn't until the road through the forest became narrower and the path tighter and curvier that he slowed down and let the horse catch its breath. Bare branches reached for him as he passed, stretching their skeleton hands after him, but Anthony was too caught up in his wretched pain to notice the scratches. Fear, like none other he had ever encountered before, made him weak and nauseous, and he knew he was riding toward a certain death.

He was done. He knew it and couldn't do anything about it. Not anymore. By refusing to pay up, Douglas had destroyed every last hope. And now he was a dead man.

As he reached the edge of the wood, he stopped, staring at the nasty manmade gash in the hillside in front of him—the Woodland Quarry. Looking down the deep hole, the coward's solution became more and more tempting. What if he took his own life? Then he wouldn't have to face the consequences of his actions.

Standing at the top of the quarry, he knew he could end his misery then and there. It was a long fall to the rocky bottom partly filled with water, and he knew it was a death trap. Last autumn a man had fallen from the very spot where Anthony stood, and the poor man had died a horrible death, his body torn into pieces by the sharp, pointed rocks.

If he rode a little farther down the road and then turned back, he could use the uncommonly straight part of the road at the top of the crest to push his horse into a wild gallop. And as the road did a sharp bend at the highest point of the quarry, before disappearing into the woods, he could force his horse to go straight forward, out into the air.

And then it would be over. No more misery.

Grabbing the reins, he took a deep breath, trying to encourage himself to sit up on the horse and make a run for it. But to his frustration he couldn't. Just as he couldn't stop himself from playing another game, he didn't seem able to take his own life. He was born a survivor and a leach, and as such he wasn't prone either to take responsibility for his own actions or to hurt himself by choice.

Ending someone else's life wouldn't be a problem for a man without conscience, but he couldn't take his own.

One thought led to another, and then another, until a relieved smile crept over his face. Why hadn't he ever thought about it before? If Douglas died, all his problems would disappear. Douglas had no offspring of his own, so Anthony, as his closest kin, would inherit Darkwood Manor, the title, and all the riches of the Scott family.

A new life. A new beginning.

Why, even Annabelle could be his. His smile

broadened more and more as he thought about Annabelle finally becoming his wife, something he had dreamt about for quite some time.

The sound of horses closing in on him woke him from his thoughts. Not in the mood for company, he led his horse back into the forest, hiding behind a crooked old tree dressed in dark green moss. His eyes narrowed as he recognized the carriage passing by. It was Douglas, and Anthony could only guess his cousin was taking Annabelle and her parents back to Gloucester.

Unwillingly, his eyes darted toward the quarry, well aware that he would never find a moment as good as this if he wanted to go through with his plan. As his cousin's carriage disappeared down the hill, Anthony stood silent, hesitating. Memories of their childhood danced in his mind, memories of the little boy who had followed him around everywhere, always looking at him as if he was the most amazing person he'd ever met. Despite their five-year age difference, they had spent much time together, especially as his father had liked to leave Anthony at his brother's house when he was on a gambling spree.

Douglas and Anthony had been close, almost as if they were brothers, not just cousins. It was the years at Eton which had parted them, made them grow apart. Douglas's father, who had been a good man with a big heart, had sent Anthony with Douglas to the school, so he too would have the education a young man of his situation should have. At Eton, they had found new friends but not the same ones—friends more like each one's own state of mind—and things had never been the same between them again.

But still…it was a long walk from growing apart

from his cousin to cold-bloodedly killing him. Although...Douglas had cut the final cord between them when refusing to help. If he hadn't, the thought of killing him wouldn't have crossed Anthony's mind. So, all in all, this was Douglas's own fault. Anthony could not be blamed for something his cousin had started.

Before he could change his mind, he walked farther down the road, until he came to the part where the road from Lydney reached the top of the hill and then flattened out, inviting a driver to increase to a more satisfying speed until the harsh bend at the edge of the forest forced one to slow down again.

The sound of hooves approaching woke him from his thoughts, and again he hid amongst the trees, planning his coup while carriage after carriage with guests from the picnic passed by. As dusk arrived, it arranged the setting for his crime perfectly, hiding him and the quarry in a coat of darkness.

When the Darkwood carriage finally returned from Gloucester, daylight was long gone. The cloudless sky was filled with twinkling stars and a full, shiny moon. Everything along the road cast shadows, spooking the already skittish horses. Just as the equipage was about to pass him, Anthony jumped out from the forest, and the horses reacted just as he had hoped. Shrieking, they wildly tried to get away from the carriage which held them down, galloping faster and faster while the coachman desperately tried to calm them.

But it was too late.

In a few breaths, the panicky horses galloped out into the quarry, their wild eyes not able to make out what was the road and what wasn't. If they hadn't been attached to the carriage, they might have made it without a scratch by following their instincts. But now, as the heavy carriage slammed behind the team, they continued straight on, blinded by fear. Just as the carriage went over the edge, the coachman threw himself off it, in a desperate attempt to save his own life, but he was too late, and his anguished scream became weaker and weaker until it was cut off. And then it all became quiet.

Deadly quiet.

Anthony's shaky breaths were the only noise heard, until the sounds of the night started anew. Slowly, he moved closer to the edge, hardly believing what he'd just done. The horses and carriage were hidden in the deep darkness of the quarry. Straining his ears, Anthony listened, but no sound was heard. No screams for help or moans of pain.

After waiting for over an hour, Anthony knew he had succeeded. All the guilt which had filled his heart when he first realized what he'd done now vanished, and he couldn't hold back a triumphant sneer. Without looking back, he got on his horse and continued down the road until he reached his humble home in Lydney. Stumbling into the small rented room, he lay down on the bed, still fully clad, and slept like a baby for the rest of the night.

It was a hard knock on the door that abruptly tore through his sweet dreams and woke him. Breathing deeply to hide the victorious smile which threatened to paint his face happy, he went to the door.

The world was finally his.

Chapter Two

Darkwood Manor, April 1815

Sir Edward Russell didn't bother to hide his unfashionable yawn as he looked up at the gray stone walls hovering above him. Even though the early morning sun hit Darkwood Manor unyieldingly, it was hard to make out the windows beneath the thick green mass of climbing ivy, and if he hadn't visited the house only ten years ago, he would have thought the former grand house abandoned for at least a couple of decades.

Reluctantly, he climbed the slippery, moss-grown, limestone steps that led to the front door, which looked as if it hadn't been opened for years. He knocked hard with the handle of his cane, waiting for any kind of response.

Just as he was about to knock again, someone called out behind him. Turning, he noticed that a smaller door farther down the side of the building was open, and a hand waved him closer. He backed down onto the courtyard again, nearly losing his balance as he slipped and almost fell. Crossing the courtyard with his usual brisk steps, he only sidestepped now and then for the piles of dirt which completely disfigured the once beautiful surroundings. As he reached the smaller door, he found an old, shabbily clad man waiting for him. Without a word, the old man ushered him into what turned out to be the manor's decaying kitchen.

"Sorry for the mess," the old man wheezed with a crooked smile, noticing Sir Edward's disgusted expression. "I completely forgot all about doing the dishes this morning."

Sir Edward glanced at the stacks of dirty plates, but decided wisely against criticizing. The old man chuckled and pointed toward a hook on the wall where dirty outdoor clothes hung.

"You can put your coat there."

"I prefer to keep it on, thank you," Sir Edward reassured politely, not wanting the only nice coat he had to get dirty.

"Don't call for me if you get too hot." The old man gave the guest another crooked smile before stepping out into a dusty hallway, where spider webs hung from the wall lamps. Sir Edward shuddered as he passed one web in which its creator sat big and black in the middle of it, staring at him as if it hoped he would get caught.

"We don't get many guests around here nowadays," the old man informed Sir Edward. "You must be the first one here for at least five years."

"Really?" Sir Edward replied curiously.

"Master Douglas has not been himself since the accident, and as he is not too fond of visitors, they tend to stay away. Only the old Duke of Thornbury persisted with his visits, until Master Douglas threatened to kill him if he was to return again."

"I have been asked to come," Sir Edward hurried to explain, and was rewarded yet another crooked smile.

"So you have."

The old man stopped at a closed door, knocking once before opening it with a loud creaking sound.

After shoving the guest inside, he closed the door again, effectively pushing the guest farther into the room. Inside, it was dark and stuffy, the only light coming from the fire glowing in the enormous fireplace. As his eyes became used to the darkness, Sir Edward could see he was in a library, the walls dressed with row after row of books.

Small movements from one of the large armchairs in front of the fireplace made him realize he wasn't alone, and he took a hesitant step forward.

"My lord?" he asked the large shadow who sat in the chair farthest away from the glowing fire, and a face clad in shadows turned his way.

Sir Edward exhaled, unaware he had been holding his breath. Finally he stood face to face with Douglas Scott, the elusive Lord Darkwood. He tried to see the scars from the wounds which his daughter Annabelle had cried about ten years earlier, but the shadows hid them effectively.

"Lord Darkwood?" he asked the shadow politely, but the other man remained quiet.

Sir Edward didn't know what to do. This was such an awkward situation. First he thought he should repeat the question, if his host hadn't heard him, but then he decided to take a few steps forward, pointing with his hand toward the other armchair.

"May I?"

When he received no answer, he decided to interpret the silence as a permission and sat down, managing with great effort not to sneeze from all the dust belching out around him. He sat silent, waiting for Lord Darkwood to acknowledge him, but the other man didn't say a word, remaining motionless, his face still hidden in the shadows, and Sir Edward wondered if his lordship was thinking about the last time Annabelle had been here, ten years earlier.

Sir Edward's oldest daughter was a relatively good girl, with a head of her own. Unfortunately for her family, she was rather vain, which originated from her astounding looks and her parents constantly reminding her of them. She embraced everything which made her look better, and had, because of this, one quite large problem with ugliness. The sight of her once-handsome fiancé, lying wounded in his bed, had not been easy for her.

What had sent her screaming had been his face, once more than attractive but now destroyed by large open wounds that started on the forehead and traced down across the right cheek to end at his chin. Annabelle had wailed for days over losing him, not once considering the possibility of marrying him despite his drastic change in looks.

In the end, Lord Darkwood had sent her a note, begging her to come and see him again, but she had refused. Instead she had sent all his engagement gifts back and cut off their relationship completely, much to her parents' chagrin. The Russell family had never heard from him again, and when Annabelle married Lord Darkwood's cousin, Anthony Scott, six months later, he had neither appeared nor sent his regards.

Sir Edward had a sinking feeling that Annabelle somehow was responsible for the condition of the property. If she had stayed on and helped her fiancé through his recovery, life at the manor would probably have continued as before the accident. However, his lovely, stubborn daughter hadn't been able to stand the thought of having to face an ugly fiancé, no matter how much both Sir Edward and his wife had begged her to.

What Annabelle hadn't stopped to consider was how the prospect of fortune and title would disappear with ending the engagement to Lord Darkwood, together with all his high-born friends and excellent connections. Her parents, on the other hand, had been all too aware of their upcoming fall on the social ladder, but no matter what arguments they told their daughter, they had not been able to convince her to change her mind.

It must have been a devastating blow to the young man in his hour of need. He had not only lost his life as he knew it, he had also lost his fiancée because of what the accident had transformed him into. He, who once had been a gentle, happy aristocrat, had turned into an elusive beast, hiding in what used to be his stately home.

"I guess you know why I'm here," Sir Edward continued as jovially as he could, in an attempt to break the ice, but Lord Darkwood still didn't answer. He sat there broodingly silent, not acknowledging his visitor in any other way than staring at him from the shadows.

Sir Edward was uncomfortable. Only the thought of what would happen if he didn't get this man on his side forced him to stay put. He got to his feet and started to pace to and fro, trying to find the right words to convince Lord Darkwood to withhold his demand.

"I received your letter yesterday," he started, with the feeling of walking on a bridge made of thin ice. One wrongfully placed step and he would fall into the depths of despair. "I have to admit I got terribly upset, as the news you had for me was not the brightest."

Sir Edward halted for a second, thinking he had heard a soft snort coming from Lord Darkwood, but wisely he continued without remarking upon his host's absence of ordinary civility. "I wasn't aware that you had bought all my debts, and if you persist with your demand, you put me in a truly awkward situation. To be honest with you, there is no way I can pay you everything I owe before the end of this week, my lord. You mentioned the total sum, and I can only admit it is vast. Therefore, I ask you to consider the possibility of receiving the money in portions, instead of all at once."

As Lord Darkwood still didn't answer, Sir Edward was starting to get desperate. "You have to think about my family, my lord. I can't get my hands on such a vast sum, even if I sell everything we own. Our home is rented, and therefore not mine to sell. I'm standing here, in front of you, begging you to please reconsider your demand. I will go down on my knees and beg, if this would make any difference."

He started to get down on his knees, with as much dignity as he could muster, when a hoarse voice suddenly broke the silence.

"Sit down."

Before he could think, Sir Edward responded to the authority in the voice and sat in the chair again. Another cloud of dust rose from the cushion, surrounding him like London fog, and this time he couldn't prevent himself from coughing uncontrollably. His host didn't offer anything to relieve the coughing. Instead he sat silent, waiting patiently for the guest to finish. When the coughing finally ended, Sir Edward's chest hurt, and he wished he could ask for a glass of brandy to soothe his burning throat. But something about Lord Darkwood's coldness made him stay quiet.

"Are you finished?" Lord Darkwood leaned forward, offering Sir Edward a better view of his face, or at least the unscarred side. He looked older, more shambled than the last time they met, the brown hair in desperate need of being taken care of by a pair of scissors.

Upon noticing Sir Edward's badly hidden interest, Lord Darkwood leaned back, disappearing into the shadows again so only the outline of his face was visible.

"You have something I want, and if you oblige me, I will remit your debts," he said quietly, and Sir Edward frowned.

"What could you possibly want from me?" he asked, knowing all too well that he hadn't anything of value, as he had already sold everything he could when he had done badly at the gambling tables before, and there were bills to pay.

"I want your daughter." Lord Darkwood didn't even flinch when Sir Edward stared at him in astonishment.

"Annabelle?" he let out with a weak voice, not believing what he'd just heard. "You want Annabelle? Why now? It has been a decade since she broke off your engagement, and, as you must be aware, she is married to your cousin." Sir Edward scratched his head. "You have not once contacted her during all this time. Why would you want her now?"

Lord Darkwood gave Sir Edward a look that clearly told what level of stupidity he thought the older man held. "Not Annabelle. I want Wendolyne."

"W-Wendy?" Sir Edward stuttered, trying to grasp

what was going on. Everything about this situation was like an intricate Greek play, and nothing could make him foresee what would happen next.

"Yes, your younger daughter, Wendy. She must be going on twenty now. Almost an old spinster, a burden of whom you will never rid yourself. So to ease the weight on your shoulders, I will relieve you of her, and you can go on with your life with one mouth less to feed."

"You want to marry Wendy?"

Lord Darkwood sighed deeply. "No."

"No?" Sir Edward was starting to feel dizzy. Lord Darkwood didn't make any sense at all to him.

"No, I don't want to marry her."

Sir Edward had to stand up again, unable to sit still. He had to move so that his brain could grasp what he was told. Not an easy thing for a shallow man.

"But you said you wanted her?"

"Not to marry."

"Not to marry?" Sir Edward stopped, his chest heaving with rightful indignation. "Are you telling me, Wendy's father, that you want me to send my daughter here, to live with you in sin?"

Lord Darkwood leaned forward, his superior grin visible in the light of the fire. "Once upon a time I was willing to marry a daughter of yours. It will never happen again."

Sir Edward gasped, outraged. "Are you out of your mind? Why on earth do you think that I, Sir Edward Russell, would give my beloved daughter to you? How can you even suggest that I leave her here unmarried? It would ruin her. It would ruin us!"

Turning dramatically, he picked up his cane from

where he had left it next to the armchair and marched toward the door. With his hand resting on the doorknob, he turned back and glared at Lord Darkwood. "This is the most absurd thing I have ever heard, and I will not stay and be treated by you in this condescending way. I bid you good bye, my lord."

Just as he again faced the door and turned the doorknob, the hoarse voice spoke again, this time filled with unmistakable mirth. "It amazes me, how lowly you think of me. Even though I will not marry your daughter, I do have a perfect chaperone to guard your daughter's good name. My great aunt will be staying with me for a year, and she is in desperate need of a companion. As she arrives tomorrow, I will give you until midnight to deliver your daughter to me. If you agree with Wendy staying here with my aunt during her visit, I will remit your debts."

Sir Edward closed his eyes, desperately trying to find the right words, but his mind became as blank as an empty page. All he could think was—what would his wife say? He knew he was a selfish coward, but somewhere in his black heart the idea of getting rid of all his debts was too tempting. Lord Darkwood was offering him an out which wouldn't affect him personally, as it was his daughter who would have to stay here, to act as a companion to an elderly woman.

It would mean a new start for him, and a new life. No more debts would mean that he and his wife could live large again and not have to think about every penny. If they didn't have to use most of their monthly income to hold the debt collectors at arm's length, they would be able to live a life filled with humble luxuries. They could move to a better apartment, or maybe an elegant house in a much better part of Gloucester.

The thought of all the servants they could hire almost made him feel as if he had been handed Paradise, as someone else would be there to take care of all those dull chores. He wouldn't have to hear his wife go on and on about his gambling, always pointing out how he was the one who had put them in this situation in the first place. Instead he would be free to gamble even more. Being without debts meant his luck had changed, and this time he would play it smart.

They would be rich.

The image of his daughter Wendy popped up in his mind's eye, and for a second he felt remorse. She was a good daughter and had never been any nuisance for him and his wife. She had done the cleaning and cooking for them, as they'd had to let the servants go a few years ago, when money became an issue. She would be missed, but if he were completely honest, he would only miss the servant part of her. He had never been a loving parent, and had always thought of his children as means to an end.

The only problem on the road to this easy solution was his wife. How would Juliet react about sending her youngest child away? His wife was a beautiful woman who loved the social swirl, and he knew she still nursed a silly hope that she would be able to let Wendy have her slightly overdue debut into society, which in the long run meant even more swirling for her. But he also knew she would do almost anything to live life as they should be able to.

The question was—would she let Wendy go?

Two seasons ago, when Wendy had turned eighteen, Sir Edward had endured a long period of bad luck, and they had ended up telling their friends a lie about a close relative dying, which had given them an excuse to mourn for a year, thus saving them from having to admit they couldn't afford the cost of a debutante.

Juliet had not spoken to him for a month, unable to hide the disdain she felt for him in destroying her chances of taking her place in society through their daughter, even though their social standing could hardly be any lower. And when they last year had to kill off another relative, she had vowed to leave him if he ever put her in the same situation again.

It had been decided that Wendy would be debuting the upcoming season, not because of Juliet's threats but for the simple reason that even though their acquaintances still believed them and gave them their time of mourning, Sir Edward had no choice but to let his wife have her way. He had run out of relatives to kill.

Juliet was something of a social matriarch, and even though their family didn't belong to the highest of social circles, the crowd they belonged to still had a large calendar, with assemblies to which Wendy and her family would be invited. A full calendar meant the need of a full wardrobe for Wendy, and too aware of their meager funding, Juliet had already spent time resewing some of her dresses into debutante dresses for her daughter.

Considering how much his wife hated needlework, he didn't think she would mind too much if Wendy wasn't there needing a new wardrobe. Instead she would be able to toss out all her old dresses, which she had worn too many times, and buy new ones with which to stun her friends.

Slowly, Sir Edward turned back again, hesitating as pictures of a smiling Juliet in fashionable outfits flew across his mind's eye. "I must talk to my wife," he said curtly, trying to sound more self-assured than he was.

"You must?" Lord Darkwood echoed, sounding remarkably astonished. It almost seemed as if he had expected Sir Edward would resist giving in to his demand and refuse to send his younger daughter away.

For a second Sir Edward felt like a cad, the worst human being to ever have set foot on the face of the earth. But the mere thought of a debt-free life quickly made him shrug it off. He knew this was the right choice if he wanted freedom.

So what if he had to sacrifice one daughter's debutante season in a selfish hunt for a better life for himself? He had already gone through Annabelle's debut, which had been costlier than he'd first expected. Considering her astounding beauty, they had been so sure she would catch a title, at least. Anthony Scott might be the son of a noble family, but all in all, he was only the son of a younger son, although the heir to his host today.

As he was a gambler himself, he had immediately recognized what kind of man Anthony was, but to no use. Neither Annabelle nor her mother listened to him, as he tried to tell them the truth about Anthony Scott. Sir Edward had known his older girl would never have a good life if she married him, which had turned out to be true.

Wendy was a pretty girl, but not as beautiful as her older sister. She would hardly attract the likes of Lord Darkwood and his league. If they were lucky, some country gentleman would ask for her hand, and then life would be even harder for her poor parents, as they would lose the only servant they had. Without money to pay a salary, they would not be able to find someone to take care of, well, everything.

How would his wife react?

She was fond of Wendy, but Annabelle had always been his wife's favorite, her precious gem. Another thought came to him—maybe it wasn't all bad that Wendy would be staying here. When she returned home, she could use the connection to the Scott family to have a very small but still recognized possibility to get into higher society.

"I will, indeed. Of course, I can't assure you that Lady Russell will think this is as good a deal as I do, but I will try to persuade her. For how long a time are we discussing? Did you say a year?"

Lord Darkwood didn't move a muscle. He sat there, still as a statue, staring at Sir Edward silently from the shadows of the room for the longest time, and not until the older man was squirming uncomfortably did he speak again.

"If you bring Wendy here before nightfall, I will give you ten thousand pounds to top off your debts. It will be for a year, to start with. If I find myself satisfied with your daughter, especially regarding her talent as a companion to my great aunt, I might consider paying you another ten thousand for another year."

Sir Edward could hardly believe his ears. Twenty thousand pounds? What an enormous sum of money! It was more than they'd ever had before. He took his hat off and bowed his head in deep regard.

"I will do my best, my lord, but it is quite a drive

from here to Gloucester and then back again," he pointed out. "Considering the condition of the roads I have to travel, I might not be able to make it by nightfall. Could we say midnight, as you did earlier?"

"No. Have her here before it gets dark, and you will have your money."

He knew he was beyond rude, but at that moment Sir Edward didn't care. Without any polite parting words, he left the room quickly, not wanting to waste another minute of the precious time he had left. As the driver of the rented carriage whipped his horses to get them to run faster, Sir Edward drummed his fingers restlessly on the worn leather seat, trying to find the right words to convince his wife to send their daughter to play nursemaid for two years.

****

Douglas sat silently, staring at the now empty doorway. He could hardly believe what he'd just witnessed. The level of the man's greed was something he'd never encountered before. Sir Edward's willingness to give away his daughter to a stranger, to force her into the simple life of a companion so he could have a life of luxury, made him sick.

For a second he felt sorry for Wendy, who meant so little to her father, but he hardened himself. He had to focus on the revenge and not let himself feel empathy for her. Wendolyne Russell was a mere pawn in the game he had set up in his hatred for her sister and his cousin, and he couldn't afford to feel remorse about sacrificing her.

Finally, revenge would be his.

Chapter Three

Looking out through the dirty window, Wendy watched the forest turn into a green blur as the carriage rushed as fast as possible toward its destination. Absentmindedly, she wiped away the tears falling down her cheeks, too emotionally numb to care about crying in front of her parents.

Not that they noticed.

Sir Edward and Lady Russell were too busy arguing about where they wanted to live, now that their situation in life was about to change, and neither of them thought twice about their daughter, who sat beside them listening to their selfishness while her heart slowly withered away.

The quiet life in their small house had been strange during these last two days, with her parents acting completely out of character. It had all started yesterday, when a delivery boy came with a letter for her father. Wendy didn't know what it said, but when her father read it, his face turned pale with shock and he rushed Lady Russell into the salon, closing the door just in front of Wendy. She had not seen her mother that upset in a long time, and not her father either. He behaved like a frightened dog with his tail between his legs.

They spent the rest of the day behind the locked door, only opening it once to have Wendy bring them some dinner. She had spent the evening alone in her bedroom, with deft fingers altering one of her mother's old gowns for herself.

The next day, Sir Edward left directly after breakfast and was gone for hours, while her mother for once didn't go out to visit and gossip. Instead, Lady Russell had been standing by the bay window in the salon, chewing on her fingernails, until her husband returned in the afternoon. Without a word, they had disappeared into the library, still not enlightening Wendy about what was going on. But this time the door was opened after a much shorter time, and when they emerged from the salon, her mother had looked determined, and her father both astonished and relieved.

With no explanations, Wendy had been sent to her room with orders to pack a bag as fast as possible. She'd just had time to pack a nightgown and one dress when Lady Russell came to usher her from her bedroom and into the carriage, with her bonnet and coat thrown onto the seat beside her. As soon as the three of them were in the carriage, her father had promised the coachman a quite hefty sum if he could get them to their destination before nightfall.

"Wendy, you have to forgive us the rush, but due to a promise we have been bestowed, we had to leave with haste. There is too much at stake right now for us to dillydally," Lady Russell had explained as the carriage raced out of Gloucester, heading northwest toward the Forest of Dean. "I am sorry you didn't have time to pack more of your things, but I am sure he will see to it that you are properly dressed."

"Who?"

"Lord Darkwood."

Wendy's heart skipped a beat as she heard the

name of the man no one had talked about for ten years. She had been only a young girl the last time they met, and she was devastated when Annabelle broke off the engagement. Douglas Scott had been very nice to her, and she'd loved the thought of having him as an older brother.

"W-What? Why?"

"You know our family is not living in the circumstances which are our right, all because of your father and his foolish gambling."

"Juliet!" Her father puffed indignantly, but his wife sent him a chilling glare which quieted him.

"Yesterday we received a letter in which we were told to pay back your father's entire gambling debts before the end of this week. I am sure you can understand how upsetting this demand was to us, as we don't have that kind of money."

Wendy had nodded, fully aware they lived on the edge of poverty. She was, after all, the one who did all the purchasing for the family. Their dire straits had forced her to learn how to turn every penny around repeatedly, in a desperate attempt to get as much merchandise for as little coin as possible. It was embarrassing to go down to the market nowadays, as most of the hawkers preferred better-paying customers. They too had to make a living and needed every coin they could get their hands on. Thankfully, a few of the hawkers still had a small space for her under their wing and let her have the food no one else wanted to buy because it was damaged or too old.

"You see, Lord Darkwood has bought all your father's debts and is the one demanding payment. Your father went to visit him today, at Darkwood Manor, to talk some sense into the man. Unfortunately, Lord Darkwood turned out to be stubborn, refusing to budge, and as we never will be able to pay off the debts, we had to give him something else which would make ends meet. And what he asked for was…you."

Wendy didn't know what to think nor what to say. Her head seemed to be spinning faster and faster, and she closed her eyes so she wouldn't faint or throw up. Lady Russell, as always, was resourceful and handed her the smelling salts, which made the nausea and the dizziness lessen.

"Me?" she whispered, after regaining her wits.

"Yes," her mother answered sternly. "As we couldn't give him the money, he remembered that he needs someone around the house, and I guess you were as good as anybody, at that moment. His great aunt, who is to live with him, needs a companion."

That was the moment when Wendy had started to cry out of disbelief and an overwhelming feeling of being abandoned. Her own mother was sending her away to become an elderly lady's companion, because Lord Darkwood had blackmailed them into it.

And now she sat here, with the darkening forest rushing by outside the carriage window, feeling cold and unwanted. Silently she put on her coat and tucked her skirt closer around her legs so no ill wind could caress them. Feeling the crispness of the raw cotton cloth against her hand made her remember the dresses she had spent the long, cold winter altering to her measurements. All those hours she had spent with a needle in the dim light of a candle had been for nothing.

Obviously, she was not getting a debut season this year either.

Not that she cared about missing another season. She had been secretly relieved about missing the previous two, only pretending to be upset about it, as Lady Russell had been furious. The fact was—she was no diamond of the first water, not like her older sister, and would only end up as a wallflower. She had absolutely nothing to offer a suitor, and therefore no one would pursue her.

At least not someone she could accept.

The only reason she had looked forward to this upcoming season had been this one chance to be in the center of her mother's attention. With Wendy debuting, her mother would have been forced to accompany her to social events and visits to other ladies of the *ton*, which had meant they would have to spend many hours together. And maybe a small chance of her mother starting to like her at least half as well as she liked Annabelle.

She sneaked a look at her parents, who sat on the seat across from her, loudly disagreeing whether Gloucester was a pond big enough for their strengthened stance in society. Then, staring out through the carriage's windows, they ignored each other and their daughter. She wished she dared to ask them more about being a companion, but she knew there was no point in doing so. Neither of her parents would feel themselves obliged to enlighten her.

Douglas's—Lord Darkwood's—aunt would inform her of her duties when it was time, certainly, but she didn't think the elderly lady could answer the most fervent question—why it was Wendy who had been chosen to be the companion. The more Wendy thought about the whole situation, or the few facts that she had been told, the less did she understand.

It didn't make sense.

Why would Douglas go to all the trouble of buying her father's debts and then merely settle for her as the companion to his aunt? She knew her father, and the sum which he owed had to be quite vast. And sums like that were not covered by someone staying as a companion for an aunt.

"Finally," Sir Edward exhaled, breaking the thick silence in the carriage as they reached Darkwood Manor just as the sun disappeared behind the trees of the Forest of Dean. Looking out through the window, Wendy looked at the large house which was to be her home for now. The gloomy building, with its row upon row of dark, dead windows, loomed high above the carriage.

Darkwood Manor looked abandoned and uncared for, and for a second she nursed a wild hope that they had arrived at the wrong house, that the coachman had taken a wrong turn somewhere—but in vain. A small door, almost hidden under the climbing ivy, opened, and an old man hobbled up to them. The coachman jumped down from his seat, opened the carriage's door, and lifted down Wendy's bag before turning to her to help her step down into the courtyard.

Ignoring the driver's extended hand, Wendy turned toward her parents where they sat stiffly, not showing any emotion. "Please don't leave me here," she cried. "Please let me go home with you again."

"You have to," Lady Russell said, pointedly. Enclosing Wendy's hand in her own, she looked at her daughter with badly hidden irritation. "Don't you want us to be happy?"

"You know I do," Wendy sobbed. "But why can't I stay with you, instead of living here with people I do not know?"

"Because life as we know it will be over if you stay with us," her mother answered, sharply. Lady Russell didn't bother to hide how annoyed she was at her daughter's questions.

Juliet Russell had never been able to take criticism in a good manner, and she was a firm believer in her own superior knowledge. Her family knew they should not disagree with her, but this time Wendy was getting desperate—she had a feeling it was now or never. As soon as she was out of the carriage, her chance of getting her parents to change their mind was over.

"Y-you can't just leave me here," she tried, and turned her crying face toward her father, trying to find some warmth and remorse, but to no avail. Sir Edward looked ready to throw her out from the carriage if she didn't get out by herself soon. "Papa, you know I have never spent any time away from you, and you know how uneasy I become when surrounded by strangers."

"As long as you keep quiet and do as Lord Darkwood's aunt tells you, there is nothing for you to worry about," her mother cut in, making a gesture to the coachman, who took a step closer.

"I-I don't understand," Wendy stuttered, looking at her stone-faced mother. "Why are you enforcing this? Our family has survived worse times before, and we can do it again. I can try harder to save money, and…and I am sure Dou…Lord Darkwood will give us more time if we talk to him. He is not a bookmaker, he is a gentleman, and even though he seems to resent our family for what Annabelle did to him when he needed her the most, I can't think that the man I remember as caring and kindhearted would heartlessly throw us out into the street. If we reason with him, I am sure he will give us respite."

Lady Russell closed her eyes and sighed. "Wendy, the respite he gives us is for you to stay here as his aunt's companion."

"But Mama! I am not the only young woman in the country. I don't think it would be so hard to find another woman who would make an excellent companion to an elderly lady. If he doesn't want to take care of the business of finding another woman to hire, we can assist him."

"He specifically asked for you."

"But Mama…"

"Wendy." Lady Russell looked as if in pain, her face stiff and her body rigid, almost as if she had been cut out of a piece of marble, her normal stance when she was utterly uncomfortable or embarrassed about something. "It is only for a year or two."

"A year or two! How can you send me away for a year or two?"

"Oh, for goodness' sake." Losing his patience with his daughter, Sir Edward stood up, and by doing so forced her to lean closer to the door. He waved his hand to the coachman, urging him to act. Swiftly the horse-smelling coachman grabbed her by her waist, hauled her out from the carriage, and dumped her quite roughly down on the ground next to her bag.

"Here you go, sir." The old man stretched his arm in front of Wendy, giving Sir Edward an envelope, which he accepted with a fanatic look in his eyes as his thumbs caressed the thick package.

The now familiar numbness spread in Wendy's heart and continued out to the rest of her body as she finally understood what it was all about. She had been right all along when she hadn't been able to add things up, knowing there had to be something more.

All the rush and the non-negotiable orders had been because of Lord Darkwood offering her parents what they yearned for the most—money. Her father's hands trembled as he slowly sat back into the carriage again, only to have Lady Russell snatch the envelope from him with hard eyes. Sitting closer than they had for years, neither of them noticed their daughter outside the open door as Lady Russell opened the envelope. Cheek to cheek, they looked at the contents before looking up at each other with big smiles, and Wendy closed her eyes in pain. To her parents, money was everything, and judging by their overwhelming happiness, they had just been given a quite hefty sum.

When had she become this insignificant? She had always known she was the second child, in more ways than by birth, but it had never been something she cared much about. She had, just like her doting parents, been in awe of the astonishing Annabelle, and spent the first ten years of her life doing practically anything to become accepted by her older sister.

But this…this was different. This was…sickening.

How could they not care for her?

She was their child. Their blood. She had done everything for them and had not once complained. Not even when her parents had gone out for family outings with their friends and their families and left her behind because she didn't have anything proper to wear, not even then had she said a word.

Instead she'd spent the hours waiting for them by sewing, altering small details on her mother's dresses so they would seem completely new. When she turned eighteen, they had brought her with them sometimes, but only when it was in their best interest, not hers. And again, she had never said one word about it.

Always the good daughter.

The coachman closed the door to the carriage and jumped up into his driver's seat. Lady Russell opened the small window and leaned out through the opening, beckoning Wendy to come closer. With a groan, she stood up, trying to ignore the throbbing pain in her backside.

"You will honor us by behaving as well as you can, you hear me? Don't you stick your little nose up in the air and refuse any chore. Whatever Lord Darkwood tells you to do, you shall obey. As long as you live under his roof, he is your master and you must fulfill his requests, no matter how small or…unheard of."

"Yes, Mama."

"You hear me, girl? You must never deny Lord Darkwood anything."

"Yes, Mama."

"Lord Darkwood is a man, and men tend to let their…bodily needs…lead the way. If you can prevail, this whole thing might have a much better outcome for us than he intended."

She didn't understand a word of what her mother was telling her, but recognizing the urgency in her mother's hard eyes, she nodded quietly. Something about Wendy's teary-eyed acceptance must have satisfied Lady Russell, as she gave her daughter a cheerful smile. "Time will pass quickly, Wendy, and before you know it we will be here again, to take you home. Stay strong and you will see this through. And remember, you are our savior."

Wendy nodded weakly, and as if on cue, the carriage drove off, leaving her staring after them until they had disappeared into the shadows of the dense forest. Slowly, she turned around and found she was now alone in the courtyard. She saw the old man disappearing into the house through the same small door from which he had emerged. As he left the door open, she could only assume she was supposed to follow. Bending, she grabbed her bag, guessing she should be grateful for not being able to pack all her things. The almost empty bag was easy for her to carry.

As she walked alongside the hovering manor, she tried to envision what it might have looked like a mere ten years ago, when its master was a happy young man not yet marred by his horrible accident. But the worn-down manor didn't give her anything to help. It was a dull old house, and there was nothing about it which could give her even the slightest idea of how it used to look before it was forgotten.

Like her.

A curtain moved in one of the windows, and she felt probing eyes looking down at her. When she looked back, the window was dark and empty. Tears filled her eyes, and she almost ran the last part of the way to the open door. She had gone through too much during this one day to be able to think straight.

After closing the door behind her, she found she had walked into the kitchen of Darkwood Manor, and the disheveled room overwhelmed her.

"How can anyone cook in here?" she blurted out,

and the old man, who stood by the stove, slowly moving a spoon in a piping hot pot, looked up at her with laughing eyes.

"It's not so hard, child. You just throw food in a pot and stir."

She let out a choked giggle, and her cheeks turned deeply red with embarrassment. "I'm so sorry, sir. I really didn't mean to offend you."

"It's all right, child. I'm not that easy to offend. And besides, you do kind of have a point."

He waved his hand toward the mess behind him, and she felt slightly nauseous. There were dirty dishes stacked everywhere in wobbly piles, and heaps of leftovers lay both on the benches and on the floor. To her disgust, she thought she saw some of it move by itself. The large windows, which faced the opposite direction from the courtyard, were so dirty that no light could reach through. The only work light was the flickering light of a beeswax candle.

"Ah, finished." The old man smiled happily as he carried the heavy pot over to the kitchen table and put it down with a loud thump. "You want some?"

Wendy shook her head. "No, thank you, I'm quite done."

The old man looked at her again with his laughing eyes, obviously not believing her for a second, but she was too tired to care.

"I really would like to go to my room, if you could show me?"

The old man put a lid on the pot and beckoned her to follow him. Holding her bag close to her chest, she followed him deeper into the kitchen and then out into a small hallway.

"The name's Quentin, by the way," he called out to her over his shoulder as they passed dusty old paintings and a hanging spider web. "I am the one to ask if there is anything you need to know."

"I am Wendy," she replied, as they climbed a winding staircase up to the second floor.

"Nice to meet you, Miss Wendy."

It was an odd feeling, but somehow his informality soothed her trashed nerves and made her feel surprisingly better. Someone had smiled at her in her new home, and it had to be a good sign, she thought, clinging desperately to anything warm in this cold, dark house.

He pointed toward the first door on her right and then quickly left her there alone in the corridor, disappearing without another word. Slowly, she opened the door and stepped into the room which was to be hers from now on. To her surprise, she found herself standing in a large bedchamber with an enormous bed at one end and a fireplace holding a roaring fire at the other. An inviting group of armchairs circled a small wooden table near the warmth.

Closing the door behind her, she shut her eyes with relief. She had expected anything but this, and she decided then and there that she would find Quentin, the first thing in the morning, and thank him for his consideration.

With tired hands, she undressed, hanging her ugly but practical dress neatly over the back of one of the armchairs. Ignoring her throbbing behind, she put on her nightgown and hurried to wash her hands and face with water from the small basin before climbing into the welcoming bed. Completely worn out emotionally, she closed her eyes and fell asleep immediately, sleeping like a baby until an angry male voice tore through her dream, abruptly pulling her awake.

"What are you doing in my bed?"

Chapter Four

The room was filled with shadows as Wendy opened her eyes, the once roaring fire now only a distant memory. At first she felt disoriented, not recognizing the bed she was lying in, but soon enough the world-turning happenings of this horrifying day came back to her.

However, she had no time to think about it, as the thick bedspread was ripped from her body. She opened her mouth to scream, but no sound came out as two large hands grabbed her waist, hauling her out of the bed. All the air flew out of her lungs as her already throbbing bottom hit the hard, wooden floor with a loud thud.

For a second she just sat there, unable to breathe. Unable to move.

In silent shock, she stared up at her attacker, who hovered above her just as the manor had when she'd first arrived, but she couldn't make out more than the shape of him. He looked large and frightening, although familiar, and she knew it was the master of the manor she was facing, the reclusive Douglas Scott.

She couldn't see any details, due to the darkness of the room, but she could sense that he was different from when she'd seen him last. At twenty he had been a tall and slender young man who held his head high and smiled easily. Whenever she'd laid eyes on him, he had looked happy.

The man standing in front of her seemed larger, as if he had broadened over the years, although with muscles rather than fat. The warmth which had been his signet was now long gone, and she shivered from the coldness radiating from him.

"What are you doing in my bed?" he asked her again, harshly. "If you think spreading your legs for me will earn you any kind of special treatment, you are sadly mistaken, my lovely."

His words made her shiver with fear again, despite the endearment. The ice-cold hatred he felt for her was all too clear in the tone of his voice. She didn't know what she had done to deserve such hostility from him, but it numbed her and made her feel small and awkward.

She was used to being overseen, to feeling neglected and unwanted. Her parents had never hidden their indifference toward her, and the only person who had showed her an ounce of love was her older sister, Annabelle. But she too was only sporadically interested in her little sister, as she had been too caught up with her own life, first with Douglas and now with her husband.

But to meet this hatred and loathing of her own person was new to Wendy, and she didn't know how to handle it, or how to handle him. Slowly, she stood up, trying not to groan too much, as the pain in her buttocks told her she would be having some problems sitting in the next couple of days.

For a second she could sense hesitation from him, as if what he had done to her dawned on him, belatedly. The Douglas Scott of her past would never have hurt anybody, especially not a woman. Somewhere in this hateful man the old Douglas hid, even though it was hard to imagine this large bulky bear had once been the slender young man of her memory.

"Gather your things and get out of here," he snarled with a dismissive wave against the door, and Wendy did not waste any time. She could feel his eyes on her person as she scurried around, collecting the few things which were her earthly possessions. For the second time that day, she violently stuffed them into the small bag.

With a murmured apology toward him, she left the bedroom quickly, shutting the door to his bedroom tightly behind her. The hallway was only dimly lit, and she turned her back to the stair, which she had climbed to get there, and instead looked down the long corridor, not knowing where to go. This house was all new to her, and as Quentin had led her directly to Douglas's bedroom, she hadn't a clue about which room contained his aunt.

She could go back down to the kitchen looking for Quentin, but just the thought of stumbling around in this dark, eerie manor sent shivers down her spine. She had never felt this scared in her life, not only because of the house but of Douglas too. He was rude and brutish, and not what she in her numb and pathetically delicate state of mind needed at the moment.

What if she chose the wrong room again?

She closed her eyes, sighing deeply as she tried to hold back the tears which hid behind her eyelids. She knew these emotions were unusual for her, but she hadn't any strength left in her. All she wanted to do was to find a quiet, out-of-the-way place where she could curl into a ball and cry her eyes out.

One small sob escaped her as she tiptoed down the dark corridor, passing one closed door after another, too afraid to open any of them. The aversion Douglas apparently felt against her seemed to ooze from his home as well, although she knew she was silly for feeling so scared. But walking around in the dark house, without company, opening door after door to find a room in which she could spend the night, wasn't something she dared to do.

Another sob escaped her, and this time the door she'd just left swung open and soft light poured out, creating shadows in the corridor as Douglas came stalking after her.

"For heaven's sake," he spat as he grabbed her hand, towing her down the hallway. "Are you so spoiled you can't even find yourself a room? All the rooms on this floor are bedrooms. Just pick one. I don't care which, as long as you don't end up in mine again. Or perhaps you would prefer to sleep in the servants' quarters?"

She shook her head, not interested at all in following him through the dark house. His snort told her that he immediately believed she had something against sleeping in the lower classes' beds, but he couldn't be more wrong. She would have loved to sleep as far away from him as possible, if it weren't for the frightening little thing about her being left alone somewhere in the house. As she didn't know the house, she didn't know where the other people who lived here had their rooms. She had always been afraid of darkness, and she felt sick to her stomach at the mere thought of being by herself in any part of this horrible, gloomy house.

He opened the door next to his and shoved her inside the dark room, and then he too stepped inside, disappearing into the shadows. She could hear him moving around, swearing loudly as he bumped into furniture before he finally found the fireplace. Moments later a fire crackled, spreading its light and warmth throughout the large bedroom. As Wendy crept closer to the fireplace, Douglas lit some candles that stood on the small table next to the bed and headed toward the door.

"I eat early," he declared hoarsely over his shoulder, before closing the door behind him, and she found herself standing there like a statue, staring after him, trying to understand what he meant.

Was she to make breakfast? Or was he just interested in her company at the table? As the latter sounded almost hilarious—her sitting there eating a nice meal with him while chatting away about this and that—she concluded that he must have meant she was to make him an early breakfast.

Her head was immediately filled with questions, and the thing she wondered most was how he ever could ask someone to prepare food in that dirty kitchen. Cooking breakfast wasn't hard; she had done it every morning since she was fourteen and the last servant had been fired. Her parents had always found something to complain about, and had to discuss whether the boiled eggs were too soft or too hard, but all in all—she knew they'd been satisfied with the meals she served them, especially as she hadn't had many ingredients to make breakfast of, due to their dire straits.

This kitchen was probably not very well stocked

either. She would have to create wonders with nothing this time too.

For the second time in just a few hours, she prepared a room for herself to stay in, all the while pondering what Quentin's position was in the household. He was an old man, dressed in simple clothes, so she guessed he was an elderly footman, taking care of the easier tasks of a household.

But who did the rest?

She hadn't seen any other servants, and considering the state of the house, she thought perhaps there weren't any. It had to be Douglas who did what needed to be done, and the thought both surprised and confused her, because it meant they had something in common.

Lying in the large, cold bed, she felt her eyes grow tired and heavy again, and her thoughts went to the man sleeping on the other side of the wall. He scared her, all the way down to her wool-clad toes. But what scared her most was the situation she unwillingly had been shoved into.

Douglas was someone she had known once, and of whom she had thought quite highly, and she found herself nursing a silly hope that somewhere, underneath the troll facade, the spirit of the happy young man rested. She had no intention of finding his hidden self, but the mere thought of who he once had been made her feel less terrified.

Her thoughts went to her family, and her chest tightened painfully as tears filled her eyes. Parents were supposed to love their offspring, but hers had clearly missed that information completely, as they without any remorse could send her away for money and a comfortable lifestyle.

She grabbed a pillow and hid her face in its dusty surface. Her agonized sobs filled the room until exhaustion overtook her and she fell into a deep, dream-free sleep.

****

Douglas sat silently at his desk, trying hard to ignore the heartbroken sounds coming from the other room, but failing miserably. Maybe it was because he could understand what she was going through, as he too had been abandoned by everyone he'd thought of as a close friend, and by family members too.

He knew he hadn't been an easy person to be near after the accident. His body had felt like it was pierced with hot swords repeatedly, and too many times he had lashed out at the innocent persons surrounding him. As pain grabbed him, he had let his agony loose and misbehaved so badly toward all his friends that he wasn't surprised they preferred not to visit him again.

The final blow had been Annabelle's shrieking refusal to be near him, and her crude ending of their engagement. The woman he had thought would walk loyally and lovingly by his side until the end of his days had left him before he had time to make room for her beside him, and all because of his damaged face. When the gifts he had given her at their engagement were delivered back with a short note in which she ended their relationship, he had lost it completely. Ransacking Darkwood Manor like a crazy man, he had destroyed every mirror he could find so he wouldn't have to see what Annabelle had seen.

A beast.

He had behaved in such a crazed manner that most

of the servants had left, finding new employment elsewhere, until Quentin was the only one left. Aware of the old man's problem with finding a new place because of his age, he had stayed out of Quentin's way.

Now, ten years later, he was thankful for his one sane moment, because he would have been completely alone if Quentin too had left. Every other month, when the yearning for release would ride his body, he would go to Gloucester and visit a young widow he had known before his accident, as her husband had been a friend of his from their childhood days.

When the young Mr. Peabody died, Douglas had left his home for the first time in three years to pay his respects to the grieving widow. One thing had led to another, and somehow he had ended up paying for her apartment so she could stay in her hometown. Whenever his need for a woman got too hard to cope with, he came to her during the darkest part of the night, and she never refused him. But then, she didn't welcome him either, or do anything but lie there like dead while he finished as quickly as possible.

He had more than once told her she didn't have to receive him and he would pay for her quarters anyway. But she always insisted that he was welcome as long as he came during the night and never asked her to do anything more than spread her legs.

He knew it was a pathetic turn of his once-golden life, but he couldn't stop visiting her. She was the only connection he had to his old life—when he had been happy. And even more pathetically, she unknowingly fulfilled his overwhelming need to feel another human body close to his, if just for a few cold minutes. So he kept silent and tried to ignore how frigid her body was beneath his.

His eyes darted to the door which connected his room to that of his newest employee, and he could feel his body respond at the mere thought of bedding Wendy. In his mind, she was his possession, and as such she had no say in how he chose to use her. She would of course refuse, and he would probably have to force himself upon her, but the thought of being able to have her as often as he wished, even every night, was too alluring, and he felt himself harden.

He closed his eyes, disgusted with himself.

Here he sat, listening to her crying, and all he could think about was bedding her. But the truth was, to feel her warm body beneath his, as he used her as a vessel for his manly needs, seemed like heaven to him.

He did of course intend to bed her; it was, after all, a huge part of his revenge plan, and he had no intention of giving it up. Even so, he could at least repress his urges for a few days and let the poor girl get used to her changed situation in life, and her new home. And hopefully she might even get used to his repulsive person.

Both Annabelle and Mrs. Peabody had made it perfectly clear to him that his good looks were long gone, and he now felt more like a beast than a young Adonis. He knew he would have to show his newest servant his face, now they were to share the same home. He would have to endure her disgust and pity for a while, but sooner or later she would at least get somewhat used to him, and then he would make his next move in his quest to destroy the life of Annabelle Russell Scott, now his cousin's wife, as she had destroyed his.

He would create a scandal no one would ever forget.

Or forgive.

Chapter Five

It was still dark when Wendy woke. For a moment she stared out into the dark room, trying to remember where she was. But soon enough yesterday's painful events came back to her, and she sank deeper into the bed with a heavy sigh.

Her parents had, more or less, sold her to Douglas in their hunt for a better life. She had always known they bore very little love for her in their selfish hearts, but they had needed her. And when there was no love to be found, being irreplaceable was at least something. She had never been anything but a cheap housekeeper to them, and even as a child she had been running errands for her mother almost before she could walk well. As a grown woman she had by herself taken care of the whole household, feeling grateful for the few crumbs of appreciation she had received.

A knock on the door interrupted her indulgence of wading in a sea of self pity. She scarcely had time to pull the bedspread up to her chin before the door opened with a bang and the doorway was filled with the frame of Quentin carrying a large tray. Without a word, he set the tray down on the end of the bed, walked over to the windows, and found a cord and pulled it hard. With a squeaking sound the curtains moved to the sides, revealing enormous windows extending from the floor all the way up to the ceiling. They probably were meant to show an onlooker a lovely view of the surrounding forest, but as they seemed to have never been washed, only dim light from the breaking dawn outside made its way through.

At least the room finally had enough light for Wendy to take in her surroundings, and she shuddered as she looked around the room where she had slept. The unusually spacious bedroom must have been utterly elegant once, with a large four-poster bed at one wall and, mimicking Douglas's room, an enormous fireplace graced by two sofas and a small table on the opposite side. A beautifully crafted desk, with a matching chair, was placed in front of the windows so one could sit and write letters while watching the scenery outside.

But now it was all in disarray, with shredded curtains, dirty smudges on the surfaces, and dust covering everything coverable. The thick oriental carpets on the wooden floor had stains, and spider webs hung from every corner. The room was in a terrible state, and Wendy felt nauseous at the thought of sleeping in the bed where she now in the light could see mouse droppings in the wrinkles of the bedspread.

"And how are you today, Miss Wendy?" Quentin smiled as he grabbed the tray again, carrying it to the table in front of the fireplace.

"Just fine, thank you," she answered politely, knowing there was no use to blame Quentin for her painful meeting with the lord of the house. It was not the servant's fault that his master was a beast who misbehaved in the worst meaning of the word.

Quentin grinned again, and she got a feeling that a smile was his usual response to most things. He was a simple man, but the warmth in his eyes made her feel welcomed, and with an almost contented sigh she left the bed, moving over to the sofa before looking down at what she guessed was supposed to be breakfast. The tray was probably made of silver, but it was hard to tell as it hadn't been polished for at least a decade. Absentmindedly she rubbed her thumb against the black surface, watching how some of the dirt came off.

Eating the odd-looking sandwich set on the tray beside a large cup of sour-tasting tea, she watched Quentin carefully shaking one of the curtains, creating a mist of dust in front of the windows. He sent her another smile as he noticed her watching him, and it came with a large dose of embarrassment over the messy bedroom.

She had to do something about it. So what if she was not here at Darkwood Manor by her own choice. That certainly didn't mean she should use her time badly. The elderly lady, Douglas's aunt whom she still hadn't met, surely wouldn't mind if Wendy spent a part of her day waking this old house up and putting it to rights.

Darkwood Manor must have been magnificent once, and a lot cleaner than it was now. It shouldn't be too hard to make the house, if not completely clean then at least livable. Even if she and Quentin would turn out to be the only available persons to work toward that goal, they could still achieve a certain amount of wonderful change. If they took one room at a time and went over it thoroughly, it wouldn't be too hard to keep each one clean later, when it was only upkeep. It would take quite some time, and many sore muscles, but honestly, time seemed to be all she would have ahead of her. She wasn't used to being idle, and this house was like a treasure box for an energetic person such as she.

Some of the devastation which had made her numb yesterday fell away, and excitement built as she considered the project. If the rest of the house was as grand as her bedroom, she could easily restore it to its normal grandeur with a little love and care. Smiling determinedly, she took a sip of the tea, and her mood was so good that she succeeded in holding her smile all through sipping on the sour liquid, as Quentin stood there, eagerly waiting for her to finish his gift.

Besides the sour tea, there was only one thing which made her feel uneasy. Douglas.

What was his plan for her?

Was she supposed to use all her time with his aunt, or would he mind if she spent her free hours on refreshing his home? Would it be okay with him if she took charge of waking up the sleeping manor? Or did he, for some strange reason, want the house to look as if it were haunted? She knew she had to do something about the house if she was going to be able to live in it without feeling constantly queasy, and she could only hope Douglas didn't disagree.

"Quentin, do you think Lord Darkwood would mind if I straightened my room a little?"

"Oh, no, Miss Wendy." Quentin chuckled. "Why on earth would he mind you cleaning? This house needs a good cleaning, and if you are willing to take it on, he should only be grateful."

"You think so?" she asked, relieved.

"I hope so."

Quentin wasn't as reassuring as she would have wished him to be, and it was only the thought of having to spend another night in this dirty room that made her decide not to care whether Douglas minded or not.

She sent Quentin to see to his lordship's breakfast, while she dressed, and then return with a couple of buckets of warm water. Grabbing the linens of the bed, she removed them in a cloud of dust. She put them in a neat pile on the floor next to the door, to later bring them downstairs and wash them. The curtains and all other removable fabric went in the same pile, and the room looked better already.

When the evening arrived, Wendy sank down into one of the now clean armchairs in front of the shining fireplace. Satisfied, she took in the loveliness of her fresh-smelling bedroom. The room seemed a little empty, with all the curtains and bedding gone, but she didn't mind, as long as all the dirt, smudges, and spider webs were gone too. It now smelled like roses and lemons, which was much better than old dust and mouse droppings. She had found acceptably clean bedding in the middle of a stack in a linen closet, and it would do for one night, to be replaced by her freshly laundered sheets and blankets the next day.

Looking down at her skirt, she winced when she noticed how dirty it had become. She had brought only two dresses with her, the one she had on and the wrinkly one she had managed to grab as her mother had dragged her out of the house. She would have to clean this dress, and that soon. The plain brown dress she wore was very practical, with long sleeves and a high collar. It was not the most fashionable dress seen in the streets of Gloucester, but it was comfortable.

Her other dress was a black thing with long sleeves too, although in the right lighting it gave a hint of some bare skin under her chin. Her wardrobe was embarrassingly small and boring, but for a companion she guessed they would do.

Her stomach growled, and she smiled faintly.

The dry sandwich Quentin had offered her for breakfast was all she'd eaten since she woke up, and now she felt almost dizzy after working so hard all day without eating. It was time to go and get something to eat, she presumed, and left her room for the kitchen, where she lost her appetite completely.

It was such a dirty room.

There were food stains everywhere—on the benches, on the floor, on the walls, and even on the ceiling. She could see Quentin walking past the dirty window, moving away from the house, and she sighed. If she were to get any dinner, she guessed she would have to make it herself. Moving around in the kitchen, she searched for anything she could use for dinner, and ten minutes later she had a pile of different vegetables and a piece of not-too-foul-smelling beef to use.

While her stew cooked, she continued with opening all the cupboards to find what edible things were in storage. It felt as if she was on a treasure hunt, she thought with a little smile, as she opened a cabinet and found a large collection of different herbs, which would do wonders to her stew.

A small mouse scurried across the floor, and she made a promise to herself to clean the kitchen the next day, when she had regained her strength. Right now she was so weary she could hardly stand up.

A sound by the door interrupted her thoughts, and she looked up to see Quentin enter the room. As soon as the scent of her stew reached his nostrils, he stopped dead. He looked at her with a peculiar expression on his wrinkled face, as if he didn't know whether to laugh or cry. He went over to the stove and looked down into the pot where the stew bubbled.

"Really?" he asked with awe.

"Yes, really." She laughed, amused at his evident excitement. "It's finished, if you want some."

"If I want?" he breathed. "Of course I want some. I haven't had a decent meal in this house since our lovely cook Mrs. Robbins left, eight years ago." He rushed to the sink to get the outdoor dirt off his person. When he had sat down at the table, he grabbed with trembling hands the full plate she offered him.

Silently, they ate their dinner in the flickering light from the beeswax candles she had lit earlier when dusk arrived. The food filled her stomach, and she could feel the warmth of the meal spreading throughout her body, making her drowsy and comfortable.

It was amazing to be so at ease with Quentin; she had just met him the day before. It was a new sensation to feel this content and unafraid with someone she hardly knew. It hadn't happened many times before, and it made her feel more lighthearted about her time here at Darkwood Manor.

"Ah." Quentin patted his belly with a contented smile. "This stew was almost better than what Mrs. Robbins used to make. And I say almost because if she heard I had said this was the best, she would come galloping from her new employment and box my ears."

"She sounds like a formidable woman." Wendy laughed, and Quentin nodded with sparkling eyes.

"There is not a man or woman on this earth who would dare to hurt her feelings. She makes the best food I have ever eaten, but I tell you—if you make her upset, you will be served something much viler."

"Oh, dear," Wendy said with feigned horror. "How vile was it?"

"I can't tell, as Mrs. Robbins has always liked me and made sure I got the very best bits. But I know a footman who refused to run some errands for her and ended up being served his own boot."

Wendy giggled as Quentin made a disgusted face, and neither of them noticed the door opening behind them.

"Who lit all the candles?" a harsh voice cut through the coziness, and Quentin flew up from the table. Hurrying about in the room, he blew out candles until only a few cast a dim light as Douglas entered the room. The master of the house sat down at the other end of the table, hiding himself in the darkest corner of the room.

"You have cleaned," he growled, as if she had done something wrong by turning the room into a place where you wanted to eat. Or cook.

Anger radiated from him, and the room felt smaller as well as darker. All her fear returned in full, and she tried to make herself as small as possible so he wouldn't take notice of her.

But it was too late.

He had already worked up a heated temper and was now blowing it all over her. "You can cook," he continued, and this time it sounded as if he were accusing her of the most horrible crime ever done by a human.

"Yes, of course I can cook," she answered, with a small, nervous smile.

"Ladies don't cook," he pronounced, not willing to let the subject go.

Before she could stop herself, she snorted over his narrow-minded opinion, and immediately his ice-cold stare fastened on her face. Mentally shriveling, she clasped her trembling hands in her lap, hiding them under the table. "I can," she almost whispered, silently praying that he would end the conversation, but he had no such thoughts.

"I don't know any ladies who can cook."

"I am not a lady."

This time it was he who snorted. "I know."

Her cheeks burned with humiliation. She wanted to run away from him as fast as she possibly could, but she forced herself to sit still. This was not how she had wanted to end her first day here, but Douglas seemed determined to make this a night for her to remember.

"Where did you learn to cook?" he continued, still clinging to the subject. She didn't want to talk about her life in Gloucester. It had been such a lonely, sad life, and he was the last person on earth to whom she wanted to admit that.

Instead she stood up and carried the dirty dishes to the sink, where she turned her back to him, hoping he would take the not-too-subtle hint. Unfortunately, life as a hermit for ten years must have made him lose some of his sense of etiquette, because the man continued as if she weren't ignoring him at all.

"It's hard for me to believe that a sister of Annabelle, a woman with no practical sense at all, knows her way around a kitchen."

Throwing the dishcloth hard into the sink—and incidentally causing dishwater to splash all over the kitchen—she turned around, indignant. Her sister had always been a trigger for her. Annabelle was supposed to be perfect. If she wasn't, there were no more excuses for her parents neglecting their younger child. A perfect older sister meant there was a reason why they had always treated Wendy so poorly.

"My sister has a very practical mind. How dare you assume otherwise!"

"The practical sense of a vulture then," he sneered disdainfully.

Wendy gasped, outraged. How dared he? How dared he!

"You, my lord, are a…a…"

"I am what?" Douglas said deceptively soft, and dread tore through her anger, shredding it into crumbs as he leaned forward, filling the room with his frightening darkness.

She turned back to the sink again, pressing her trembling lips together as she frantically dried the water off the wooden surface. Lord, what a spineless woman she was! She knew she acted like a scared mouse, but old habits die hard. All her life she had lived in constant fear of her mother's unforeseeable wrath, her arms constantly adorned with bruises after being dragged through the house and locked into the cellar when she, in her mother's eyes, had misbehaved.

If a small woman like her mother could handle her that easily, what could not a large man such as Douglas do to her? Closing her eyes as she gathered the last strength she had left, she knew what she had to do. She had to go back and be the good daughter again. The good and humble servant.

She had to compose herself and thicken her skin

against him, because she knew she would never prevail if she ended up on his bad side. A single tear ran down her cheek as she remembered that small moment earlier, before Douglas had entered the kitchen, when she had sat there, content and unusually giddy. Almost…happy. For a moment she had forgotten how worthless she was, instead feeling quite smug over her own achievements.

With a deep breath, she turned, composed.

"Would you like some stew, my lord?"

"Thought you'd never ask."

Ignoring his biting tone of voice, she filled a bowl and set it on the table, knocking a glass over as she withdrew her trembling hands.

"You clumsy wench," Douglas spat. The water ran over the table and down into his lap. "Can't you do anything right? My God, you are the most useless person I've ever met. No wonder your parents had no problem sending you here."

"I'm sorry," she whispered, too aware of her own shortcomings to be offended, instead handing Quentin a towel to give to the master.

"Now, now, Master Douglas," Quentin soothed. "It's only water. It will soon dry up again. Why don't you taste that stew our girl here cooked? It's like manna for your stomach."

Drying his lap, Douglas glared at the older man. "Don't you have anywhere else to be?"

Quentin, who looked torn between an urgent need to stay and act the mediator and the need to go and continue with his never-ending list of chores, hesitated.

"Oh, for goodness' sake." Douglas sighed. "I am not going to kill her. You can leave."

Mumbling to himself, Quentin disappeared through the doorway, and Wendy found herself alone with Douglas.

Nervously, she started to clean the dishes, her hands shaking so much she almost dropped the bowl she held. She could feel Douglas's eyes on her back, and she shivered in response.

"That's right," he drawled. "You should be afraid of me. I am the master of this house, and as my servant, you have to live by my rules."

"Yes, my lord," she agreed, hiding behind her composed facade.

"Oh, stop the crawling." Douglas snorted. "Both you and I know you are anything but humble."

"If you say so, my lord."

"Wendy…"

It was an odd revelation, but the man seemed to really dislike when she didn't stand up for herself and answer him back. If she hadn't known by experience that it was the worst thing one could do, she would have thought he preferred her to use the spine in her back and glare at him with her arms crossed over her chest rather than cowering in fear.

She had always been treated as though she had no brain and no feelings, and her parents had in the end had the most annoying habit of talking about how useless she was, even when she was standing next to them and could hear every word. Sometimes they had even wanted her to join in, as if finding fault with her own person was something she wouldn't mind at all. She had always thought it was a rather strange conclusion, but her parents had never thought past their own conversation.

But then, they had never minded walking all over her repeatedly, either.

"I mean it," Douglas continued grimly. She could tell he was getting a little too irritated with her, and immediately her heart skipped a terrified beat.

Oh, come on, she thought. Where is my spunk? Where is that righteous anger I should unleash upon him? Had years of behaving like a dog, too used to an angry hand, destroyed her will to stand up for herself? Had her parents done such a good job with turning her into an obedient, grateful servant that her first instinct was to throw herself to the floor and beg for mercy?

She was pathetic.

Taking one long, deep breath, she turned to look at what she could see of his frowning face, which was mostly hidden under the hood of his cloak.

"Staring at the beast, are we?" he snickered, before he stood up so quickly his chair fell to the floor behind him with a crash. "I guess your sister told you all about me?"

"No," she answered in a squeal, moving backward and away from him. "Annabelle never talked about you again, after she sent you the letter in which she ended your engagement."

"Right," he drawled, apparently not believing a word.

"She didn't. Y-you were no longer a part of her life, and so she didn't waste any time repeating everything that had happened between the two of you. You were history to her, and thus not interesting."

"Right," he drawled again, but this time the contempt was gone.

And no wonder.

He too had known Annabelle closely, and there was no way to hide the truth: Annabelle was a spoiled, selfish minx who would never spend time thinking about something which didn't concern her own person. Ending the engagement had been a final act for her, and afterward she had thrown out every thought about Douglas and his fate, instead continuing with her own life. Annabelle was born a survivor, and nothing ruffled her feathers, at least not for more than a moment.

How would Annabelle respond to the news about her younger sister being sent to live with her old fiancé? Would that upset her? Would she want to come and get Wendy back, or would she just shrug and demand her part of the money? Her husband of ten years, Anthony Scott, was just as much a gambler as their father, and Wendy was no fool—she knew her sister had a hard time keeping up the appearance of riches and an easy life.

The façade presented to society was everything to her sister. Nothing else mattered, and Wendy guessed she had the answer to her question: she was here to stay, and there was no one who cared enough about it to do anything.

She had no friends. She had lost contact with her few childhood friends when her parents had lost all their money the first time and moved the family to Gloucester to start anew. Wendy and her friends had promised each other to keep in touch, but as time passed she had received fewer and shorter letters, until they had stopped completely. She had continued writing for a couple of years, but no one replied.

She had not been able to make any new friends in Gloucester, as her parents had kept her under lock and key, preferring to keep her in their home as a free servant rather than having to pay for her debut into society. And there weren't many young women for Wendy to make friends with under their rented roof.

"Why are you sighing?" Douglas interrupted her thoughts.

"I-I was only remembering old times, my lord," Wendy answered quickly, turning her back to him again, continuing with the dishes.

"It must have been hard for you to grow up in the same house as Annabelle."

Wendy looked at him over her shoulder, startled at his insight, but he still hid his face in the shadows of the hood, and she looked away again, not wanting to show him her vulnerability.

"You are nothing like your sister at all, are you?" he asked quietly. For once his voice had lost all anger and contempt. "You possess none of her self-awareness, her egoistical behavior, or her large and exquisite wardrobe."

"There is nothing wrong with my wardrobe."

"Really?" He snorted. "I saw your bag, and it certainly didn't hold more than one dress, perhaps two. Annabelle has been married to Tony for what, ten years now? If your parents had spent even a tenth of what they used to spend on her when we were engaged, you would have brought more than one bag. You would probably have had twenty bags like that one with you. It must have made you envious, knowing how they gave Annabelle everything she wanted and you nothing."

Silently thinking of every curse she had learnt when at the market, Wendy didn't understand why he persisted with this interrogation. She had led the most boring life there was, and it would take her not one minute to tell him all about it. So why did he persist? If he wanted to know more about her, he could simply ask her. She would tell him anything, or at least everything which wasn't too personal. Like how much she liked the way his large, tanned hands carefully held the delicate silver spoon.

She cursed again, but this time she forgot to keep it quiet, and Douglas leaned back in his chair with a snicker, and even though she couldn't see his face, she knew he was smiling at her.

Bloody hell.

"Envy is not something I can afford," she answered quietly, hoping the small admission would end the conversation. She could feel his eyes on her, but she refused to turn around, and instead she started to energetically scrub the bench.

"Tell me," he demanded softly. "Why can't you afford envy?"

"Why?" she snapped. "Because if I do, I will realize how much I will miss. Do you honestly believe that I would rejoice over my new situation? Do you think this is what I wanted with my life? Is it so strange that I, like most young women of today, want to be a part of the social life among my equals, to enjoy my first season?"

She took a deep breath, trying to calm herself down.

"You can still have your season," he replied, and if she hadn't known better, she would have thought he sounded a bit ashamed. But this was Douglas, the heartless beast. He could walk over babies or kittens without caring.

"Can I? When? When I am thirty? Don't you understand how hard it will be for me to find someone to marry by then? I am not different from other women. My goals in life are the same. I want to meet a good man and have a home and a family of my own."

Tears blurred her vision, but she was too upset to care. How dared he patronize her? It was he who had made her a companion for the still unseen aunt, and it was he who had offered her greedy parents more money than they would refuse. It was his money that had made them send her away.

Her attraction in the marriage market decreased every year she became older. She was well aware she wouldn't have been anywhere close to landing one of the most eligible bachelors of her acquaintance, even if she'd had her debut when she was eighteen. But the truth was she would have settled for any man as long as he wasn't too old. Just as long as he was her man, and they would have a home and a couple of children she could adore.

"You are all the same," Lord Darkwood spat out, not hiding his cynicism. "All women only want one thing, and it's a man stupid enough to marry them."

"That is not true," she gasped, outraged.

"Oh, no?" he asked sourly. "Then why can't a man turn around without finding an eager mama standing there with a young daughter or two in tow, waiting for him to make a mistake so she can haul him in and force him to marry her ugly daughter?"

Before Wendy had a chance to answer, he stomped out of the kitchen, disappearing into the hallway. Trembling with anger, she sat down at the kitchen table.

Of all the simpleminded men in England...

He did have a point about women and marriage, she had to give him that. The marriage market was like a war zone, all coming down to who would catch the biggest fish in the pond of eligibility.

What infuriated her most was how he didn't seem bothered about how he had put her life on hold. She had been completely honest, confessing her feelings to him. But instead of acknowledging them, he had gone on and on about women and marriage. He had not cared enough to answer her about her situation.

And furthermore, he still hadn't introduced her to his aunt, whom she was there to accompany. As far as she knew, it was just the two of them and Quentin in the manor house. If that would become common knowledge, how unchaperoned her life here at Darkwood Manor really had been, she would be out of the marriage market permanently.

Lonely for the rest of her life.

Chapter Six

Wendy's second morning at Darkwood Manor started much like the first one had, with Quentin entering her bedroom carrying a large tray. The only difference this time was that he had brought two cups instead of one.

Filling the cups with hot tea, he sat down in one of the chairs, encouraging her to join him with a wave of his hand. She moaned as she climbed out of bed, her aching muscles protesting loudly. Ungracefully, she stumbled across the floor and sank into the other chair with a very unladylike groan. Ignoring her company's chuckle, she accepted the cup offered to her.

They sat silently, but it was a contented silence that didn't bother her. Instead she felt at ease and comfortable, as she found she always was with Quentin.

"How are you feeling today, Miss Wendy?" he asked smoothly, trying to sound as if he wasn't worried about her. She hid her smile behind the curtain of her hair, deciding to use this time alone with him to get some answers.

"I am just fine, Quentin, all because of you." She praised him warmly, and his leathery skin turned red as he blushed with delight.

"The kitchen sure is looking fine today. It was a pleasure to make your morning tea."

"Quentin," Wendy said, not answering his kind

words, "do you know when I am to meet the elderly lady I am here to accompany?"

"Miss Lila?" Quentin frowned. "She probably won't need you for a couple of days yet. She is in bed with a terrible cold. Her old maid has had me running up and down the stairs with hot water, and soon I think I'm going to pretend deafness. She is such an old hag."

"Miss Lila?"

"No, not Miss Lila." He chuckled. "She is as sweet as a plum in August. No, I was thinking of Hastings, the maid she brought with her."

Well, at least there was a Miss Lila, and she did reside in this very house. Thank the Lord. Now she could only hope no one would ever hear about how Miss Lila had been kept to her bed during Wendy's first days here at Darkwood Manor, leaving Wendy alone with Douglas.

"Anything more you need, Miss Wendy?"

She shook her head, and Quentin stood up, ending the conversation. He took the tray with its dirty dishes and disappeared just as silently as he had arrived, leaving Wendy alone again.

Humming, she put on her black dress, as the brown one was now too dirty. She almost ran downstairs in search of somewhere to wash clothes. She found Quentin in the kitchen, where he was cleaning the dishes they had used, and he showed her where she could do her laundry.

Soon two large barrels were filled with hot water, and, still humming, she took care of her stained dress before continuing with all the curtains and bedspreads that she had stripped from her room yesterday.

When she was done with her own clothing and

linens, she made Quentin collect his dirty things, and when she had washed them, she asked him to fetch Miss Lila's and Hastings' dirty laundry and soon had a new mountain in front of her.

But when she asked him to fetch her Douglas's things, he refused, most stubbornly. Apparently, he didn't think that was such a good idea, and before she could use mild force and have him do it despite his objections, he scurried away faster than she had thought it possible for him to move.

She frowned at his disappearing back. What was she to do now? Taking care of the laundry wasn't a part of her position as a companion, but it felt such a waste to not do everyone's clothes when she had the hot water ready. It wasn't as if she looked forward to doing Douglas's laundry; she mischievously enjoyed the thought of him having to wear dirty, itchy clothes.

But in the end she decided to do them regardless. Who would take care of them otherwise? Quentin was an eager servant and did his best, but he was still an old man, and she didn't want to wear him out. He had the infamous Hastings to run around for and didn't need Wendy to send him scurrying as well.

Douglas's door looked as angry and foreboding as its master, and she hesitated slightly before knocking on the hard wood and waiting for his response. To enter without being given permission was not a part of her plan.

When he didn't answer, she knocked again, although much harder, and this time she heard his voice from the other side of the door. As she couldn't make out what he said, she took his response as invitation and resolutely opened the door.

The bedroom was as dark as night, the thick curtains hiding the daylight effectively. Again, just as on her first night at Darkwood Manor, the fireplace was the only light source in the room, and she took a few steps into the darkness, straining her eyes as she tried to locate Douglas. Her eyes had not got used to the room's gloominess yet, and so she could see only shapes that were darker than the room.

"My lord?" she asked as she squinted toward the bed, trying to see if he occupied it.

The door shut behind her with a sharp bang, and she jumped with a yelp before twirling to find him standing right behind her. Although she couldn't see his face clearly, she was certain he was snickering.

The man was a beast.

"You scared me," she squealed, trying to sound untouched but failing miserably.

He didn't answer her but instead stepped closer, and she took an unintentional step backward. With a soft chuckle, he passed her and went to the fireplace, where he threw some logs onto the fire. The fire grew with a roar, lightening the room enough that she could see him and the furniture almost clearly. Mesmerized, she stared at him as he stood with his back toward her, looking down into the blazing fire. Tall and well-built, he didn't look like the scrawny aristocrats she had seen surrounding Annabelle. Clad only in a shirt and tight breeches that showed every twisting muscle on his fit body, he looked more like what she would have fancied a highwayman or a pirate should look like.

As he turned, she momentarily forgot to breathe.

The shadows of the room still hid the horrendous scars for her, but she could clearly make out the handsomeness she so vividly remembered from ten years ago. Then he had been a very beautiful young man, almost exquisitely so. Annabelle had, during their short engagement, gone on and on about them being the perfect couple, and especially about how beautiful they both were. She had even compared her fiancé to famous statues from past times, claiming him to be almost as perfect as she.

The Douglas standing before Wendy now had lost all the prettiness and slenderness. Instead he stood broad-shouldered and manly in front of her, and an odd sensation tingled deep inside her stomach as she watched him.

She still found him utterly beautiful.

"What do you want?" he asked, precariously soft.

"I-I came t-to collect the laundry," she stuttered, her heart beating wildly.

A slow smile quirked his full lips. "Did you now?" he replied with a voice as smooth as velvet, and again she forgot how to breathe as he gave her a look from the corner of his eye that had her legs turning to butter.

"Y-yes…" she whispered.

"The bed," he purred, and she looked at the large four-poster bed with a strange mix of fear and longing.

"The bed?" she repeated, dumbfounded, generating another amused chuckle from him as he left the shadows, seeming more like a predator closing in on his prey than a master moving toward his servant.

He halted just a step away from her, grabbing her chin with his strong fingers and forcing it gently upward until she could feel the heat of his breath against her face. Mesmerized, she stared into his vivid blue eyes, the sensation in her stomach growing to a crescendo. With a smug smile, he leaned even closer to her, touching her ear lightly with his hot lips.

"The laundry is by the bed," he whispered into her ear, before moving back, away from her, leaving her shaking with a need that she didn't know how to deal with. Hastily, she collected the clothes and almost ran toward the door.

Mumbling inaudibly, she shut the door and leaned back against it, too dizzy to move without falling as his amused laughter came from the room on the other side. But this time it wasn't her stomach which made her unnervingly close to fainting. No, when she had stood there looking back at him, she had noticed something even odder than her fluttering stomach.

The man had no scars.

The light in his bedroom had been dim, but she had still managed to make out his face's features, and she had not noticed any bulging scars at all. After hearing her sister whine about how horrendous he had become, Wendy had been prepared for the worst.

Only—he had looked just fine to her. The only conclusion she could make from this was that either he had healed completely from his wounds or the scars were too thin to notice.

So why hide? Why live under the hood of his coat as if he were a beast in a fairytale? He had managed with the achievement to turn himself into a man known only by name, instead of the vibrant young man she so clearly remembered from her childhood.

They had met a couple of times, during the time of his courtship and engagement with Annabelle, but except for the engagement party, only in her home, never in his. Annabelle had confessed to Wendy that

Douglas preferred for their parents to stay as far away from Darkwood Manor as possible.

"But just you wait until after the wedding," Annabelle had gloated. "As soon as I am the new countess, I will have the three of you brought to Darkwood Manor."

It hadn't mattered how much Wendy had loved the thought of moving in with Annabelle and Douglas, she still had found her sister's plan...dishonest. To the romantic ten-year-old, love meant caring for each other and showing one another respect and honesty. Of course, in the end, Annabelle had showed them all just how little she had loved Douglas when she abandoned him after the accident.

The door she was leaning against opened suddenly behind her and she fell backward, slamming hard into his torso.

"Why are you still standing here? Go, and hurry up. And when you are done with the laundry, you can return to me with a bottle of wine."

She stumbled into the hallway as he shoved her away from him and closed the door between them again. That man wasn't a beast, Wendy thought as she washed his clothes a little more roughly than necessary. No, that man was a warty toad. He made her, the most even-tempered person in England, feel ready to kill him. She banged the wet clothes even harder, and the feel of the poor, innocent fabric under her hand was extremely satisfying. Especially as it was his.

What game was he playing now?

He was up to something, but she didn't know what, and it made her uncomfortable. Her knowledge of the stronger sex had up until yesterday consisted of her father and Anthony, and frankly, she didn't think it would do her any good to treat men in the same patronizing way that her mother and sister treated their husbands. The men whom she had met and greeted at the few social assemblies she had attended didn't count. They had probably forgotten all about her as soon as she left their side, if not sooner.

Douglas was a completely different kind of man than the men she had met and dealt with before. He was rough, straightforward, and seemed to have no limits at all when it came to bad behavior. For the first time ever, she wished someone had told her more about having social intercourse with a man. Or what one was supposed to do if he touched you. Or threatened to.

Wendy had asked Annabelle once what it was like to be kissed by a man, and her sister had said it wasn't so exciting. In fact, Annabelle had confessed, it was just wet and messy, and not likable at all. Wendy had agreed with her sister. After all, who wanted to taste someone else's lunch?

But moments ago, when Douglas had moved closer to her, placing his lips against her ear, she had wanted to do just that…taste him.

Sighing ruefully, she at last emptied the laundry barrels, watching the dirty water disappear into the sink. She did most definitely not want to go up to his lordship again with that bottle of wine he had ordered. He would undoubtedly continue with his new game of making her feel awkward and uncomfortable.

Considering his smug behavior, she could only surmise that he intended to offer her some wine too, and that would not do. She could not drink wine with Douglas, and especially not in his secluded bedroom.

She had once heard her mother gossip with her friends about a woman of their acquaintance who'd had too much wine to drink and done something so scandalous that her husband had sent her to their country house up north.

Not that she could become more sent away than she already was…

Although, considering her silly heart's somersaults when Douglas was near, he would probably not have to use wine to get her to act scandalously. The man was simply too attractive for his own good. Or rather for her good.

Quentin entered the kitchen, and before she could change her mind, Wendy sent him to Douglas's room with the requested bottle of wine. She couldn't stop a smug smile of her own as the servant disappeared with a knowing chuckle. The beast upstairs had not said a word about taking advantage of her, but his predator's walk had been easy to interpret.

Lord, it felt good to vex him.

Humming a happy tune, she started to peel a potato energetically, feeling quite satisfied with herself. She might be a scared little mouse in the lair of a lion, but now and then even the smallest mouse could roar. Or at least make a sound other than a scared little squeak.

"Mission accomplished," Quentin said as he reappeared in the kitchen. "Although I must admit Master Douglas was a wee bit surprised to find me entering the room. The boy almost scared me to death, standing behind the door, slamming it shut behind me when I arrived."

"Oh, I'm so sorry." Wendy hid her smiling face under the curtain of her hair, wishing she had been able to see the scene Quentin so vividly painted for her.

"Don't be." Quentin chuckled as he filled a pot with water for the potatoes. "That young man should know better than trying to trap old men in his bedroom."

She couldn't stop surprised laughter, and Quentin wiggled his thick eyebrows at her, just as amused as she. What a wonderful man he was, she thought tenderly. She had not been at Darkwood Manor long, but already she trusted the servant with all her heart.

Perhaps it was his complete acceptance of her person or how he seemed to trust her ability around the house that made her so at ease with him. She wasn't used to feeling appreciated, even though she had spent most of her life doing everything her parents asked her to do.

"I think I will go and see if I can find something to serve with the potatoes," Quentin mumbled after rummaging through the cupboards. "I think I saw something edible in the pantry earlier."

His voice trailed off as he disappeared down the hallway in search of something more to put on their plates, and Wendy found herself alone with the potatoes and her sad thoughts of yesteryears. As the pile grew in front of her, she again, as too many times before, wondered what horrible thing she'd done to make her mother so indifferent toward her. Sir Edward had once told her they'd never planned to have her, that she was a mistake. Even though she didn't know the whole picture of what he'd meant, she still got the message: she was unwanted.

Lord, she was one pathetic woman, she thought as she put the potatoes in the pot Quentin had left for her.

If she had received a penny for every time she spent time dwelling on her parents, she would have been a rich woman by now. With a grunt she lifted the heavy pot and turned to put it on the stove, only to walk straight into the hard, unyielding torso of Douglas.

"Ouf," the beast grunted as her forehead hit his chin.

"I'm sorry," she squealed, managing to save the pot and the potatoes from falling onto the floor as the impact made her lose her grip slightly. Only a little water sloshed over the edge onto her hand...and his shoes.

"You should be," he answered, rubbing his chin with his hand. It was such a nice hand, Wendy thought irrationally. It looked strong and able. And manly. Absolutely manly. No one would ever think of him as having a lady's hand, even though his fingers were long and slender.

"Staring at the beast again, are we?" Lord Darkwood drawled, and Wendy tore her gaze from his hands, confused. And then it hit her: she could see his face clearly.

In the sharp light, he showed her his whole face, including the wounded side. Her mouth opened slightly as her eyes darted over the scars which had forever transformed his face, and all she could think was...*Is that all?*

She had thought it earlier, when she saw him in the dim light of his room. The side of his face was lined with scars, but they were so thin they were almost invisible. If she hadn't known to look for them, she wouldn't have noticed them at all.

Douglas Scott was just as beautiful as ever, and the

only thing the scars did was give his face some character. He didn't look scary at all. However, he apparently thought so, which was very easy to see in the defensive way he was staring at her, silently daring her to react badly to his wounded face. Last time he had shown his face to a Russell woman, she had left the manor screaming.

"Y-your s-scars," she stuttered, and immediately he took a defensive stance.

"What about them? Are they horrifying, awful, or just plain scary?"

He leaned closer to her, and she felt his hot breath against her forehead. Unwillingly she took a step back, not appreciating his obvious attempt to make her feel small and scared.

"Are you going to do an Annabelle on me?" he growled.

"A w-what?"

"Your sister, bless her black heart, took one look at my face and threw away all her fake love. I have never seen anyone move as fast as she did that day, when she promptly ended our engagement and barged out of my sorry excuse of a life."

He was trying hard to get to her, to find her weak spot, and he was doing a bloody good job of it too. Anger filled her veins, racing wildly throughout her body, filling every part of her with a desperate need to defend herself, and she had to use all her will power to calm herself, to stop herself from launching into a discussion she never would win.

Her antagonist apparently didn't suffer from bad conscience, and her refusal to take his bait clearly frustrated him. Wendy pressed the pot of potatoes closer to her bosom, bracing herself for his next attack, which she was sure was only seconds away.

"Master Douglas, perhaps you should wait in the dining room. We will serve you dinner as soon as possible." Quentin had arrived quietly, his gaze jumping between the two of them indecisively.

Douglas sent Quentin a look over his shoulder that had the servant scurrying from the room. The dismissal in the master's eyes was too obvious for the servant not to obey. Looking back down on Wendy, a wicked smile crept over Douglas's full lips as he grabbed the pot from her numb hands and placed it on the counter behind her. The movement made him come even closer to her, forcing her to tilt her head back, so she could meet his eyes.

"So," he said calmly, which scared her more than his earlier anger. "What do you think of the beast of Darkwood Manor?"

"I see no beast," she whispered, and took a small step back, only to find herself pressed against the counter. Douglas immediately followed, lifting his arms to put one hand on each side of her head, building a human cage in which she was trapped.

"And yet you try to get away?"

"Y-you are t-too close," she breathed, more honest than she wanted to be, but something about his closeness rendered her unable to breathe. She could smell the soap he had washed himself with, and the musky scent overwhelmed her. The whole room started to spin, and the only thing standing still was his hard, unyielding body, which only needed to move an inch to touch hers.

"So I affect you?" he asked, in a voice as smooth

as velvet.

Her cheeks started to burn as his hot breath played over her skin, and she couldn't stop a small whimper. Something in his eyes changed. The darkness turned into a burning fire, and she knew there was nothing she could do to stop him. She was caught in his web and could only stand there, petrified, waiting for his next move.

When his lips landed on hers, her knees started to wobble, and she had to grab his arms for support so she wouldn't turn into a pile at his feet. He took her touch as an invitation and pressed his body against hers, catching her between him and the cupboard. Again and again his lips slanted over hers, causing her to feel sensations she hadn't thought possible.

No man's body had ever been so close to hers, and the feeling was unbelievable. His warm skin pressed against hers, and she could feel her heart follow his heart's rhythm. Slowly she let her trembling hands travel up his arms, and he let his circle her back, pressing her even closer to him until they felt as one person instead of two.

She closed her eyes as his lips momentarily left hers and instead moved over her cheek, leaving a track of small kisses on the soft skin. He kissed the back of her ear, and she shivered in response. One of his hands moved downward, gently pressing her closer to him, and she heard him growl low, as if in pain.

His lips left her ear, following the line of her jaw back to her mouth. Just as gently he pressed his lips against hers, forcing her mouth open with his tongue. Her hands on his shoulders must have left bruises, so hard did she grab him as the sensation of a real kiss hit her confused mind.

It was wonderful. It was hot. It was…unexpected…

The surprise of his tongue forced reality back into the bubble of passion he had created around them, and before he had a chance to react, she slipped under his arm and ran away from the kitchen with her hands pressed against her burning cheeks. Not until she stood inside her bedroom, with her back against the closed door, did she let herself breathe again.

She couldn't believe how wanton she had been. This was not how a lady should act. She had heard what Lady Russell had told Annabelle on the day of her marriage to Anthony Scott. Her mother had made it very clear that a wife's duty was to lie still until the husband was done with his manly needs. She should never make a sound, and she should never, ever, make a movement to encourage him to prolong the wife's duties.

Wendy had, at her very first encounter with a man's needs, broken every one of her mother's rules. But Douglas had overwhelmed her. She had not been prepared for how wonderful it would feel to have his body so close. His warmth and manly scent had turned her into a living doll, unable to think about anything but him.

She put her hand against her mouth, not knowing if she wanted to mentally take away the kiss or savor it. A part of her desperately wanted to wipe her mouth with a cloth until every sweet memory of his kiss was gone. And yet another part of her desperately wanted…more.

She lost her breath as she heard his footsteps closing in. Closing her eyes, she tried to brace herself from turning and unlocking the door so she could relive the sweet sensations he had woken inside her. Silently, she stood there as he stopped outside her door, and it felt like an eternity passed before he knocked lightly. It was not what she had thought he would do. He was after all more the kind of man who wouldn't let something as easy as a closed door stop him. He was such a large and muscular man, with a temper to match.

Should she open the door? What should she say?

Before she could make up her mind, she heard his footsteps leave. Relief washed through her at not having to face him yet, with her whole body in turmoil after the kiss in the kitchen, and the only thing destroying her moment of joy was the drawling voice coming from the other side of the room.

"Did you really think I would give up that easily?"

Chapter Seven

She had forgotten about the adjoining door.

He hadn't, obviously, and was now standing inside her bedroom with a triumphant grin, oozing a silent promise about more kisses to come. A small part of her treacherous heart shivered with excitement, and she cursed between her teeth, angry with herself for reacting to him.

With an amused chuckle, Douglas moved closer to her with slow, victorious steps. "You must forgive me, my lovely, but a lonely beast like me is not giving up so easily when I've got a kissable beauty under my roof."

She felt an overwhelming urge to roll her eyes at him, and she savored the feeling, afraid she would turn into that motionless, wanting wanton again if she didn't. "Please get out of my room," she said, trying to sound indifferent as he stopped in front of her, looking down at her with a knowing, lecherous smile.

"No."

"No?"

His smile deepened as he shook his head. "No."

Again, she wanted to roll her eyes at him. Or perhaps just slap his mouth to make that wicked smile of his disappear. She felt cornered and wanted nothing more than to escape before he did something she would regret for the rest of her life. Douglas was tall and muscular, where she was slender and of average height for a woman—if she stood on her toes—and if he would choose to use his strength against her, she wouldn't stand a chance.

But, to be honest…what scared her the most was not Douglas. No, what scared her the most was her own inability to stay unaffected by him.

He might be a brutish beast who seemed to have lost his ability to be even the slightest bit polite or considerate. A grumpy hermit who roamed through his ruined manor like an ogre in a fairytale. And yet her silly, treacherous heart still sang whenever he was around. Why, he'd even managed to spark enough anger inside of her composed person to make her want to throw something at him.

Or at least just pinch him.

Hard.

It was such a strange urge for someone who had grown up in the household of her parents and had managed to learn enough serenity that she had forgotten she even had a temper. Or a will of her own, for that matter.

But things had changed. Her whole situation had changed, and now she had to change too. Douglas was not going to leave her alone just because he should. He would persist, and she simply had to prevail. She, who had never stood up against anyone, would have to find a way to keep herself as far away from scandal as she possibly could.

Although…

A faint memory of her mother's last words when her parents had dropped her off here at Darkwood Manor, came to her mind. *Whatever Lord Darkwood tells you to do, you shall obey.* Remembering her mother's order killed off her small spark of defiance. What was she doing refusing him? She was in no position to deny him, and even if she did and he pushed the matter, there was no one who would come and save her.

Swallowing hard, she clasped her hands in front of her stomach and forced herself to look up at him, to meet his burning gaze. "As you wish, my lord."

His chuckle was warm like the sun in May as he lifted his hand and softly put a tendril of her hair, which had come loose, back in place. "What is your game now, my lovely? Are you trying to lure me into letting you go? If so, you can give up that thought immediately. I am here to stay…"

"No, my lord, I don't play games with you. I was told to never deny you anything, and I am trying my best to fulfill that request."

His hand fell to his side as he took a step back, frowning at her.

"Wh-what?"

This time it was he who stuttered, sending her one of his dark, brooding looks, and she shivered in response. As much as his warmth made him irresistible to her, his darkness filled her with reluctant dread. He was anything but mellow in his moods. It was as if she threw herself from a cliff not knowing whether the waiting ocean would greet her with warmth or coldness.

"Who told you that?" he demanded, hoarsely.

"My mother," she whispered, humiliated over having to admit the truth and thus letting him know how little cared for she really was. But she had nothing to win, nothing to gain, by not telling him the truth.

"Your mother?" he repeated, astonished, and she

nodded solemnly.

He started to pace, moving from the door to the fireplace to the bed and then back to the door again. He drew his hand through his thick, dark hair, and again she couldn't help staring at his strong fingers, which seemed able to rule the world. He was such a beautiful man. She almost sighed, but caught herself in the last second. This was not the best time to stand there and stare at him in awe.

"Your mother told you to give yourself to me?" He seemed astonished, as if what she told him was unheard of.

"No, my lord, she told me not to deny you anything."

"I don't believe you."

"I'm sorry."

He glared at her over his shoulder. "You are such a timid little mouse, too scared of your own shadow to even look me in the eye and tell me the truth."

"I'm sorry."

"Bloody hell, Wendy," he sighed, frustrated. "If you are going to lie to me, you have to do it better than that. No one in their right mind would ever believe that a mother would tell her beloved child…to…to…"

Douglas stopped at the bed, staring at her with unreadable eyes. She wondered what was going on inside that handsome head of his. The man was clearly annoyed with her, otherwise he wouldn't be glaring at her that viciously, with narrowed eyes and flaring nostrils.

What she'd said had angered him, and she felt herself shrinking in front of him as he took a step toward her. For the longest time, he stared at her silently. And then suddenly, out of nowhere, he muttered something under his breath, and left her there, alone in her bedroom, staring at the now closed adjoining door.

Not daring to move a muscle, she waited for him to reappear. But he didn't. The other door stayed firmly closed, and she finally realized that Douglas was not coming back into her bedroom.

With numb fingers, she changed into her nightgown, all thoughts of food gone, though the potatoes and whatever Quentin had found in the pantry had been abandoned. As she lay there in her dark bedroom, she could hear Douglas moving about in the next room, and she couldn't help but wonder what he was thinking about her admission. He had not believed her, that was obvious, and really, she couldn't blame him.

When she thought about it, it did sound like a fabricated story. Parents were supposed to, if not love and cherish their children, at least want to keep them away from scandals. A child with a damaged reputation could harm a whole family's chances to climb socially.

Oh, how she wished she could say that she probably had misunderstood her mother, that Lady Russell hadn't meant for Wendy to let Douglas have his way with her. But the simple and humiliating truth was that she had.

And now Douglas thought her a liar.

She closed her eyes as quiet tears ran down her soft cheeks. Hiding under her bedspread, she cried over chances lost.

****

Douglas sat in his armchair, staring into the dying

fire with a glass of port in his hand. This evening had not ended up in any way near what he had thought it would.

Oh, he had planned the whole bloody thing, right down to the surprisingly hot kisses in the kitchen. That beautiful little mouse had turned out to be quite intoxicating, with her innocent response to his touch. She had, as he had foreseen, hidden in her bedroom, which was the sole reason he had made sure to place the key to the adjoining door between their bedrooms on his side.

But what he hadn't planned for was Wendy's confession.

Juliet Russell didn't know it, but she was a lucky woman. Had she been anywhere near Darkwood Manor, he would have throttled her by now. How could that old hag tell her youngest daughter to not deny him anything?

Juliet Russell didn't know the person he was today. Bloody hell, she hadn't even known the real him ten years earlier, as he had disliked her most intensely and had made sure to stay as far away as possible from her, and from her sniveling husband.

That woman didn't have a clue about who or what he was today, and yet she had, so easily, sent Wendy to him. And with such advice. Her youngest daughter, for goodness' sake.

Her baby.

When he had been engaged to Annabelle, he had only had one objection against her, and that had been her parents. They had behaved like vultures whenever they met him, asking him all sorts of questions about his financial status, which was against every known etiquette rule.

You never talked about money.

Sir Edward had been the one asking the most questions regarding his annual income, whereas Lady Russell had been more interested in what connections he had and his family ties, even the most obscure ones. Shamelessly, she had poked and poked at him to launch them into the *ton*, to introduce them as family.

Only the admiration he had felt for Annabelle had made him stand fast with his promise to marry her. His only relatives were his cousin Anthony and his Aunt Lila, and he had looked forward to starting his own big family, not once considering Annabelle's lowly status.

His godfather, the Duke of Thornbury, had mentioned it, as was his duty, but Douglas had already made his decision. Annabelle was a diamond of first class and would fit straight into the social swirl of the *ton*. As long as her parents weren't around, no one would believe she was unworthy of a countess's tiara.

He did remember Wendy well, too—the sweet little sister, who had looked at him with stars in her pretty eyes. He had enjoyed her company and, silly enough, appreciated her young admiration for him just because he liked her version of him: a knight in shining armor.

After the accident, he had come to realize he'd never loved his fiancée, only been blinded by her beauty. The resentment he felt toward Annabelle now came from how callously she had left him. Her preposterous screaming when she had found him lying in bed badly wounded still echoed in his mind.

That only a couple of months later she had married his cousin had been the definitive nail in the coffin for his already lukewarm feelings for her. Annabelle had hurt him more in his hour of need than he had thought possible, and somewhere deep inside him he recognized a call for revenge. It wasn't like him to feel a need to avenge himself, but after the accident nothing was as it had been before, and so it seemed the right thing to do.

The only thing to do.

He had spent almost a year in bed recovering from his physical injuries and constantly working out his plan on how to accomplish his private mission regarding the emotional injury she had done to him. What he would do afterward, when he had fulfilled his plans, he didn't know. He only lived for the moment when Annabelle would feel the same pain he had felt when she gave up on him.

However, time had its special way of healing wounds, even broken hearts. He hadn't thought about his former fiancée, or her family, for years, not until one day when he had been visiting Mrs. Peabody, his mistress. As always when he had been with her, he felt dirty and more like a rapist than a lover. He had just left her house when he bumped into his cousin and his wife.

They had not recognized him. As a matter of fact, they hadn't even bothered to look at him, as they had been too deep into their argument to notice someone standing in their way.

Something ugly had started to grow inside him when he saw his former fiancée, who looked just as lovely as ever. The exquisite vision of her made it too clear to him what he had lost the day he went into the quarry, especially as he had Mrs. Peabody's silent endurance fresh in mind.

All he had wanted was love, and here he was, ten

years later, lonely and unloved. Without thinking, he had followed them, too curious about them to care about being caught.

Anthony hadn't changed much over the years; he looked as rugged and bloated as he had ten years ago. As the subject of the heated discussion was money, it wasn't too farfetched to believe that marriage hadn't removed his lust for gambling. Apparently, his cousin owed some lowlife a rather large sum, and it was all due to be paid back with an obscene interest to top it off.

Annabelle had been quite upset, showing more emotion than Douglas had seen during their whole engagement, which told him how deeply in debt they were. Anthony's desperation had been obvious, and for a moment Douglas had a flashback of ten years earlier, when his cousin had been on his knees, begging for salvation in the form of money.

Their desperation made him a very satisfied man.

At least until their conversation turned to him and it became perfectly clear what lowly thoughts they had about him.

"It couldn't be a more perfect time than this," Annabelle had said, sternly. "Douglas has been sitting there in his mansion, alone for ten years, and knowing how much he used to love good company, I think he would be more than happy if you came and visited him. Judging by the way he has made himself into a hermit, he will probably shower you with money and gifts, just to make sure you will come back and visit him again."

"I don't want to," Anthony had whined, which earned him a look so patronizing, from Annabelle, that a shot of relief had flown through Douglas. Bless the good Lord for making sure this woman never had become his wife. Seeing her overbearing, contemptuous demeanor toward her husband made him almost sad for his cousin, who was trapped with her.

"You must," she had insisted, and Anthony had sighed and nodded, solemnly, his whole body screaming out his resignation.

"I wish you could go," his cousin had mumbled, and Annabelle had stopped to stare at him with horror written all over her beautiful face.

"Me?" she had shrieked, still not caring who saw her outburst. "How can you even consider sending me into that monster's lair? Don't you remember how repulsive he was, and how crushed I felt for a whole week after our last meeting?"

Repulsive? Monster? Douglas had felt the old pain again, and his heart screamed in agony. As the married couple moved farther down the street, Douglas stood there, staring at their disappearing backs. All the old hatred came back, knocking him hard, and he had to sit down on a nearby bench for a few minutes to find his breath again.

Repulsive.

When he returned home that same night, he had been a changed man. Gone was the hurting hermit, and instead a stone-hearted avenger had made plans so egoistical he had almost changed his mind.

But only almost.

Annabelle had once been everything he'd ever wanted, and the woman with whom he had seen a future with a family of his own. Now her words had sent him over the edge. He had to do something to repay her selfishness, or he would never be able to come out of his self-inflicted loneliness.

The unplanned meeting had restarted the need for revenge, and he had been sure to plan it as watertight as possible. However, there was one small thing he hadn't considered while plotting his revenge: Wendy.

Something about her made him curious, and he wanted to learn more about her life with her family. It had been a really nice surprise to find out she had grown up to be a very lovely young lady, with beautiful honey-colored hair and stunning olive-green eyes. She wasn't as overwhelming as her sister, but for that he was only grateful.

He'd had enough of too much beauty.

What intrigued him the most with Wendy was her complete lack of coyness. She was behaving more like a humble servant than a beloved and cherished daughter of a middle-class couple.

When she'd arrived at Darkwood Manor, she had immediately started to clean and cook, tasks which a well-bred young lady wasn't supposed to know anything about. A lady should know only how to order the housekeeper regarding tasks to be done, not how to do them herself.

Even so, without a single complaint, she had taken care of her own room, cleaning it meticulously, before doing the same to the kitchen. The dinner last night had been divine, especially considering what she'd had to work with.

And such divinity came only with practice.

He still found it outrageous that Lady Russell had, more or less, thrown Wendy into his bed. But considering how coldhearted her mother had been ten years earlier, he could easily imagine her sacrificing a daughter for a luxurious lifestyle.

The thought about cold women made him think about Mrs. Peabody, and he suddenly remembered that he had an appointment with her in a couple of days. Before changing his mind, he penned a quick note, ending the affair. He didn't feel any remorse over breaking up their one-sided affair with a letter. Mrs. Peabody had never hidden from him how disgusting she found his person.

He had more than once told her that she didn't have to go through with it if she didn't want to, but she had insisted. He guessed spreading her legs for him once a month had been the easiest way for the poor widow to keep her comfortable life. Without income, she would probably have to go and live under the roof of some far family member, who would use her like an unpaid servant. Her other alternative was throwing herself into a new marriage with any decent man who was willing to marry her.

To make sure she wouldn't be thrown out on the street, he enclosed enough money to last her a year. The poor woman had endured him, even though filled with disgust, and such stamina should be rewarded.

Wendy hadn't reacted with disgust.

He looked at the adjoining door, remembering her face earlier, in the kitchen. She had stared at him, yes. But not with disgust or contempt. No, Wendy had stared at him with…surprise.

And she had not disliked him kissing her. In fact, her passionate response to him had almost made him take her then and there, on the kitchen counter. Only the thought of her innocence had stopped him. A virgin needed a bed and a slow and sweet introduction to making love, not a hard thrust against a counter.

He felt secretly relieved at the fact that she was a virgin. If he'd had any suspicions of her being deflowered, they had disappeared when he had deepened the kiss. Her innocent reaction made it quite clear that this was new to her. A virgin had no other man to compare him to. No perfect man who was as far from being a beast as he was from being unblemished.

He went to the mirror, which Quentin stubbornly carried back every time his master banned it from his bedroom, and looked at the image of his face. He tried to see beyond the scars, instead looking upon himself with Wendy's eyes, but all he could see were the ugly lines deforming him.

Closing his eyes, he took a deep breath, cursing his own stupidity.

What had he thought? That he would be back to his old handsome self, pre-accident? The person that he had been ten years ago was long gone, and now there was only the beast left. An angry, self-loathing, hateful man who had nothing to live for.

All he had wanted was to find someone to love, someone who would love him back. But that ship had sailed, because, honestly…who could love a beast?

Chapter Eight

Darkwood Manor, June 1815

Wendy sat in the garden, enjoying the warm morning sun, feeling that odd sense of contentment which had become a regular occurrence these past few weeks.

It had all started when Lord Darkwood kissed her in the kitchen. Something within her had changed when his lips touched hers, and now she was starting to enjoy life as it was.

So what if she would miss another season? The season itself didn't mean anything to her personally. She had only looked forward to it because it meant she would be spending time with her mother. That lonely part of her had rejoiced at having her mother to herself and being the one her mother would take to outings and parties, just like she had with Annabelle. Wendy had never cared about the rest of polite society.

The strange thing was, now as she was living in this manor hidden deep in the dark woods, she had more people to socialize with than she'd ever had before. Her life before Darkwood Manor had been more than lonely. She had spent most of her time alone, waiting for her parents to come home, yet when they did, they only dismissed her as soon as they could.

But now she had Miss Lila, who finally had sent

for her, and who had turned out to be a very fragile, bedridden lady. She was the sweetest person, even though still suffering immensely from the cold which had sent her to bed immediately after her arrival at Darkwood Manor.

The elderly lady was very upset at not having any need of Wendy for the moment, and even more upset over not being able to act as the chaperone she was supposed to be. She made Wendy promise not to do anything stupid or reckless, but as she blushingly refused to explain what exactly a stupid thing was, Wendy still lived in blissful ignorance.

Hastings, the rigid maid of whom Quentin was deathly afraid, had ushered Wendy out of Miss Lila's bedroom and told her that she would be sent for when needed. In the end, that had meant reading for Miss Lila every morning and having tea with her in the afternoon. The chaperone was a very chatty lady, who loved to tell Wendy all about her life, starting with her very first memories and working forward from there.

So far, they had gotten to when Miss Lila was a chirpy five-year-old and had been given the outstanding gift of reading by her precious Papa. Considering how many weeks it had taken them to reach that point, Wendy had a feeling she would need a year or two to get the whole story.

Two happy birds interrupted her thoughts, and she sighed with pleasure, listening to their tweeting in the blooming garden. When had the worst thing ever to happen to her turned into the best?

Wendolyne Russell was happy.

A whistle cut through the warm air, and she waved to Quentin, who passed the opening in the high wall surrounding the lovely herb garden. She had started to spend most of her free time here, ever since the weather had changed from drizzly and gloomy to warm and light.

Spring had turned into summer.

Looking up at the mansion hovering over the north part of the wall, she realized even the house seemed warmer and more welcoming, not as dark and forbidding as when she first had arrived.

Now it felt like home.

A movement in one of the windows caught her eyes, and she saw Douglas standing there, looking out at something on the horizon, and she sighed again. She knew she was behaving like a little girl, silly in love, but it seemed she just couldn't help herself. The man was so beautiful.

Something had definitely changed that day when he kissed her. She didn't know what had affected him, but whatever it was, she was forever grateful for it, as he had become a changed man. Gone was the beast, the disdainful ogre, and instead the polite gentleman from her memories had returned.

He had modified lots of things, which made her life at Darkwood Manor easier in a way she'd never experienced before. He hadn't said much about it to her, which didn't mean anything, as he didn't speak to her more than an occasional greeting when they happened to meet. But the day after the kiss in the kitchen, he had taken the worn carriage to Lydney, returning with a large number of servants she was supposed to command.

Quentin had been speechless at first, and she had more than once found the old man standing staring at his master with his mouth wide open. But he too must have understood the good in what had happened, as he lately walked around with a cheerful smile on his lips.

Life at Darkwood Manor had turned out to be a pleasant experience, as most of the servants whom Lord Darkwood had hired were people who had been there earlier. They all thought she was an angel sent from heaven, the one who had made it possible for them to return to the home they had left most unwillingly.

Mrs. Robbins, the cook, had even hinted about seeing a wedding in the future, and when Wendy understood she meant between her and Douglas, she had blushed fiercely. All the servants in the kitchen had seen her red face and immediately thought there was some truth in the cook's words. It didn't matter what Wendy said; they still thought of her as their future mistress and treated her with all the respect that she as such would take for granted.

The manor quickly came back to its old grandeur. There wasn't one spot left that hadn't been gone over repeatedly and cleaned until it glistened. At first, she too had tried to take her part of the harder chores, but she had been faced with a wall of indignant servants. As a companion and housekeeper, she was supposed to oversee, not do anything.

So Wendy started to work in the garden, which apparently was a chore a companion and housekeeper was allowed to do, because no one stopped her from it. The only cloud on her bright blue sky was Douglas and the way he secluded himself from everyone.

Including her.

She wished there were some way she could make him come back to life too, just as Darkwood Manor had. But Douglas was unreachable, spending the days in his bedroom and the nights on horseback, galloping through the surrounding villages.

She sighed again, there in the garden, and as if he heard her, he turned his head and looked down at her, startled. She felt a horrifying blush color her cheeks as he caught her staring at him. Noticing the blush, he lost his melancholy momentarily and gave her one of those gorgeous wicked smiles that turned her into a warm pile of heart-mush.

She was glad she was sitting down; the man was too magnificent when his eyes twinkled with mirth. All she could do was stare at him in awe, he was such a splendid-looking man.

As always, her eyes darted to his lips, and she could almost feel them pressed against hers, as they had been that evening when he had kissed her in the kitchen. As if he knew what she was thinking about, his smile vanished, and his eyes became darker, hotter, forcing her silly heart to beat faster.

For one breathless little moment, there was no invisible wall between them, and she desperately wished she had an excuse to go to him, just to see what would happen. Maybe he would kiss her again…

But she hesitated too long. Something interrupted the moment, and he gave her a cold nod before leaving the window empty. She knew she wasn't acting as a companion and housekeeper should, but there was something about him that mesmerized her. She was drawn to him like a moth to a light, and she knew, deep inside her heart, that she was dangerously close to falling in love with him.

On the other hand, maybe she was falling in love

with the man she'd slowly made him out to be while listening to the servants' stories about the old days. Douglas Scott was their hero, and most of them had known him since he was a little boy. They didn't care much about his hermit ways or his beastly reputation.

"Heartache can make one do the oddest things," Mrs. Robbins had told Wendy, while her nimble hands kneaded dough. "Master Douglas has been trying too hard to turn himself into the villain in a fairytale to realize it is he who is the prisoner in need of finding his savior." She looked pointedly at Wendy, who had understood that she was supposed to be that savior and had felt her cheeks growing all warm and red again. Blushing seemed to happen too easily whenever they talked about the master of the manor.

The sound of a carriage arriving woke her from her thoughts, and she brushed away the dirt from her skirt before walking through the gate that took her to the courtyard. A hack halted in front of the staircase leading to the renovated front door. The driver gave Wendy a winning smile, which she ignored. Instead she walked to the small door in the carriage, where a young woman peeped out with an astonished look on her pretty face as she gazed up at the façade of the manor.

Wendy could see the guest had expected the view that she herself had seen when arriving over a month earlier. Darkwood Manor had transformed drastically, and now all the withering ivy and broken windows were gone. The country house now gave the impression it should, that this was the home of the rich Earl of Darkwood.

"Can I help you?" Wendy asked politely, not knowing how to greet the young woman. They had not had any guests to the manor before, as Douglas had done a very good job of secluding himself from everyone, including his friends.

Lovely blue eyes looked down at her, took in every part of Wendy's dirty skirt and tousled hair, and placed Wendy as the servant she was. Dismissing Wendy with a disdainful snort, she instead viewed the manor again with a triumphant smile.

"I am here to see Lord Darkwood," the woman said with a soft voice of sweet velvet.

"Is he expecting you?" Wendy dared to ask, and was immediately punished with a hard stare.

"No, he isn't. But he will receive me. Take me to him."

Wendy didn't know what to do. If there was anything Douglas had been straightforward about, it was to not disturb him under any circumstances. However, this young lady wasn't so easy to dismiss, especially as she had been eager enough to see him to travel through the forest, which was a rather bumpy journey.

Wendy couldn't send the carriage away again, not without at least informing him about the guest. With a strange mix of dread and exhilaration, she brought the young woman to the salon and sent one of the footmen to get a tray with tea and biscuits before asking the guest for her name.

Hesitating outside Douglas's bedroom, she took a few deep breaths to calm down. Finally, she had an excuse to see him. She didn't care if it was because of one too-lovely visitor, as long as it meant she would spend some time with him. Knowing he would only dismiss her, she didn't wait for him to answer her knock on his door. Instead she opened the door and hurried to get inside before he had time to close it in her face.

He sat at his desk by the window and gave her a disgruntled glance as she came closer. The sunlight played with his dark hair and made it shine with nuances of red, and again Wendy lost track of her thoughts and words as her eyes drank in the image of him.

"Did I not tell you to never disturb me?"

"Y-yes, my lord."

"And still you are?"

"Are what, my lord?"

He gave her an impatient look, and she woke from her stupor. She must make such a sad figure in his eyes, she thought. Always staring at him with stars in her eyes, unable to think an intelligent thought whenever he was around.

"Disturbing me," he hissed.

"Oh." She blushed, and his annoyed face changed as his eyes began to twinkle.

That slow, wicked smile that made her heart beat faster graced his lips. He stood and came close to her, to stand just in front of her. She had to tilt her head back in order to meet his eyes. He lifted his hand and let his index finger slowly follow the line of her chin before grabbing it gently with his large hand.

"Could it be you want me to finish what we started the last time we were alone, my lovely?"

Oh, my God. He was going to kiss her, and she had to brace herself so she wouldn't throw her arms around his neck and drag his head closer to hers.

"Or maybe," he continued smoothly, "maybe you

want to show your gratitude for the last time and kiss me right back, and if that is your wish, be my guest. My lips are yours."

The word "guest" cut through Wendy's daze, and she took a step back to put some distance between them. Something odd, almost resembling devastation, flickered in his eyes, but she had no time to think about it. The word "guest" had brought the woman in the salon back into her mind.

"You have a guest, my lord," she breathed quickly and caught his attention immediately.

"I have a guest?"

"Yes, my lord, and she is waiting for you in the salon as we speak."

"She?" He frowned. "Does she have a name?"

"Mrs. Peabody, my lord."

"Mrs. Peabody? Are you sure she said her name is Mrs. Peabody?"

He didn't wait for her answer. Instead, he left the room quickly, heading down to the salon. Wendy followed as fast as she could, but when she reached the salon, Douglas closed the door in front of her, and she stood there staring at the painted wood.

Who was Mrs. Peabody?

She knew she was reacting irrationally, but she couldn't stop the little thorn of jealousy cutting deep into her heart. She wasn't in love with him; how could she be? She hardly knew him, after all. But somewhere during the last month he had turned into something natural to her life, something important, as she had settled into her new environment, and this unannounced guest turned Wendy's world upside down again.

When a footman arrived with a tray, she sent a

silent "thank you" to the Lord above before grabbing the tray. The very amused footman opened the door to the salon for her without knocking, and she hurried to get inside before anyone called out to her to close the door from the outside.

She found them sitting in the smallest sofa, side by side, staring at each other. Mrs. Peabody's tiny, elegant hand rested in his big brawny one, as they apparently drowned in each other's eyes.

Wendy ignored the other woman's irritation over the interruption, and put the tray down on the small table next to them. She felt Douglas's eyes on her, but she refused to look up at him. Instead she kept her eyes on the tray as she poured hot tea into the two cups.

"I can take it from here," Mrs. Peabody snapped dismissively, and Wendy cursed silently. She had no choice but to put the pot down on the tray again and head for the door.

"You may remain," Douglas said, curtly, and gratefully Wendy took a stand next to the door, trying to make herself as small and invisible as possible.

Mrs. Peabody looked even more irritated, and Wendy bit her lip hard to stop herself from smiling. She looked quickly at Douglas, afraid to meet his disapproving gaze, only to find that he was still looking at his guest, who served him a cup of tea with a sweet smile.

Mrs. Peabody was so pretty, Wendy thought sadly. Not beautiful, like Annabelle, but pretty enough she must be accustomed to being admired and courted. Her friendliness toward her host told Wendy more than anything that they had some sort of relationship. Some sort of friendship.

"I must say I was surprised when I saw your home." Mrs. Peabody smiled as she lifted her cup, gracefully, her back correctly straight. "You have always described it as more of an old ruin, but this is a most stately home you have."

"I wasn't aware of ever describing my home to you."

Mrs. Peabody's smile faltered as his harsh answer cut through her sweetness, but only for a second. Almost immediately it returned, brighter than ever.

"Oh, you have, my lord, but maybe not in so many words."

She put her hand on his again, but this time he stood and walked over to the window. As he turned his back toward his guest, he missed the frustrated look she gave him. Wendy couldn't help but feel sorry for her, knowing exactly how it was to be ignored so completely by him.

Mrs. Peabody must have sensed that she didn't have much more time with him before he would dismiss her from the manor, and his life, and she put down her cup before going gracefully to his side as he stood looking out at the courtyard.

"I got your letter," she said softly, and put her hand on his arm.

Wendy could see the muscles in his arm flex, but he didn't remove it. "So why are you here?" he snapped, impatiently, making Wendy feel much better. This Douglas she knew all about.

"Because I don't want it to end," Mrs. Peabody replied, with even more sweetness in her smile than before. But in vain, as Douglas didn't bother to look her way. Instead he snorted, as if he found what she said highly amusing, and effectively erased the smile from her face.

"Really," he drawled. "You don't want it to end?"

"No," she replied, her voice trembling, and this time he looked down at her. Immediately she turned on her sweetness again, as she had his full attention. What she didn't realize, as she was too full of herself, was how he was already lost to her.

"But I do know that you don't want it to continue, so please stop this charade," he sneered.

"W-what do you mean?" Mrs. Peabody stuttered. "I want it to continue. My gratitude to you is endless. You saved my life when no one else cared, and I can never repay you for it."

"Consider it fully repaid," he snapped, and without excusing himself, he stalked from the room. Mrs. Peabody looked about to cry as she watched his disappearing back.

"You can't do this to me," she screamed to the empty doorway, with tears in her voice. "This is not what was supposed to happen!"

"Then what was supposed to happen?" he demanded harshly, as he reappeared in the doorway. "In all the time we spent together, you looked like you couldn't wait for me to leave, so why are you not happy when I finally do leave you?"

"You were supposed to marry me," Mrs. Peabody shrieked, completely forgetting her sweet façade.

Douglas froze, staring at her with disbelief written all over his handsome face. "Marry you?" he whispered.

"Yes, marry me."

"But you loathe me."

Mrs. Peabody became still, looking at him with astonishment written all over her. "Why would I loathe you?"

"Because you looked like you were in pain every time I came to you."

This time it was Mrs. Peabody's time to snort. "Of course I did. That is how a lady is supposed to be, when it comes to the more private parts of a relationship."

"W-What?" Douglas was completely lost for words, and Mrs. Peabody immediately grabbed the chance she was bestowed. She hurried to his side, pressing his hand to her heart.

"I wanted to be more passionate with you, but I didn't want you to be disgusted with me. My late husband made it perfectly clear that a lady shall not be a part of the act, and I was to lie there still and just be the receiver of life."

At first, Douglas stared at her as if she were a simpleton, but then his eyes started to twinkle. He looked from Mrs. Peabody to Wendy, and then back again, before he started to shout with laughter. Shaking Mrs. Peabody's hand off his arm, he walked out of the room, leaving his guest staring after him.

Wendy didn't know what to say to the poor woman. In the end, she didn't have to do anything, as Mrs. Peabody found her wits again. Grabbing her purse, she rushed from the house. She almost dove into the carriage, and soon it had disappeared into the dark forest.

Wendy left the window, where she had watched the woman leave, and sat down on the empty sofa with her hands neatly folded in her lap. So that was what a mistress looked like, she thought, and she felt an overwhelming urge to throw herself onto the sofa and cry her eyes out. She saw the beautiful face of Mrs. Peabody in front of her, with her lovely blonde hair and her eyes like a summer sky.

Wendy knew she had nothing to compare with the other woman—a woman who apparently had shared with Douglas the most intimate thing a man and woman could do, something Wendy was completely ignorant about.

She sighed again.

Why was she caring so much about him? He didn't mean anything to her, other than being her employer, and God only knew how little she meant to him. She knew she was special to him somehow, judging how much he had paid her parents for her to come and work for him. He had claimed it was because of his aunt's desperate need of a companion, but she knew that was only an excuse. Aunt Lila didn't need a companion; she needed a nurse.

That bedridden old lady was supposed to chaperone Wendy, making sure there would be no scandal as she, an unwed young woman, lived under the same roof with a confirmed bachelor. But Aunt Lila was never around, and even though Douglas mostly wasn't either, they had still spent enough time alone together to be forced into marriage if anyone were to find out.

And besides, she knew Douglas would never marry her, even though his actions would have caused her ruination. It wasn't because he didn't want to get married; he was after all an aristocrat with the need of an heir. The truth was that she was simply not the right choice for a wife—she didn't think he would find his next fiancée below his own class.

Wendy sighed deeply, and felt lonelier than she ever had before.

No one wanted her.

Not Douglas, not her parents, and apparently not her sister.

Come to think of it, she wondered what her parents had told Annabelle about Wendy leaving home just as the season was about to start. Her sister must have missed her by now, one would think.

The rest of the day she spent in a daze, and afterward she couldn't remember a single thing that she had said or done. As she entered her bedroom later that night, she felt exhausted emotionally, and all she wanted to do was to curl up in her bed and sleep. Hopefully she would be her usual composed self again when the new day arrived.

She looked at the door which separated her bedroom from Douglas's, and she shuddered slightly at the mere thought of experiencing another kiss like the one they had shared a month ago. She closed her eyes and relived the sensation of his lips pressing warm and hard against hers. She felt a little ashamed for her heart beating faster just from thinking about it, but more than anything she felt disappointment over her own reaction when he had deepened the kiss. She had more than once tried to imagine what would have happened if she had stayed, but her innocence put an end to how far her imagination could take her.

She now knew a man and a woman could use their tongues when they kissed, a knowledge which had shocked her down to her toes, but then…what? Both her parents and Annabelle and Tony had separate bedrooms, and she had never thought more about it. But when Douglas more than once had made it clear that he wanted into her bedroom, and preferably into her bed, she guessed that was where it all happened.

In her bed.

She opened her eyes, and looked at the large piece of furniture which stood there, prepared for her to climb into it, and she tried to see herself and Douglas in it, kissing, and the mere thought made her blush. As if on cue, a sound was heard at the adjoining door, and she could see the doorknob turn. She took a deep breath as the door unlocked, and when it started to open there was only one thing she could think of.

This time she wouldn't run.

Chapter Nine

He was such a magnificent man, Wendy thought, as Douglas came through the doorway. His dark hair framed his strong, tanned face, with its bright blue eyes, straight nose, and full lips. His body was broad and muscular, and the only piece of clothing he was dressed in was his breeches, leaving nothing to her imagination. His body was in full view, and he was practically giving himself to her on a plate.

He had a bottle of wine with him, and two glasses. Without a word, he filled one of the glasses with the red liquor and handed it over to her. She accepted it with shaking hands, and he gave her a satisfied smile, which made his eyes sparkle wickedly.

Nervously, she took a big sip and started to cough as the taste hit her with all its alcoholic strength. The second sip made her head spin, and she had to sit down to be able to try a third time.

He sat down beside her, his hand following lightly down her spine, barely touching the thick fabric of her dress until it landed on her hip on the opposite side from him. Gently, he pulled her closer to him, until the side of her body was pressed hard against his. He took the now empty glass and set it on the floor before taking her chin and turning her head so she would look up into his eyes.

"You are so beautiful," he breathed, and the truth

of his words was undeniable. His awe of her was fully visible.

"So are you," she whispered back, and he smiled again, oozing with satisfaction.

Even though he thought of himself as a beast, he was more than pleased that she didn't. He bent his head, and when his lips finally landed on hers, she sighed with delight. Another soft chuckle slipped through his lips before he let his hand hold the back of her head steady as he thrust his tongue into her mouth. The heat of the kiss was overwhelming, and all she could do was hold on to his shoulders as the kiss deepened until she thought she was drowning in the pleasure of it.

His hands moved over her body, but she didn't realize he was removing her gown until the unfamiliar sensation of his hot skin against hers woke her up.

With a squeal of surprise, she jolted backward, but this time he didn't let her go. Instead he followed her, and as she landed flat on her back in the large bed, he moved on top of her. Before she had a chance to react, or even a chance to take in what was happening, he kissed her. Repeatedly, he let his lips slant over hers until she didn't care about anything but his lips.

The heat was wonderful, and her body sang under his hands. When he came into her, she was more than ready for him. A prick of pain made her wake for a moment from her passionate dizziness, but it lasted for only a second, and then the passion of the act took over again.

His mouth, hands, and body moved over hers, until all her feelings escalated into a tornado of heat, and she screamed when she felt as if she was sent to heaven and back. Then, as she lay there with him beside her, she felt her heart return to a more normal pace, and she couldn't stop a sigh of satisfaction. He rolled over to his side and leaned over her, his cheek in his hand.

"Satisfied, are we?" he drawled, and she couldn't stop the blush from reddening her cheeks.

She had never been this close to anyone before, and the mere thought of his naked body so close to hers made her even more embarrassed.

"No, don't," he whispered, and let his free hand cup her cheek gently. "There is nothing to be ashamed of. You and I… What we just did was bound to happen sooner or later. And even though I would have preferred sooner, I must say later was just as good."

"I'm not ashamed," she whispered, as the need to tell him the truth took over the embarrassment. "Only, it-it's a little unusual for me to be this…"

She grew quiet, not knowing how to continue.

He gave her a soft, tender smile, which made her heart ache, and she knew she was dangerously close to falling in love with him. Loving him would cause her more pain than she ever wanted to live with, but in this moment, in her bed with him, she didn't care. All she wanted to do was to lift her head and kiss him. She wanted to make him feel what she had felt moments before, and so she did just that.

She kissed him.

He spent the night in her bed, and they made sweet, passionate love so many times that she lost count. When morning came, he gave her nose a gentle peck and climbed out of the bed. Naked, he walked across the room, grabbing his pants as he passed them on the way into his own room. As the door closed behind him, all the warm emotions left her, and she started to shiver as she sat there in her rumpled bed.

What had she done?

What had they done?

She hid her face in her hands, devastated over her actions. She had been sent over the edge. She was now a persona non grata, and nothing that she did would ever change the fact that if the truth became commonly known, she would be a scandalous outcast.

The only thing that could save her in this new situation would be Douglas marrying her, and she had already come to terms with herself about that; it was something that would never happen. He had once been engaged to Annabelle, and everyone had known he was marrying a woman beneath his class. The Russell family was of no importance, but the Scott family was. The whole engagement had been like a fairytale, but no one had been too surprised when it ended.

It had been Annabelle's beauty that had brought him to accept her as a fiancée. If she hadn't been such a diamond set in the ordinary surroundings of their acquaintance, he would never have noticed her and would not have felt the attraction to her that had made him consider marriage the perfect ending.

Wendy was no great beauty and had nothing to offer him. She had no one else but herself to blame for giving him her virginity, and now she probably had no other choice but to pray that he would want her in his life as long as she lived. While he still wanted her, she would have a home and somewhere she would belong. However, as soon as he grew tired of her, she was doomed. She couldn't tell her parents about her foolishness, and she would never be able to marry. Any man who married an unmarried young woman would expect a virgin, which meant she would have to spend the rest of her days as a spinster.

What if he met someone he wanted to marry?

At the mere thought of him marrying someone else, she felt like a spoon was slowly digging her heart out of her chest. Climbing out of the bed, she dressed quickly and straightened her room, erasing every evidence of Douglas's presence. She needed something to take her mind away from Douglas and the night of precious passion they had spent together.

Quentin looked at her, surprised, when she came into the kitchen. Usually he brought her breakfast upstairs, so that she could eat it in her room before starting her day. Without a word, he handed her the tray he had been preparing, and she sat down at the table, filling her empty stomach with tea and the delicious sandwiches.

"Enjoying your breakfast, Miss Wendy?" Mrs. Robbins, the cook, stood by the stove, large and rosy, and Wendy nodded her approval, her mouth too full to be able to speak.

"Of course she enjoys the sandwiches, you daft woman," Quentin rolled his eyes in the cook's direction. "Who wouldn't? They are almost too delicious to eat."

Pursing her mouth slightly, the cook let the near-impertinence slip by, as it had been a part of one quite lovely compliment. But Quentin still got a very pointed look, which had him scurrying away, too aware of the cook's well-known temper and good aim with her rolling pin.

"Men," Mrs. Robbins snorted after him. "If it wasn't for the gift of life, they would be completely useless. Just look at that Quentin. He likes to have us all thinking he is such an old, fragile man, and yet he can run faster than the footmen if needed. Liars are they, the bunch of 'em."

"Aye," Agnes, the kitchen maid, agreed wholeheartedly. "If it weren't for that little snake in the grass, I wouldn't go near one."

The rest of the servants in the kitchen giggled, but not Mrs. Robbins. The formidable cook turned and glared at her helper. "Agnes, you silly wench. You just silence that trilling tongue of yours. We have ears in this kitchen who are too innocent to hear you talk like that."

Agnes threw her hands out in front of her. "Who? Miss Wendy? I say that girl needs to hear the truth about men. Have you not noticed the master staring at her like she is one of those delicious scones of yours?"

"Agnes!"

Ignoring the glaring cook, Agnes sat down beside Wendy, who looked back, her eyes like big saucers. So even the servants had noticed Douglas's staring? Oh, this didn't bode well. She had enjoyed these last couple of weeks, for the first time meeting people who accepted her for the person she was and who appreciated her efforts. If they were to learn she now was a fallen woman, she knew all the warmth and respect they felt for her would disappear, leaving only disdain and disgust.

"Now, you listen to me, Miss Wendy," Agnes said, her pretty face serious. "Never let a man fool you into something you shouldn't do. They are snakes, the lot of them, and all they want is to get under that skirt of yours."

"Well, not all men…" Mrs. Robbins started.

Ignoring the input, Agnes leaned closer, as did the rest of the young servant girls, eager to hear the words of wisdom from the wildly experienced kitchen maid. "Especially the noblemen. They are the worst. They think they can have whomever they want, and the worst thing is, you can't deny them when they beckon you."

"Of course you can deny them," Mrs. Robbins puffed indignantly. "They are not all monsters who will throw you out on your fanny if you say no."

"Oh, rubbish," Agnes snorted, just as scornful. "Perhaps not Lord Darkwood, but I assure you, there are plenty of men out there who don't care what becomes of you when they finished with their fun. They simply move to the next girl who catches their lusty eyes. And then you stand there alone, with the rest of the servants looking at you as garbage."

Mrs. Robbins huffed and puffed again, but it was clear to them all that the cook agreed with Agnes. A scandal was a scandal, no matter what class you came from, and Wendy felt herself frowning as she took another bite of her sandwich.

If the servants found out about her night with Douglas, she would be devastated. It would be too hard for her to live with them behaving with condescension toward her, knowing all too well already how it felt. She had lived so for twenty years.

"Looking a bit worn today, are we," Mrs. Robbins said in a motherly fashion, changing the subject as she sat down next to Wendy.

"I'm all right." Wendy tried to smile back. "I am only a bit tired today, as I didn't sleep too well."

"You poor girl," Mrs. Robbins cooed with

compassion. "You aren't coming down with something, are you?"

Wendy patted the older woman's hand, shaking her head, and Mrs. Robbins let the subject go. "Well, I guess we all have our better or worse nights," she admitted with a grimace. "I, for one, can't sleep very well knowing Quentin is out there lurking around the kitchen. You know what the kitchen looked like after he had done his so-called cooking in here. If I ever find that man anywhere near my utensils, I can't be responsible for my actions."

Agnes rolled her eyes behind the cook's back, making a lovesick face, and Wendy had to bite her lower lip hard to keep from giggling.

Mrs. Robbins, who hadn't noticed the girls' exchanged look, poured herself a large cup of tea, and Wendy felt her heart beat faster with giddy expectations—it seemed to be time for a trip down memory lane. The cook loved to tell tales of old days' glory, and she couldn't have a better listener than Wendy, who couldn't hear too much about how life had been at Darkwood Manor when Douglas was a little boy. Without realizing it, the cook told Wendy all about how Douglas's life used to be, and what kind of person he had been back then.

"There was not another boy in the whole county who was as dear as Master Douglas," Mrs. Robbins said with a loving smile. "He did his share of pranks, of course, but so have all the little boys I have known, and I guess it's just in their nature. A little boy must play pranks, or else he will probably explode with the need of it."

Mrs. Robbins laughed heartily at her own joke, and

Wendy's heart ached with love for the older woman. The cook had taken her under her wing and kept her feeling close and cared for.

She would have to beg Douglas to not let the servants know about their changed relationship. The mere thought of asking him for anything was like a large stone on her shoulders. She would rather clean the whole house again, by herself, rather than talk to him about feelings.

"Once he took his mother's lovely diamond earrings and gave them to one of the maids, who was suffering because of a heartache. He told the maid that the diamonds would make her eyes sparkle again. He sure had his way with women."

"What did his mother do?" Wendy asked, interested, and the answer came, not from Mrs. Robbins as presumed, but from the doorway behind her.

"She told me that a man only gave the woman he intended to marry jewelry, and then continued by asking me if I intended to marry Nell. I was quite the gentleman in those days, and not wanting to take the earrings back from Nell, I told my mother that I was indeed going to marry her. My mother clapped her hands and told me she was glad to hear about my engagement. Then she ordered a large wedding, to which all the servants were invited, and where I was to be married to Nell."

Mrs. Robbins looked at Douglas with tears in her eyes, cherishing this moment of memories with him. Ever since the servants had returned to the manor, he had been avoiding them as much as possible, just as he had Wendy, treating them politely, but at arm's length.

"Did you marry her?" Wendy asked, intrigued, and

he shook his head with a chuckle.

"No, one of the footmen disagreed, as he was engaged to the pretty Nell and didn't want her to marry anyone else, even if it was just for fun. My mother gave me a comforting hug, and then made me promise never to give jewelry away again."

"It was such a wonderful party," Mrs. Robbins sighed, before standing up and bestowing Douglas that special smile she saved for him and him alone. "Is there anything you need, Master Douglas?"

"I wouldn't mind some breakfast brought to my study," Douglas said, sending Wendy a look which unmistakable told her to be the one bringing the meal to him.

"I will have someone come with a tray for you. Now, off you go and let us do our jobs," Mrs. Robbins encouraged, pushing him softly toward the door. "You go to your study now, and let us take care of our chores."

"I can take it," Wendy offered, when the tray was finished, and the stressed cook gave her a grateful smile as she passed.

"Oh, thank you, dear girl. You are such an angel."

If the cook only knew, Wendy thought, walking down the hallway. There was nothing angelic about her person anymore. Now she was a used woman, a fallen woman. And the worst thing was, she could hardly stop herself from running to the study, ready to throw herself into Douglas's arms and relive the amazing passion of last night.

But she had to harden herself. She had to talk to him about her need of secrecy as soon as possible, before he said or did something which would tell the servants the truth. However, the lord of the manor had other plans, and as soon as the door closed behind her, he relieved her of the tray and grabbed her hand. As he dragged her into his arms, all thoughts of the other servants were lost. Repeatedly, his lips slanted over hers, and she threw her arms around his neck to come even closer to him. Grunting with satisfaction, Douglas opened his trousers with one hand while still pressing his mouth against hers, before carrying her across the room to the desk, where he set her down.

She moaned with disappointment as he ended the kiss, and tried to lean forward to continue with the kissing. With a low, manly chuckle he slowly pulled her skirt up over her legs, caressing her soft skin as it became visible.

Wendy couldn't look away from the heat in his eyes—it overwhelmed her. Eager to play this game with him, she let go of his neck, helping him with his task until both her legs were bare in front of him. Silently he pushed her legs apart and she forgot to breath as he took a step closer, slipping his hands under her buttocks. She felt the hardness of him throb against her, and she couldn't stop a sound of excitement as it escaped her throat.

With a groan, he lifted her slightly so he could thrust deep inside her. The feeling of him was magic, and she pressed her face against his chest in an effort to muffle the moans of pleasure escaping her. Harder and harder he pushed until he had lifted her to heights she hadn't known existed.

Caught into the passion he created between them, she leaned her head back and screamed as her whole body climaxed together with his.

For what felt like eons of time, neither of them moved.

In the end, it was Douglas who, with a rueful sigh, let go of her and took a step back. Without acknowledging her, he straightened his clothes with a thoughtful frown marring his forehead. Sitting down in the chair at the desk, he poured himself a cup of tea and grabbed a stack of papers, which he began to search through. The man was clearly dismissing her mentally, and not being the least bit subtle about it.

Awkwardly, she stood and let her skirt down, straightening it with trembling hands. She didn't know how to act toward him after what they had done, and if it hadn't been for her urgent need to talk to him, she would have left immediately. Silently, she waited for him to acknowledge her, with her hands clasped in front of her. When he realized she wasn't leaving, he waved his hand dismissively toward the door.

"You can leave now."

Gone was the passionate lover. Instead, he looked just as forbidding as he had when she'd first arrived at the manor. With an angry frown, he glared at her from the other side of the desk, threatening her with his eyes, but to her surprise she found he didn't scare her anymore. She, the most frightened person in England, was no longer afraid of him. But she was irritated.

"I have to talk to you," she said, ignoring the blunt order.

He arched an eyebrow in surprise. "You do?"

"Yes, my lord."

"About what?"

She took a deep breath to calm herself down. "About what has happened between us."

"That is nothing to talk about," he cut off, turning his gaze back to the papers in front of him.

"How can you say that there is nothing to talk about?" she objected angrily. "How can you dismiss what we did only minutes ago?"

"Oh, for goodness' sake, Wendy!" He sighed in frustration. "I don't dismiss the lovemaking. I am dismissing you, because I really need to concentrate. Could you please leave, so I can have some peace and quiet?"

Silently, Wendy watched him continue with his work, mentally erasing her from the room. How could he so easily pretend she wasn't there? Completely engrossed, he was searching through the stacks of paper, muttering as he tried to find the right sheet.

Was this how the rest of her life would be?

Would he use her when he felt so inclined, only to turn his back on her as soon as he was done, and continue with his life, while she stood alone, staring at him with empty hands? He had made it very clear he was not inclined to marry. And even if he did change his mind, she would not be on his list of presumptive brides.

The worst was that she had only herself to blame.

She had not been brought up to throw away her future just because the man of her dreams opened his arms for her. It was as if he had put a spell on her when she first arrived at Darkwood Manor, forcing her to forget what was important. And as a consequence thereof, she had without hesitation fallen into Douglas's waiting arms, sending all etiquette rules into oblivion.

She had been devastated by her parents' betrayal and had not had the opportunity to rebuild her self-confidence before she met Douglas that first night. Beautiful, mysterious, and obnoxiously overwhelming Douglas, with his scars and broken heart. The beast who nursed his hatred and wounded soul, but who was the kindest, most lovable man she'd ever met, although he quite deftly hid the last part.

Had she not known him before the accident, when he was a very different person, she would probably not have looked at him twice. Not because of the scars, but because of his malicious behavior and his objectionable habit of threatening her. But she had known him through Annabelle, and even worse—she had idolized him. She had been such an easy target, and unfortunately a target without regret.

Her only fear now was that, despite his claim to the contrary, he would marry. If he expected her to live here, under the same roof as he and his wife, she would need to leave. She would rather marry the meanest and ugliest man on earth than be forced to stay and watch Douglas live happily with a family of his own.

He had vowed never to marry, but she knew that one day he would want more in life. One day he was going to be able to let his scars go, and when that day arrived, she would leave. To stay and watch him lose interest in her because he had found someone else to open his heart for—that would be self-torture.

It amazed her that he found his scars so horrifying. It was easy to tell, as he was always turning away the scarred side of his face from whomever he was talking to, and it made her cry when she saw how insecure and vulnerable he was. She had a sinking feeling that nothing she could say would make him understand how insignificant those scars were. He clearly lived under the impression that he looked the same as he had soon after the accident, ten years earlier.

For being an intelligent man, he was rather stupid, she thought with a slow smile, just as Douglas happened to look up.

"Why are you laughing at me?" He frowned.

"I'm not laughing at you."

"I saw you standing there, snickering."

Lord, how self-centered was he? She rolled her eyes, and turned her back to him, deciding it was probably better to talk with him later. She needed to have his full attention, so she could make him understand that secrecy was a necessity.

He was amazingly fast for being such a large man, she thought, as she bumped into him. The man must have flown past her. Looking up at him, she could tell he was not pleased with her, and a very small part of her applauded it. She wasn't so easy for him to handle after all.

"Why are you leaving?"

"You told me to."

"I did not," he bit out, towering over her with his hands on his hips.

With an indulgent sigh, she patted him on his arm in an attempt to make him move to the side, and let her pass. But the man had to be created out of a large chunk of marble; he didn't budge an inch.

"Yes, you did," she scoffed, impatiently, "and quite rudely too."

"No."

Lord, how he made her blood boil. It was a miracle she hadn't set herself on fire yet, with all this frustrated anger flaming through her.

"Yes, you did," she repeated, between her teeth. "Could you please let me pass?"

"No."

"No?"

Leaning closer to her, until their noses almost touched, he stared at her, sternly. "No."

This was going nowhere. The man was as fickle as a summer breeze. She decided to change her plan of attack, and awarded him her sunniest smile to confuse him. But to no avail, the beast simply smiled back, and she found herself sighing again, as the smile transformed him from handsome to utterly magnificent.

Lord, he was such a splendid-looking man.

The wrinkles in the corners of his eyes deepened, and the smile changed from artificial to cordial, which immediately made her heart skip a beat. Lifting his hand, he put it gently against her cheek, and she savored the feeling of his warmth against her soft skin. The tenderness of his smile made her whole chest ache, and she knew she was lost.

"I never told you to leave, I simply dismissed you."

"Most people would say that those two things are the same."

"But I'm not most people."

Breathless, she gazed up at him. "No, you are not."

"Do you mind?"

Unable to speak, she shook her head, and with a slow smile he kissed the tip of her nose, tenderly. She couldn't remember anyone touching her so lovingly before, and the thought hurt. She had spent most of her life trying her best to make herself irreplaceable, and yet Douglas, who wasn't the least in love with her, showed her more tenderness than her parents ever had.

"But I am like most people," she whispered. "And I want you to promise me one thing."

"Anything," he breathed, his lips placing small kisses all over her face, wherever he could reach.

"Please don't touch me in front of others. I don't want them to know."

The gentle smile was replaced with a frown as he took a step back, releasing her. "Excuse me?"

"You say that I am here to stay, and if that is the truth, then I have only one request. Please, don't take away the respect the other servants show me. That would be unbearable."

"You find me unbearable?" he asked, hoarsely.

There he went again, making it all about himself.

"That is not what I said. I was merely asking you to…"

"Enough," he cut her off. "Just leave."

"Douglas…"

"That's 'my lord,' to you," he sneered as he barged over to the door and opened it for her. "Get out."

She closed her eyes and tried to swallow down the anger rising inside her. Why was it so hard for him to think about someone else, to not always focus upon himself? "Not until you have listened to me."

"Oh, sweet Lord, save me from stupid women. What in the short phrase 'get out' did you not understand?"

Oh? Now she was stupid?

His eyes narrowed. "Are you snorting at me?"

"Of course not," she said with a sweet smile. "I am too stupid to understand when I am being insulted."

"What are you talking about now?" he asked angrily, and she rolled her eyes toward him, without saying a word. Instead she made a big fuss about walking around him to the open door. In the doorway, she turned and looked back at him where he stood staring at her, bewildered and disgruntled.

"I will be in my room, when you feel you are ready to apologize to me," she said haughtily, and then she closed the door hard behind her.

Pausing for a moment, she eagerly waited for him to react, to chase after her, demanding an explanation. But not a single noise was heard from inside the study, and all the hot air went out of her with a pouf.

What had she done?

Why had she let her anger win over her better judgment? She knew from experience that one never won anything with anger and insults, something Douglas himself had shown her from her first day here at Darkwood Manor. Had she in her anger pushed him even farther away from her? Had he even understood the meaning of what she'd just asked him to do?

Sighing deeply with distress, she went back down to the kitchen.

What had she done?

Chapter Ten

Douglas glared at the closed door while pouring himself a large glass of brandy. Women, he thought with uttermost disdain, were impossible at intelligent conversation. What had she not understood? It was she who had disturbed him, and then, from out of nowhere, she had turned it into his fault.

And then she'd had the nerve to ask…no…to demand an apology?

Walking over to the window, he looked out without really seeing the scenery. No other woman had confused him like Wendy did. That daft woman didn't play by ordinary rules. She made up her own, and then became upset with him for not following them.

But how could he? He had not a clue what it was she wanted from him. Although…she had been quite forward about what it was that she wanted this time, and that was an apology.

The question was…for what?

Did she want him to be sorry for making love to her? If so, she could forget it. Making love to Wendy had been surprisingly fulfilling, and every time he lost himself inside her, he had wanted her even more. He knew he was behaving like a young man who'd just had his first woman, but he couldn't help it. It was different with Wendy, but not in a bad way. He knew it sounded silly, but somehow it had felt like coming home. He wanted to climb into her bed and stay there with her forever.

Her innocent response to him was honest and fresh, and the knowledge that he was the first to enjoy her curves was extremely satisfying. His hands rejoiced when touching her, and her body was a perfect match against his.

When had it changed? When had she stopped being a vessel for his revenge and instead turned into a necessity to him? He hadn't known her for such a long time, only a mere month or so, and already he couldn't imagine life without her.

Bloody hell, who was he lying for? The truth was that he felt nauseous just thinking of her leaving him. Tasting her sweet body had made it even more difficult for him to keep her as far away as possible emotionally. If she would ask him to release her, he would have to let her go. Whatever he had said to her father, and whatever his plans had once been, it all had changed when he got to know her.

When he had started to care.

This past month, life had turned into something wonderful. With all the servants back in place, Darkwood Manor had once again become the embracing home he had grown up in. Under Wendy's careful hands, the house had awakened, and he could never thank her enough.

Not that she had done so much by herself. As soon as the servants had returned, they had lifted all chores from her, treating her as if she were the mistress of the house, not a lowly companion. Not that the wench appreciated the respect they bestowed upon her; it was almost as if she felt useless and slighted.

At first, he had wondered why she seemed to take it so hard, as most other young ladies didn't want to clean and cook by themselves, but then the truth hit him. The Russells had probably never had any servants since her childhood, as money was something Sir Edward couldn't hold on to. As Wendy wasn't against making an effort, he could only assume she had been used as a servant, and the thought saddened him.

He had already felt disgust over how easily her parents had set her aside, but to her it must have been their normal behavior. How quickly her childhood must have disappeared, he thought with a heavy sigh. She had probably been caught between being an unloved daughter and an unappreciated servant.

And just as her situation was about to change, when she finally would have had her season, he had shown up. He, with his ego, had put her in an even worse situation. Without remorse, he had used her as a pawn in his revenge, ignoring her innocence. It wasn't Wendy's fault that her sister was a selfish, calculating, stone-cold witch.

He had not thought twice about Wendy or her feelings about the matter when he dragged her from her home, the unloved yet respectable daughter, and turned her into his whore, with no regard about her future. About her life. She would never be able to live anywhere else, not without being another man's personal toy.

Suddenly, after pondering the subject off and on all day, he remembered what she had said about the servants, and keeping their new relationship from them, and a slow smile grew upon his face. At last he realized what she had been asking him earlier.

She wasn't rejecting him. No, she had only asked him to not cause the other servants to resent her. Relief, like none he'd ever felt before, flooded through him, and with a light smile he walked up to Wendy's bedroom, ready to beg the little wench for forgiveness. If he was lucky, she would withstand him for a while, and he would have to kiss her into forgiving him.

Without knocking, he opened the door to her bedroom, only to find it almost completely dark, the heavy curtains covering the windows effectively keeping the bright daylight away. The only source of light came from a small candle on the nightstand, but it was enough for him to find her in the bed, hidden under the bedspread.

Standing at the side of the bed, he looked down at her. She lay on her side, her pretty face resting in the palm of her hand, sleeping soundly. Tenderly he lifted a tendril of hair lying across her cheek and placed it on the pillow, next to her thick braid. She wasn't as astoundingly beautiful as Annabelle, who'd had crowds gaping when she walked into a ballroom, but to him Wendy was the winner when comparing the two of them. He found her ten times more beautiful than her sister, and with the warmth of her generous heart shining through, the most magnificent woman he'd ever seen.

Without waking her, he snuck into the bed, curling up behind her. He put his arms around her, gently pulling her sleeping body closer to his. Again an overwhelming feeling of contentment swept over him, and he knew she was becoming more important to him by the minute.

How would he ever be able to let her go?

He knew that, despite all his selfishness, he couldn't force her to stay with him for the rest of her life. She was worth so much more than this. With her caring heart, she would be a loving wife, and a wonderful mother.

The only thing he didn't like with that picture was that it wasn't going to be his ring on her finger, and those children wouldn't be his. Someone else would be the one who could sneak up on her like this, and someone else would see his features mixed together with hers in a small child.

The pain in his heart was horrible at the mere thought of Wendy with another man, and he closed his eyes. Somewhere, deep inside, a wish to be the one who would marry her and share the rest of his life with her started to sing, but he knew it was something that wouldn't happen.

He could never marry Wendy because he couldn't marry anyone.

No woman would marry a man who looked like him. With his nose in the crook of Wendy's neck, he fell asleep.

****

"You need some new clothes."

Wendy smiled at Mrs. Robbins, shaking her head. "I really don't. My wardrobe is perfect for a companion."

Mrs. Robbins frowned at her. "You have two dresses, child. Whereas one is your Sunday best, the other even a homeless old woman wouldn't want. You are young and beautiful. You should be dazzling us with your lovely clothes instead of hiding behind those ugly things."

"But Mrs. Robbins, you keep forgetting I am just a companion, and I don't need lovely clothes. What I need is practical clothes, easy to wash, that will look just as good although washed frequently."

"Humbug!" Mrs. Robbins spat, and the other servants, who had been listening covertly to their conversation, scurried away in every direction. They all knew the cook well enough to avoid her when her dark temper began to arise.

She was the sweetest, dearest person most of the time, embracing everyone with all the love her huge heart could manage. But now and again she would have a fit of outrage, and all one could do then was to hope you weren't the one she found upsetting.

Looking around the now empty kitchen, Mrs. Robbins chuckled as though deeply satisfied, and a sense of dread rose in Wendy's heart. The cook had clearly wanted privacy, and now, without any warning, Wendy found herself pierced by Mrs. Robbins' blue eyes, and she swallowed hard.

"So," Mrs. Robbins said, curtly, "it's just me and you then."

Wendy nodded, sending a longing look toward the kitchen door.

"First, I just want to make something very clear to you, Miss Wendy. I have known his lordship since the day he was born. Except these last years since the accident, I have been at his side all his life, and I think it gives me the right to now and then say whatever is on my mind. Furthermore, in my opinion, it gives me the right to ask the questions no one else among the servants can, or want to, ask."

With a sinking feeling, Wendy knew there was no

escape. Her respect for the dear cook was deep, and as she couldn't find it in her heart to simply stand up and leave, she could only make a shivering wish about the questions not being too difficult for her to answer.

"I have a few things I would like to come clean about," Mrs. Robbins continued, while pouring them some more tea. "And I think I would like to start with you enlightening me about what exactly you are doing here."

Accepting a cup with a shaky smile, Wendy tried to find the right words, so that she could answer without telling the whole story. She didn't know whom she was protecting. Except for what had happened between her and Douglas, she had done nothing wrong.

A part of her knew she could tell the cook anything, without being judged for it. Even so, to say it all out loud made it all too real, and deep inside her, she still nurtured a silly hope that it was all simply a bad dream. The little girl inside still wished she would wake up in her parents' house and find that she was cared for. Loved.

"I am Miss Lila's companion, a humble servant, just as you," she tried, but Mrs. Robbins just snorted. She didn't believe one word of the thin explanation.

"You are not a servant, Miss Wendy, and even my own son, the footman, who never has been known for his great mind, knows this."

"But I am," Wendy protested, desperately trying to find the right words to persuade the cook. "You are almost correct about me not being a servant, because I was born as a member of the gentry and was also raised as such. Nevertheless, things have changed for me, and now I am here to work as Miss Lila's companion.

Maybe for a year, maybe for two, maybe for more. I don't know. What I do know is that today I am Lord Darkwood's humble servant."

"Both you and I know that Miss Lila has no need for a companion. Besides that dragon of a maid she has, she needs nothing more. You have done nothing for her other than converse with the lady. So my question still stands unanswered. What, my dear child, are you doing here?"

Wendy had to blink a few times to keep the tears from streaming down her cheeks. Mrs. Robbins had found the core of her problem without any trouble, and Wendy didn't know how to answer her.

"I-I don't know, Mrs. Robbins," she finally admitted with a sigh. "I really don't know why he brought me here. He just…did."

"Where are your parents?"

"I-I don't know," Wendy stuttered, her cheeks turning red, and Mrs. Robbins shook her head.

"You, Miss Wendy, are one very bad liar. I guess this means they are not dead?"

"No, they still have their health. At least as far as I know…"

"Are they homeless?"

Wendy shook her head, unable to think one straight thought, still caught in her own befuddled mind. "What? No, we live in a rented house. Or at least they did when I lived with them. I…I don't know where they live…now."

Good Lord. Wendy grasped her hands under the table, away from Mrs. Robbins' see-it-all stare. In her misery, she had been completely absorbed by her own situation, and had not once considered that things must have changed drastically in her parents' lives, too, during this last month or so. It was an awful truth, but she didn't have a clue where they stayed now. Considering the thick envelope Douglas had given them, she could hardly think they had remained in the small, rented house in the wrong part of town where she had spent most of her life.

She didn't even know if her parents still lived in Gloucestershire.

"Is your home in Lydney?"

"Gloucester."

Mrs. Robbins frowned at her. "Gloucester? Why would Master Douglas go and find a companion for Miss Lila all the way over in Gloucester?"

"I don't know."

"Yes, you do. You are blushing."

Wendy felt her cheeks grow even redder and decided against denying. It had been too obvious a lie anyway.

"Where were you born?"

"In Lydney."

"Aha." Mrs. Robbins looked like a cat that had just caught a mouse. "Finally, a real answer. But then again, it doesn't say much. Because if you had lived in Lydney, I would have known you, and honestly, I don't recognize you at all, Miss Wendy. Lydney is the closest town for us here at Darkwood Manor, and where we go for all supplies. Lydney is not that big. I would have known you."

"We moved to Gloucester when I was a little girl," Wendy said, hoping this truth didn't reveal too much. Gloucester was a big town, not as huge as London, but large enough for its residents to stay estranged. When

Douglas had collected all his servants again, he had just introduced her as Miss Wendy, Miss Lila's companion, and never mentioned her family name.

"Ah," Mrs. Roberts let out, her probing gaze not leaving Wendy's fiercely red face. "Well, that explains why I don't know you."

Wendy didn't have time to exhale, relieved, before the cook continued.

"Although I would still have known you when you lived in Lydney. I have always loved children and have made sure to know the names and faces of most children during my years. I don't think I would have missed you if you were in Lydney as you claim..."

"Perhaps we never met?" Wendy tried. "I can't say I remember you, Mrs. Robbins, but I was only ten years old when we left for Gloucester, and I didn't meet that many people when we lived here."

Mrs. Robbins froze on the other side of the table. "Ten years old, you say?"

"Yes."

For the longest time, the cook stared at the squirming Wendy with unreadable eyes, until she thought she couldn't take it any longer without running screaming throughout the house. Just as Wendy thought she would fall into a pile of nervous pieces, the cook stood up.

"If you'll excuse me, child, I just remembered I have something I must do. Let us finish our tea another time, shall we?"

Unable to believe her luck, Wendy nodded, not trusting her voice. Without another word, the cook left the kitchen, and Wendy sank back into the chair. Good Lord, that had been a close call. If the cook hadn't stopped, Wendy would have spilled it all out, without exceptions.

Grateful for the unexpected blessing, she grabbed a scone and hurried toward the gardens, knowing she didn't want to be anywhere around the cook when she returned.

****

The door to the study burst open just as Douglas was about to finish an extremely long calculation, effectively ruining his fourth attempt to come to the correct amount. Angry over the rude interruption, he looked up only to find Mrs. Robbins standing on the other side of his desk, looking more like an avenging amazon than a plump country house cook.

"I need to speak with you, Master Douglas," the cook informed, sternly.

"Mrs. Robbins, you are disturbing me. Please remove your person from the study."

The cook didn't respond to his harsh demand. Instead, she crossed her arms over her ample chest, pinning him with hard eyes.

"Who is Wendy?"

The question took him by surprise. "W-what?"

With a disrespectful snort, the cook lifted her chin, looking down her potato-shaped nose at him. "You heard me."

It was a look Douglas had seen many times before, especially when he was a curious little boy who constantly upset the cook with his mischiefs. He knew he should fire the cook for her offensive behavior, but he couldn't. When she and the rest of the servants had returned, he realized how much he'd missed them. They were his only connection to his childhood now that his family was gone. And therefore he bit back his anger and clenched his jaws in a threatening manner but was otherwise silent.

The cook wasn't affected at all by his weak attempt to intimidate her. She lifted her expressive eyebrows, seeming almost amused by his anger.

"Mrs. Robbins, please. This is not your business."

"As long as the wench is a part of my staff, it is my business."

Her staff? By God, if he hadn't been this annoyed with her he would have laughed out loud. But he let the comment slip by. "She is not your concern. To you she is Miss Lila's companion. Who she is and where she is from is not your concern. Please leave Wendy alone. She doesn't need a nosy cook prying into her life."

"One doesn't need to be nosy to understand that the girl is not what she pretends to be. I know many young women from the upper classes have been forced to become companions and governesses due to their parents' empty wallets or other dire circumstances, but that is not why I am asking you, Master Douglas, about who Wendy is. You see, my lord, I think I know exactly who the little gem is, and if I am right, I think you'd better run as fast as you can out of here before I can lay my hands on your behind."

Douglas gaped dumbfounded at the cook, and to his own surprise he felt a prick of fear. "You don't understand—"

She cut him off. "No, I certainly do not. What has that little sweetheart ever done to you? She is not the one who ran from here screaming her head off. She is a sweet, dear girl who has nothing to do with what happened ten years ago."

Douglas sighed and put his head in his hands. "I know," he whispered.

"So why? Why destroy this sweet young girl's life? Treat her like a servant, eh? Does it make you feel better?"

"No."

"Then why?"

"An eye for an eye."

Mrs. Robbins snorted, shaking her head in disbelief. Douglas didn't know what to say. All his arguments about why he needed his revenge and why he should use Wendy for it were already long gone. They had disappeared when he got to know the chit better. If he couldn't convince himself anymore, how would he ever be able to convince Mrs. Robbins?

"You have completely destroyed her life, bringing her here. I have seen how you look at her, and that girl's virtue is long gone. Oh, don't you even try to deny it. Wendy will never be able to live a life amongst her peers again. She will have to spend the rest of her days being spit at, and all because of your wrongdoing."

"Darkwood Manor will always be her home…"

Mrs. Robbins took a step back, with a silencing hand against him. "Damn you, Master Douglas. Damn you!"

With more contempt in her final glance than he had ever met before, Mrs. Robbins left the study, leaving Douglas feeling just as crushed as he had ten years earlier, when Annabelle had left him.

He stared at the closed door, listening to the footsteps stomping off. He had known this time would come, the time when he would have to decide about

Wendy and her…their…future. But like an ostrich, he had hidden his head in the sand, mentally holding the need of a plan as far away from the surface as possible.

The time had come to decide what to do about Wendy.

Should he marry her?

Ignoring the little prick of happiness at the mere thought of tying the knot with her, he instead began to think about sending her away. She would make an excellent governess, with her caring heart and soft approach. She would make some children very happy.

However, would the children make her happy?

For a while maybe, but sooner or later they would grow up, and then she would no longer be of use to the family. Where would she go then? To another family, who would keep her only until she was of no more use to them?

Was this how he wanted her to live her life? Always looking at others' happiness and not being able to have some of her own?

But what other options did he have?

Finding her a husband, one who wouldn't mind that she wasn't a virgin anymore, was a possibility, but it wasn't one he would choose. He'd already concluded that last night.

The only thing to do was to marry her, but there was one rather large problem with that solution.

How could he make his beauty marry a beast?

Chapter Eleven

Kneeling in the dirt of the herb garden, Wendy pulled the weeds out with such harshness the poor plants probably would have screamed if they'd been able. Something was going on with Douglas, and Wendy had not a clue what. He had behaved in the strangest way the last couple of weeks, and she didn't know what to think about it.

It had begun very quietly, and at first she didn't notice the change, even though he surprised her when he told her to get ready to go for a drive. She was so excited, as she hadn't been outside the manor's premises since she first arrived, and she rushed to get ready.

Unable to sit still out of excitement, she climbed into the carriage and bounced up and down on the seat next to Douglas as Quentin drove them through the forest. Laughing, Douglas dragged her into his lap and kissed her silly until the carriage came to a rocking stop. Quentin opened the small door for them, and they climbed out.

To Wendy's surprise, they had arrived in Coleford instead of Lydney, which suited her just fine. She didn't know anyone in Coleford, and wouldn't be recognized while traveling alone with a man. It was dusk when they arrived, and as the carriage was unmarked and Douglas hid his face in the hood of his cloak, no one recognized him. They were strangers in a strange town, and it felt oddly comfortable.

Douglas told her to go with Quentin, as he had some business to take care of, and obediently, Wendy followed the old man, who took her to the local seamstress. The sour-faced woman read the note the old man gave her, and turned into pure sunshine. She was to make Wendy a new wardrobe, and there was no limit to the costs. It wasn't long before Madame Coux realized the young customer had no knowledge of fabrics nor fashion. Ignoring Wendy completely, she started to mumble instructions to her assistants,.

Wendy didn't mind. In fact, it gave her ample time to ponder why Douglas insisted on hiding his face. There was nothing wrong with his face, so why continue with this silly charade, pretending to be hideous? Someone who had never met him before and didn't know his background wouldn't even see the thin scars.

When the fitting was done, Madame Coux told her to return in a week's time to try on the half-finished clothes. Relieved to leave the stuffy air of the seamstress shop, Wendy then followed Quentin to the Flying Rascal, the local inn, where Douglas awaited her in the darkest corner.

"You really didn't have to," she started, as she sat down on the bench next to him, but he dismissed her with a shake of his hand.

"It is nothing. Mrs. Robbins was rightfully upset over how tiny your wardrobe is, and she asked me to have you some new clothes made."

"Some new?" Wendy said, hoarsely. "B-but Madame Coux has plans for more than some! I should go back to her and…"

Douglas grabbed her arm just as she started to stand, and drew her to sit back down. "Madame Coux only did what I told her to in the note Quentin gave her. You have nothing to worry about."

"Are you sure? It sounded expensive."

"Well, it better be expensive." Douglas laughed, and Wendy decided to drop the subject, because it made her feel both excited and ashamed, and it was an odd mixture of feelings.

She smiled at the waitress who came to their table with a large tray filled with delicious-smelling treats. The food tasted just as good as it smelled, and they ate silently until Wendy leaned back, patting her belly. "I couldn't fit in one more bite, even if I tried," she purred with a satisfied smile, and Douglas chuckled in response.

"You are so beautiful," he whispered, leaning closer to her.

"I'm not beautiful," she said, quietly losing her smile.

"Yes, you are."

She shook her head over his stubbornness, but decided against arguing with him. If he found her attractive, so be it. She was woman enough to appreciate it, even if it was just a lie. What could be better than to hear the man you probably almost loved tell you that he found you beautiful?

"Are you often in Coleford?" she changed the subject to more comfortable grounds.

"No, I come here only once a year maybe. I prefer going to Bristol or Gloucester."

Big cities where you can hide in the masses, she

thought, and again wondered why he hid himself when there was no reason to. But still lacking the courage to ask him why, she didn't seek an answer. She liked this lighthearted Douglas, who seemed determined to make an effort for her to enjoy this unexpected trip.

"Why not Lydney? It is closer, after all."

He gave her an unreadable, slow smile that made her a little squirmy. He was such a difficult man to read sometimes, and it made her nervous when she couldn't. It was at those occasions one never knew what he would say or do.

"I only do errands once a month, and as Mrs. Peabody lives in Gloucester, it felt a better use of my time to do all my tasks in one trip."

Of course he would bring up his mistress. That awful Mrs. Peabody, who wanted most desperately to marry him. When first meeting Mrs. Peabody, she had not become jealous when she was told that the woman was his mistress. She hadn't cared about the other woman at all until Douglas introduced her to what a mistress did, and then she could hardly think about her without wanting to kill her.

The mere thought of him making the same sweet love to Mrs. Peabody as he did to her was tortuous. And what was even worse was the feeling that he knew about it, because he looked very smug as he sat on the other side of the table.

The toad.

"How organized of you," she said between her teeth, and he chuckled softly, placing his large warm hand upon hers where it rested on the table.

Jealous anger took over, and before she could stop herself she pulled her hand from his, putting it on her knee, out of his reach. Immediately, all the warmth in his eyes disappeared, and they turned dark and cold.

"Don't like my touch, do you?"

"This is a public place," she snapped, feeling smaller by the second. Why had she removed her hand? He obviously withdrew himself from her after her open cut.

"Too ashamed to admit to anyone about cuddling with a beast like me, are you?" he ground out between his teeth.

"Stop it," she hissed back, too aware of the curious gazes looking their way, but he only snorted at her.

"Why don't you just admit how ashamed you are of me, so we can leave?"

She gasped, unable to believe what he'd just said. So she was supposed to feel ashamed of him, was she? Why did everything end in his belief about being the ugliest man on earth?

He put some coins on the table, preparing to leave and effectively ending their meal together. Without thinking about the consequences of her actions, she moved over to his side of the table, in one swift movement placing herself in his lap. Putting her arms around his neck, she passionately kissed his full lips with all the anger and excitement roaring through her.

At first it was as if she were kissing a statue. Then he softened, lifting his arms to put them around her, pressing her body closer to his. The crowd in the inn howled with laughter, demanding they get a room, but Wendy didn't care. Lost in the wonderful kiss, she felt warm all over.

It wasn't until the innkeeper came and asked them to leave that the kiss ended. But that was only a temporary ending. As soon as the door to the carriage closed behind them, they continued, only it didn't end with kissing.

Douglas threw a blanket on the floor of the rocking carriage, and soon they were lustfully exploring each other while the carriage slowly brought them home.

That had only been the beginning.

Douglas had changed toward her since she kissed him at the inn. It was as if some secret wall had been brought down. As if her public display of her feelings had made him believe they were real.

Even the servants seemed to feel the change between them, and she was now treated as the mistress of the manor. Thinking about it, she guessed she was, in every way she could be without being married to the master. Sometimes she let herself get lost in a wonderful fantasy in which they were married, happily so. Living in the secluded world that Darkwood Manor was, she could easily hold on to the dream for days, until something happened or someone said something that took her down to earth again.

She wasn't the lady of the manor and the wife of Lord Darkwood. She was Wendolyne Russell, the servant and mistress of his lordship. Nothing would change the awkward situation, as Douglas would never marry her. He had made it clear too many times before that he wasn't in this for marriage.

It was a thorn in her side, knowing she was his possession in every way except the most important, but there was nothing she could do about it. The only thing she could hope for was that he wouldn't find someone else to marry, because such a situation would be horrible. Living under the same roof as the man she loved, watching him and his wife thread through life together, would be like walking through purgatory.

Douglas seemed satisfied with their relationship as it was, not contemplating any changes, and so she decided to restrain her own wishes. As long as he was pleased with her, he was her man. She would be lost if he became bored with her and searched elsewhere for company.

So she laughed and kissed, and made love with him whenever and wherever he wanted. They had made love in so many places that she blushed just thinking about it. What if they had been caught? Luckily for her, Douglas had been more than cautious, making sure there wasn't the slightest risk they would be caught in the act.

She had been so happy these last weeks, and she was terrified something would happen to change everything. It was a good thing Darkwood Manor was quite secluded, and that no one ever came by, not even by mistake, and they barely left the house at all.

She had been back to Coleford to visit Madame Coux, who had her try on dozens of half-finished dresses, promising to send the new wardrobe to Darkwood Manor as soon as they were done. This time Douglas had driven himself, and he had brought a picnic basket, which they had emptied, sitting in the grass, soaking the sun. For the first time, they made love outside, and the feeling of the hot sun against her skin was remarkable, but the feeling of Douglas was so much better.

He had started to whisper things to her, as he slowly moved inside her, inaudible little things, which drove her wild during the act, and crazy with curiosity afterward, as she didn't know what he had said. She had told him once that she couldn't hear him, and he had given her his most wicked grin and kissed the bridge of her nose without answering, and she had not had the nerve to ask him again.

When the coffers with her new wardrobe arrived, Douglas insisted she wear a new dress every day. He even made her change from morning dress to promenade dress, and then to evening dress. He had mentioned hiring a maid to take care of her, someone who could help her put on the beautiful dresses, but she refused, solemnly. She didn't want someone to come and see things for what they really were, and thus destroy the fragile bubble they had created for themselves.

Instead she got one of the scullery maids to help her with the buttoning, and took care of the rest by herself. Douglas shook his head against what he thought stupidity, but thankfully enough he didn't persist.

Maybe he too understood how fragile their life was.

After a while, she noticed that he stopped hiding his face to her, and after a few weeks it was easy to see that he didn't think twice about it anymore. It made her immensely glad, because it told her how safe he felt with her. It gave her hope that one day he would reconcile with his scars and finally realize of how small importance they were. But she didn't mention it to him, and he never said a word about it.

She spent a lot of time in the garden, pruning, and had a lot of help from Quentin and a few of the other servants who liked to work outdoors. Slowly they started to wake up the sleeping manor's exterior, and when summer finally arrived, the garden was filled with beautiful flowers in every size and color imaginable.

At midsummer, the manor looked just as good as ever, so when Annabelle Scott climbed out of her carriage, she thought she had travelled ten years back in time, to when she still was engaged to Douglas and her life had been light and easy.

The only thing different was that she hadn't come for Douglas.

This time she had come for her sister.

Chapter Twelve

Wendy sat silently, sipping on her delicious cup of tea, listening to her sister chatting away about the social life of Gloucester. Annabelle especially lingered over discussion of her admirers, what clothes she had bought recently, how many invitations she got every week, and how she had been named The Queen of Beauty for the last ten years in a row.

Wendy had never thought of Annabelle as self-centered and egotistical before. Not until now. As she sat there, staring at her gloating sister, who was telling a most colorful tale of two beaus almost dueling over the last spot on her dance card, she was amazed at how selfish Annabelle really was. It wasn't that she didn't care about Annabelle and her life, because Wendy had always loved to hear her elder sister's stories of her social life.

But…Annabelle might at least have mentioned Wendy's current situation before throwing herself into an endless monologue about her own life.

"Lord Hampton even wanted me to leave Tony and marry him instead. Have you ever heard such a thing? If I had been unmarried, I would have accepted immediately, because this specific lord has a very large income. A friend of mine told me he has twenty thousand pounds a year. Twenty thousand! It is such an incredible sum of money. It certainly makes one forget he is such an ugly little man. Do you know he always sweats? Dancing with him is a prelude to a visit to the ladies' restroom, as you really need to freshen up after socializing with him. Thank the Lord my Tony doesn't sweat as much. I would have been too embarrassed if he ever had even the tiniest bit of moisture covering his complexion."

Wendy mumbled something indistinguishable, too aware that her sister didn't listen to what she said anyway. As long as she said something which made it sound as if she listened to every last word, Annabelle would be completely satisfied with the meager response.

The older Russell daughter kept on with her one-sided conversation until a footman came into the room and effectively quieted her.

"Mrs. Scott, your husband asked me to remind you about how fast the night falls here in the deep wood."

Immediately, Wendy stood up, aghast. "Annabelle, you didn't tell me Tony was accompanying you. Please, you must tell him to come inside and at least have a chance to freshen up. And the two of you must be starving, if you have come all the way from Gloucester to visit."

"We didn't come straight from Gloucester," Annabelle said in a rather surly tone, not too pleased with her husband for interfering with her visit. "We have been visiting an old friend of mine, who still resides here with her husband. They are the nicest of friends, even though not too highly ranked. But they did welcome us to their very modest home with open arms."

Wendy knew she was silly, but it was starting to

feel as if her sister were walking all over her. Was she so unimportant to her sister that Annabelle could make a stop to visit some friends instead of driving straight to Darkwood Manor, where her sister now resided as a companion?

Wendy's life had changed drastically in the months since her parents had left her here. It wasn't as if Wendy needed someone to save her, but one could think that Annabelle would come rushing as soon as she heard about it, if only to make sure her younger sister was all right.

The sisters had made lots of plans for the Season, before Wendy was sent to Darkwood. Annabelle had spent the winter going on about all the assemblies they would attend and the shops they would visit. To Wendy, it had sounded like heaven to spend time with her sister, even though it meant she would have to join the social circle. And even though knowing how utterly silly she was, she had hoped and prayed Annabelle felt the same.

But considering how little her sister had missed her during the Season, which had now passed, she could only assume it had all been about Annabelle, as usual, and not an unimportant little sister who was only a means for getting more invitations to more parties.

"Annabelle," Wendy interrupted, "why are you here?"

"To take you home, of course," Annabelle said, her smile sweet as sugar. "You can't stay here as a companion forever. We were supposed to spend the Season together, and now I had to endure it alone, without you. If you only knew how slighted I felt, when there were parties to which I wasn't invited, just because you weren't there as a debutante. If you knew how much I have missed, these last months, all because of your absence, you would beg me for forgiveness."

"But I can't go home, either," Wendy replied, trying hard to hold back her tears. She didn't want to cry in front of her coldhearted sister, who probably would laugh with disdain instead of showing any compassion.

"Of course you can." Annabelle sniffed. "You can always come home to your family."

Really, Wendy thought, could she? Why would her family greet her with love and understanding, after sending her away so selfishly? Could her parents be regretting the rash decision they'd made in their desire for a better and more luxurious life for themselves?

Her heart screamed yes, but her head said no.

There had to be something that would make it lucrative for her parents to bring her home. Otherwise they would never have sent Annabelle here, straight into the lion's den. Furthermore, there had to be something in this for her sister. Otherwise she would never have made the uncomfortable trip willingly.

"Our dear parents have missed you sorely, Wendy, and they just want you to come home to them, to where you belong."

Somehow Annabelle succeeded in making it sound as if it was Wendy who had left, not her parents who had brought her here forcibly to Darkwood Manor.

"It's because of our parents that I am here," Wendy said, hoarsely. "And I can't leave. They accepted a sum for which I was supposed to stay here at least one year. It has only been a few months."

"Of course you can leave," Annabelle scoffed.

"Stop the dilly-dallying and go up to your room and collect your things. We are leaving as soon as possible."

"Why?"

If Wendy hadn't been staring so closely at her sister, she would have missed the flash of something which strongly resembled embarrassment as it flew across Annabelle's beautiful face. The look disappeared as quickly as it had come, and for a moment Wendy thought she'd had it all wrong. It was odd to even consider Annabelle feeling something as human and awkward as shame. That would mean she recognized her own wrongdoings, and that had never happened before, as far as Wendy knew.

Shame was not a feeling Annabelle was used to. Had she changed over the years she'd been married to Tony? Maybe she had finally realized that every action had a reaction, and that she couldn't treat people just any way she felt, not without them turning their backs on her.

A commotion at the door interrupted the moment of tension, and seconds later Anthony Scott rushed into the room, two angry footmen following him closely. With a yelp, her brother-in-law hid behind the sofa where his wife sat, and while trying to hide an amused smile Wendy stood and put herself between the footmen and their prey.

"Giles. Alan. Mr. Scott is a part of both his lordship's and my family, and therefore an appreciated guest here at Darkwood Manor. Please leave and let me catch up with my relatives."

Glaring angrily at Tony over her shoulder, both footmen reluctantly withdrew toward the door, and she knew she would have to apologize to them later for her harshness. She couldn't let them interfere now, even if it meant staying up all night baking every cake those two yearned for.

She desperately needed to hear Annabelle tell her what her parents' new plan was, so she wouldn't be building up hope for something that would never happen.

Straightening his clothes, Tony gave the two footmen a disdainful look before turning toward Wendy and giving her a sweet smile that sent shivers down her spine. She had never liked her sister's choice of husband. The man had a way of looking at her like she was a pudding, all his to eat.

She had always wondered why Annabelle had given such a man her hand in marriage when she could have had her pick amongst the most wanted of the eligible bachelors society had to present. Tony was infamous for being a poor man without connections, and with a gambling habit which had his creditors chasing him down the street.

"Tony," Annabelle snapped, "you were supposed to stay in the carriage and wait for us."

Her husband, who'd just spotted the tray on the table, ignored his wife, instead joining her on the sofa and pouring himself a cup of tea that he sweetened with five full spoons of sugar.

"It was too warm in the carriage," Tony mumbled, filling his mouth with chocolate cake. "And I was getting hungry. You have been inside here for ages, and just the thought of you eating and drinking in here made me almost faint from starvation."

"Tony," Annabelle hissed.

"What?" her husband snarled, spitting breadcrumbs all over the sofa. "Can you please calm down, Belle? So what if my cousin comes? I don't care. We have been avoiding him for ages because of your irrational fear of him, and now I don't care anymore. I'm worth so much more than living in poverty, and it is my right to come here. It's my right to be here!"

Annabelle gasped, outraged. "You must be crazy, Tony, if you think you have any right to this house, because you don't. Douglas is the rightful heir, and you are just the poor cousin who lives on any crumbs you can find. If it weren't for me, you would be crawling in the gutters. Crawling!"

Tony stood up so fast the sofa fell backward with a large crash. The footmen, who still lingered at the door, unanimously took a step forward, but Wendy held up a hand, stopping them. With a nod of her head toward the door, she sent them out into the hallway again, not wanting to interfere in the war between husband and wife.

This was starting to become too interesting, and she didn't want anything to stop the married couple's unusually open argument. That Tony thought he had the right to this house interested her immensely. Even if he was Douglas's cousin and heir, he still had no right to this house as long as Douglas was alive. And should Douglas get married and have children, Tony would fall farther away from the Darkwood wealth with every baby born.

The disdain in Annabelle's blue eyes when she looked upon her husband was saddening. Was this how a married couple of ten years behaved? Wendy didn't think so. If she could marry Douglas, she would be just as much in love with him after twenty or thirty years of marriage as she was at this very moment.

"How dare you," Tony hissed, and Wendy's heart skipped a beat as she recognized the unmasked hatred on his face. "You would be nothing if it weren't for me, nothing. You, who are not of noble blood, only gentry, and without any consequence, are you standing here, in front of me, patronizing me? I'm a Scott of the Darkwood family, and that is nobility, my dear. Not being a mere sir."

"How dare you?" Annabelle shrieked, aghast. "My father was honored by the king for his duty in the war, and he…"

"Duty in the war?" Anthony laughed, sounding more like a madman than a humble peer. "What duty? Did he manage to impress the king with how much he lost while gambling? Your father is a selfish bastard and would never put his life in the line of fire. You can never convince me that he did something to be honored for. I would guess he blackmailed himself into it rather than earned it."

"Why aren't you knighted then? You have gambled away so much money during the years that you should have made yourself worthy of a dukedom by now."

The looks of loathing passing between them were awful to see, and again Wendy wondered why. When they married ten years earlier, they had seemed happy, or at least Tony had. Everyone had seen how madly in love he was with his astoundingly beautiful wife, and even though no one had been able to figure out why she had chosen him, she still had looked satisfied with her choice of husband.

But now all the love was gone, and only harsh

words and hatred were left. It wasn't so strange that Anthony wanted this house. He needed something that would give him the upper hand against his wife.

Thinking about it, Wendy realized he had been very close to having his every wish fulfilled, with Douglas's accident. If Douglas had died, Tony would have inherited everything, including the noble title and vast holdings. And Annabelle would have been the lady of the manor.

Was this the true reason her sister had said yes to Anthony?

As far as Wendy knew, everyone had still thought Douglas was dying when Annabelle accepted Tony's proposal. Maybe she too had assumed her former fiancé only minutes away from death, and by accepting the cousin's proposal, she would still be able to have what would have become hers as Douglas's wife.

If so, the plan had failed when Douglas survived, and instead of becoming the lady of the manor, Annabelle had found herself married to a loser of her father's kind. Wendy almost felt sorry for her sister, but as she didn't know if this was the truth, she decided to harden herself.

"Can I offer you some sandwiches?" Wendy asked, in an attempt to soothe the hurt feelings filling the room, but all she accomplished was putting herself into the midst of the war between the spouses.

"And who do you think you are?" Annabelle snickered. "The lady of the manor, perhaps? You are nothing but a disgrace to your family, living here with him without being married. Do you think you ever will be anything but a servant in his eyes? You are nothing compared to me, and when he couldn't have me, he went for the second best…you."

Wendy hadn't thought her heart could break into more pieces, but the pain in her chest told her it was possible. What had she ever done wrong to cause her family to treat her this way?

"Why are you here?" she whispered. "I can't for my life understand why you would want me to come with you."

Annabelle walked over to her still puffing husband and placed her hand in the crook of his arm as if she needed extra strength. "Because you are my sister."

"But you don't want me. You just admitted you think I'm a disgrace."

"I did not say such a thing. How dare you suggest it?"

This time it was Wendy's turn to snort, which had Annabelle's lips turning into a small sour bud in a very unattractive way, and she looked older and more worn as fine lines appeared around her mouth.

"Well," she drawled, obviously trying to find the right words to convince Wendy otherwise. "You misunderstood me completely."

"How can I misunderstand being a disgrace to my family?"

"There is no use in discussing this any further. You seem inclined to put words in my mouth, woeful words that I'd never say."

"There's nothing more illogical than a woman," Anthony chuckled. "And I'm married to the worst of them."

Annabelle's sweet, convincing smile faltered slightly as she tried to ignore her insulting husband. "Mother is devastated over how things ended between the two of you, and yes, she wants you to know you are always welcome at home to continue with life as if this little…interlude never happened."

Wendy had done nothing wrong. It was her parents who had insisted she come here and be Lila's companion. So why did they want her back now? And then it dawned on her.

"Is the money gone already?"

At that, Annabelle got all flustered, which told Wendy all she needed to know.

"I can't believe this. Are you here to take me home because father lost all the money?"

"Wendy," Anthony whined, in an attempt to sound sincere. "You are the only one who can save us all from being thrown out into the street. The creditors are chasing your father and me because we did a little bet with a friend, which we lost. We too need a home and food on our table. How can we give away the only money we have?"

Wendy didn't know what to say. How could they have lost all that money already? It had been only a few months since they had become debt free and in possession of a large sum to start anew besides. "There is nothing I can do to help," Wendy tried, frustrated. "Our parents left me here at Darkwood Manor to work as a companion to an elderly lady. They made a deal with Douglas about it. At least a year, they said. You can ask Mother. She knows this."

"Wendy, Wendy," Tony scoffed, with an amused snort. "You have been here for a couple of months, and I think Douglas must be pretty tired of your little face by now. If we help him get a new girl to play companion to his aunt, someone much prettier than you,

I am sure he will let you go without regrets."

"What Tony means," Annabelle continued, trying to soothe the effect of her husband's words, "is that you are not the most attractive girl, and you are rather boring to talk to. Even though it is the aunt you are here for, I can only guess Douglas must be fed up with you by this time, and not too hard to persuade to let you go."

"W-what?" Wendy stuttered, not believing her ears. So now she was both boring and unattractive?

Using her moment of confusion, Tony left his wife's side to walk up to her and grab her cold hands in his sweaty ones. "Wendy, there is a way you can help us out of our predicament. Your mother has a friend who knows of a very rich man up in Yorkshire. He wants nothing more than to have someone to share his life with, and as he lives in a very secluded part of England, he needs a wife who is not afraid of leaving her home and her loved ones. According to your mother's friend, he is now in his thirties and desperate for an heir. As he has lots of money, and a nice home, we thought this could be your chance to redeem yourself in the eyes of your family."

As Wendy stared, dumbfounded, at Tony, Annabelle quickly took over from her not-so-diplomatic husband. "This is your chance to regain control of your life, to become a married woman, instead of living here as a mere companion. You would be something more than just a person of no consequence. You would have your own home, and you could have children of your own."

Wendy hated to admit it, but Annabelle struck a chord with her there. She really did want a family of her own, and especially children that were hers to love and cherish.

Sensing Wendy's hesitation, Annabelle increased the pressure. "Think about it, Wendy. Even though Mr. Wetherby isn't the best catch, he still is perfect for a person in your situation. You are turning into a spinster, and as long as you stay here, buried in the deep wood, you will never find a man to settle down with. Marrying Mr. Wetherby would mean that you will have your own family. He seems like a good man, and if you give him a child or two, he will probably be thankful enough to leave you alone. You would be respectable, Wendy, and could be a part of your village's social life. A matriarch."

Wendy looked around the room, trying hard to focus on something other than Annabelle's smooth voice, but it was hard to ignore the longing for a child of her own which filled her heart, her body, and her soul. Closing her eyes, she saw the picture of herself sitting with a small child in her lap. It was an adorable little girl, with her hair and Douglas's eyes...

"You would not only save yourself," Annabelle continued, eagerly, smelling victory. "You would save your whole family."

Closing her eyes, and thus effectively removing her sister's and her brother-in-law's eager faces, she tried to make some sense out of what they were telling her. What did she want to do? Did she want to save her family again?

Was she an ungrateful daughter if she said no? Her heart belonged to Douglas, and even though he didn't want it, or even know about her feelings, she still felt sick at the mere thought of leaving him. The thought of never seeing him again hurt more than the thought of never having a child of her own.

Maybe one day she would regret it, but this day she wanted to stay by his side. Maybe one day Douglas would wake up from his stupor and realize what he had in front of him. Maybe he would find something inside him that could resemble love.

Looking at Annabelle and Anthony, who stood there eagerly waiting for her to promise them she would solve their problems for them, she knew she couldn't do it.

Not for them.

If they'd had even the smallest thought for her feelings in their plans, she might have agreed, but they thought only about themselves and of their own happiness. They had not once thought of her, other than the excuses they offered, and they definitely hadn't been reluctant to sacrifice her for the second time in less than six months.

To them she was just something they could bargain with, so they could save their own future. As soon as she had given them what they wanted, they would never think twice about her again. Douglas had bought her for her father's vast debts and ten thousand pounds, and she couldn't help but wonder how much poor Mr. Wetherby would have to pay to have them deliver her to him.

"How much?" she asked before she could stop herself, and her sister looked at her, not understanding.

"I'm sorry," Anthony said, just as confused. "How much what?"

Wendy took a deep breath before she continued. "How much will Mr. Wetherby have to pay for me?"

"Wendy!" Annabelle cried out. "This is definitely something I don't want to talk to you about. Please don't you think about it anymore. It is of no consequence for you."

"But I want to know how much I'm worth this time."

"Wendy!"

Annabelle looked pointedly at Anthony, silently pushing him to confront her surprisingly obnoxious younger sister, and he cleared his throat to buy some time.

"Well... Ah... Money is not the issue here, my dear. Your future happiness is all that matters."

"My happiness, or yours?"

"Why, yours, of course!"

"How can it be my happiness, if you are paid for it?"

"All you have to care about is saving us all from a fate worse than death," Annabelle sighed, her patience growing thinner by the minute. "Do you want us living in some small, dirty cottage, surviving only on what other people give us out of pity?"

"Of course I don't," Wendy whispered. "But I still want to know. How much will Mr. Wetherby have to pay to get me for his bride?"

"That's it," Annabelle exploded, and grabbed Wendy's arm harshly. "You are coming with me, and I don't want to hear another word about it."

Wendy tried to rip her arm loose, but Annabelle was stronger than she looked and held tight. Tony grabbed Wendy's other arm, and without a word, they dragged her toward the door, not stopping until a voice cut through the silence.

A voice they both had once known very well. "What is going on here?"

Chapter Thirteen

Annabelle froze as she heard the too-familiar voice, and with dread she looked up at the man standing in the doorway, frowning at them. A shriek worked its way through her body from somewhere deep inside until it left her mouth.

It was a ghost from her past come back to haunt her. The ghost of the man to whom she'd once been engaged and who had turned into a beast, forcing her to turn her life into the mess it was today. Gone was the horrifying monster from ten years ago, and instead an older version of the man she'd once loved stood in front of her.

Even though his appearance was a bit disheveled, with dirty clothes and mud covering his boots, he still looked magnificently handsome. When the fright and surprise were gone, only regret was left. Regret over leaving him.

Why had she been so stupid and hurriedly broken off the engagement? If she had waited, she would have realized it hadn't been so bad, and then she would have been married to a real man, a gorgeous man who was rich beyond her imagination, and she would have had anything she wanted.

But instead she had cut off their relationship as fast as she could, and ended up in the hands of Douglas's poor cousin, who had made it his mission to make her as unhappy as possible.

Wendy grasped the moment of surprise and ripped her arms free from her relatives' hands, running across the room to hide behind Douglas. The look they shared when she passed him filled Annabelle with anger and resentment together with one quite unhealthy dose of jealousy. It should have been she who stood there beside Douglas and was bestowed that look of love and contentment, not Wendy.

But it was too late for her. Ten years too late.

****

Hatred riveted through Anthony's body until he hardly could breathe as he looked at his cousin for the first time in ten years.

Why hadn't he died? Why was the tenacious bastard still standing there, looking just as fit as before the accident? Anyone else would have died in the crash, but not Douglas Scott. The wealthy Lord Darkwood had proven to have more lives than a bloody cat.

He could still remember that moment, ten years ago, when he had opened the door, ready to receive the lawyers' condolences, but had instead met the scared eyes of a footman who had been sent to inform him about his cousin's accident after getting the doctor to go and tend the injured man.

How was it possible that Douglas had survived that awful crash?

The quarry was a hellhole, and the carriage had been broken into tiny pieces, spread all over the rocky bottom. Anthony had been there, investigating the crash site after the footman had brought him the bad news of Douglas's survival. The coachman had died a horrible death, his blood painting the scene red.

But Douglas had survived, and even though he had been severely injured on the outside, the doctors' still thought he would be able to live a healthy life until old age, as the wounds weren't deep and he hadn't broken even one bone.

He had made yet another attempt to kill his cousin while he was still unconscious after the accident, but Quentin unknowingly interrupted the opportunity before he'd had a chance to put a pillow over his cousin's wounded face.

He had never seen Douglas again.

Too afraid of what his cousin might have known or understood, he had set out to start a new life with the money he'd been able to find in Douglas's study, before he left Darkwood Manor behind him. For the moment debt free, he found a refuge with the determined Annabelle, who had brushed Douglas and their engagement aside and was now searching for a new wealthy man to marry.

Determined to grab what he could that was Douglas's, Anthony made sure he and Annabelle were found in a situation that could be interpreted as too intimate, and her parents had no choice but to give their treasure to the worst husband possible.

He would regret that decision every day from then on.

Annabelle was a self-centered bitch who loathed any human touch. Her frigid body was stiff and dry beneath him, and with her harsh words of resentment echoing in his ears, even he couldn't find fulfillment when thrusting deep into her seeming loveliness.

Three times he tried, before giving up—three awful attempts which had erased all warmer feelings for her, leaving only contempt. An emotionally free man, he started to gamble again, not caring that he lost not only the money they had but his wife's respect as well. He didn't care anymore, and in the end her parents didn't care either. Caring meant helping the young couple with money, and money wasn't something a gambler and his wife gave to someone else.

Not even to their own child.

Through the years, he'd thought about visiting Douglas, but he was too afraid. What if Douglas knew something? What if his intelligent cousin had put two and two together, and understood that Anthony was the culprit behind the accident?

But as time passed, Anthony started to relax. Had his cousin found out the truth about the accident, Anthony would have known by now. But Douglas never came to accuse him of his crime. And when rumors of the elusive beast at Darkwood Manor reached his ears, he couldn't have been more grateful. With Douglas hiding in the depths of the Forest of Dean, Anthony continued with his life, almost forgetting the deed he had done.

With Douglas staying hidden from the world, he wouldn't find someone to marry and, oh, terrifying thought, breed an heir. Anthony would remain the presumptive heir, and, as soon as Douglas did the right thing and died, he would have his dream come true—all the money in the world and a rank no one could deny.

But he had made the mistake of believing that the reason Douglas stayed away from everyone and everything was that he was too badly damaged, and that he was getting closer every day to finally dying. Nevertheless, all those speculations came to a dead end as he looked at the man who had interrupted the kidnapping of Wendy, and he realized three things:

One—Douglas looked as fit as ever.

Two—Douglas wasn't going to die anytime soon.

Three—Anthony would have to kill his cousin, again, before Douglas came around and married Wendy, or any other woman, for that matter, who could give him a child, an heir.

****

Looking down at the top of Wendy's head, Douglas silently exhaled in relief. Thank the Lord he'd arrived when he did. If the two bastards standing on the other side of the room had succeeded with their attempted kidnapping, he would have lost Wendy forever. It didn't matter that he had paid thousands upon thousands of pounds to get her here in the first place.

Lawfully, he had no rights to Wendy. She would have been in the hands of her parents, who, considering how easily they had sold their daughter to him, probably would sell her as a wife to the highest bidder as fast as possible.

He would have his revenge anyway, forcing Sir Edward and his wife into the poorhouse. But Wendy would have been lost to him, if she had been married off to someone else, and that thought scared him immensely. The last couple of months had changed his life from purgatory to a life worth living, and the thought of spending the rest of his life alone, without Wendy, made the future seem bleak and dull.

Looking at the married couple across the room from him, he realized that perhaps he had put too much into this whole thing about marriage. If those two, who clearly loathed each other, could stay married, why couldn't he and Wendy? He knew she loved him; she was such an innocent, and so transparent he could see straight through her. And even though he didn't love her back, as he didn't know how to love, he still had tender feelings for her.

It would be a good life, on his premises.

"Douglas, how wonderful to see you." Annabelle interrupted his thoughts, moving closer with her elegant hand held out gracefully for him to take.

Looking at the still-astonishing beauty, the reason for his revenge, he was surprised to learn he didn't feel anything. Gone was all the resentment and hatred. It was as if he looked at a statue with no meaning for him, a costly piece of art that he would walk by without noticing, any day of the week.

All the time he had spent thinking about having his revenge against her for leaving him, and now, when he finally had her in his house again, he couldn't care less.

"Is it?" he asked, ignoring her hand.

"Of course it is." Annabelle's voice was strained as she let her hand fall to her side again, but she maintained her friendly smile.

Douglas forced a smug smile back. He knew he was behaving rather childishly, but so what? Some smugness now couldn't be that wrong, especially when one considered the revenge he had planned from the start and now had skipped.

"It has been a long time since we last met," Anthony tried with tense politeness, his face flushed and uncomfortable.

"Yes, it has."

Annabelle's laughter was forced, and she sounded

more as if she were being strangled rather than letting out honest and hearty laughter. "I must say you are not a man of many words, my lord. At first it felt as if you hadn't changed at all since we were engaged. But then you were quite mouthy, constantly whispering sweet things in my ears."

The picture she painted was true, and Douglas too remembered all the pathetic nonsenses he had whispered to her, little things that were meant for nothing more than to amuse her. "What do you want?" he asked, eager for them to finish this visit and leave and let him forget all about them again.

"We have come to save Wendy," Annabelle said, scraping together the last small crumbs of the spine she had left, and Douglas had to admire her brutal honesty. She knew what she wanted and didn't pretend otherwise.

"She doesn't need to be saved."

"Of course she does. She is a gently bred lady, born to live in polite society, not wither away in some faraway house in the middle of the forest."

Anthony stood behind his wife, nodding to show Douglas that he agreed with his wife's every word, but he looked more like an overweight parrot, bobbing on its branch.

"She stays here," Douglas said with a weary sigh. "And that is final."

Annabelle moved closer, her hands reaching out to him again, and from out of nowhere he got a feeling that this was her grand gesture, the one she used when nothing else worked. "Don't do this, my lord," she begged. "Don't be this selfish. To force a young lady to live here, with you, is beyond the worst scandal imaginable. The Douglas I used to know was above such selfishness."

"Many things can happen in ten years," Douglas replied icily, aware Annabelle had successfully moved all the blame to him. But he wasn't the one who had put Wendy in this situation. Her parents were. He had just shown them a new door and then patiently waited for them on the other side.

The choice had been theirs. He had just given them the option.

"I can't believe you have changed this much, my lord. You were the most decent man I knew back then, and I think you still are. Please let Wendy go. Let her live a good life. A quiet life without scandals, instead of forcing her to stay here and become a social pariah."

"So marrying her to anyone who will pay for her will make her life better than the life she has here, amongst friends?"

Annabelle's smile faltered for a second, and Douglas mentally patted himself on the back. This was an easy game to win, as long as he didn't underestimate his opponent. He knew desperation for money could make a man, or a woman, do the most astonishing things. Considering what he had heard thus far, he could only come to one conclusion—Annabelle didn't play a fair game. She had all to gain with a marriage, and nothing by leaving her sister a maiden.

"I think she would be much happier married to…to a farmer and having a family of her own, than spending her life here as a companion to an elderly lady."

"So you think that your gently bred sister, born to live in polite society, should end up dividing her time between childbirth and farming?" Douglas snarled. "I am not sure I follow you."

"There is absolutely nothing wrong with farming," Anthony said cheerfully. "I have many friends who have told me that farming is a most wonderful way to spend some time. Get your hands dirty, now and then. Be one with nature. And everyone says that fresh air is good for your health."

Annabelle gave her husband a look that clearly told she doubted his sanity. Douglas seized the opportunity and pushed Wendy toward the door. He mouthed to her to go to her bedroom, and even though it was obvious she wasn't at all pleased with his orders, she still left the room silently, without her sister and her husband noticing.

"She is staying."

"No. She will come home with us. You can't force her to stay."

"You can't force her to go with you."

"I don't need to force her. If she wants to go, she is free to leave you. You don't own her just because you paid my parents' debts."

"Yes, I do."

"Are you insane?" Annabelle shrieked, losing her composure in a most unattractive way. "You can't force anyone to stay here with you if she, or he, doesn't want to, and that includes my sister. She is coming with me."

Douglas leaned forward, until his nose almost touched Annabelle's.

"No."

"No, what?" she asked, her voice hard and unbending.

"No, you cannot take her with you. Wendy's life is here, with me, and I will never, ever, let you take her with you, just so you can save your own asses by marrying her off to anyone who is willing to pay for her."

"You will get your money back."

She would never give up, he realized. She almost had her carrot in her hand and wouldn't give up until she did. With a weary sigh, he stomped to the door and summoned the footmen who stood waiting in the hall.

"My cousin and his wife are leaving. Please make sure they do."

With a nod of his head, he left them there, staring at his retiring back, without believing what he'd just said. The footmen didn't hesitate, though. They used the guests' confusion to advantage, and before they knew it Annabelle and Anthony were placed in their carriage, heading back toward Lydney.

Douglas didn't stay to make sure the carriage left. Instead he ran up the stairs, three steps at a time, and didn't stop until he came to Wendy's bedroom, where she awaited him.

"Are they gone?" she asked with a small voice, and his heart hurt over the obvious pain she suffered.

"Yes."

Wendy chewed on her lower lip for a while, thinking about what had happened, and all Douglas could think about was kissing her. But one didn't have to be a mind reader to see that she wasn't ready for kisses just yet. However, he didn't mind. He had all the time in the world to kiss her. As a matter of fact, he had the rest of their lives to make sweet love to her, and all he had to do was to make sure she would stay his forever and ever, and he knew just the thing to do.

He would have to marry the chit.

Chapter Fourteen

Anthony Scott sat silently in the carriage, his unseeing eyes staring out through the window at the passing woods surrounding his family's ancestral home. Ignoring his wife's nagging, he struggled with the problem of his cousin.

What was the matter with Douglas? The man had more lives than a cat, and it didn't matter how his world was turned upside down, he still stood securely on his two feet. It was frustrating, and it made Anthony boil with envy.

Why had he not been born the heir?

The life he would have had, the money he would have been able to spend... He wouldn't have had to care about how much he gambled, as even he, one of the worst gamblers the London brokers had ever met, would never have been able to lose all the money in the control of the Earl of Darkwood.

Douglas had never cared about the wealth. He was content as long as the household ran smoothly and he could buy a good horse now and then. Even as a young man he had rarely traveled farther than Gloucester or Bristol, the social season in London never tempting him. His preference of the quiet country life had been the only thing he and Annabelle had argued about during their engagement, other than his rejection of her parents.

Being the eldest daughter in a family without funding, Annabelle was desperate for a life in the polite society that Douglas was a part of by birth. He, on the other hand, didn't want that life, as he had spent a couple of seasons in London before he met Annabelle and was too aware of the decadent lifestyle and shallowness which ruled among the *ton*.

In a strange way, it was the same yearning for inclusion in the *ton*'s society that had made Anthony and Annabelle friends in the first place. It was the one thing they'd had in common—the desperation for a better life. And now they sat here, in their friends' ugly carriage, dressed in clothes which had been in style at least three years back. They had no wealth, no social life, and no means to be somebody.

As the carriage passed the deep hole in the ground in which Douglas had been supposed to end his life, Anthony couldn't keep from fantasizing about how life would have been if his plan had succeeded all those years ago. He would still be married to the same woman, as he had been too much in love with her not to marry her.

But instead of this shabby carriage, they would have been traveling in a new, luxurious carriage that would make everyone who saw it green with envy. They would have been dressed in the latest of fashions, from top to toe, and they would have been sitting here gossiping about their friends in the *ton* instead of fighting over what they didn't have.

"We deserve so much more," Annabelle whined, as if she had read his mind. He nodded, agreeing with her silently. She gave him one of her sweet, honest smiles, and he enjoyed the warmth of it. She was usually very restrictive with her true smiles, so he knew to make the most out of every last one she bestowed upon him.

"If he had died ten years ago, all of it would have been ours," Anthony said quietly, still thinking about the outcome of the staged accident.

"But he didn't die," Annabelle said slowly, not really listening to her husband. "Instead he survived, and all his horrible wounds ended up in scars you barely can see. If I only hadn't been so rash with my judgment, ending the engagement before I had a chance to think things through, I would still have had it all, and I wouldn't sit here with you in these old clothes, in this stinking carriage."

Luckily, Anthony didn't listen to her either. To hear his wife that easily dismiss him from her life would not have been something to enjoy, no matter how little he now cared for her. Instead, he nursed a small, lingering thought that had popped up inside his head and didn't go away again.

What if Douglas had another accident?

He still had no children, and therefore no apparent heirs. If he died, Anthony was the next in line and would have it all. Just the thought of the money that came with the earldom made Anthony sweaty, and considering how Douglas scarcely used any money at all, he knew the wealth must have grown even more during the last ten years.

The thoughts raced, making his head ache, but he didn't care. Instead he could have hit himself—hard. Why had he not thought about it again earlier, before all these years had passed? When he still was young and still had his looks? Now he was in the end of his thirties, on the brink of becoming an old man.

Even so, if he became the earl now, he would still have a few years to be one of the dandies he'd always admired from afar. And Annabelle would hang on his arm, beautifying him even more, and all the other men would be so envious of him, of his life, and of his fortune.

"Do you know what," Annabelle interrupted his thoughts, "I think Douglas will marry Wendy soon."

Anthony sat up, staring at his wife, his face white with shock.

Douglas marry Wendy?

Not as long as Anthony was around to stop it.

But what if Douglas did? What if he impregnated her before Anthony had a chance to take care of him? Then the child would be the heir, not Anthony. He wouldn't have the right to anything more than he had now.

But Annabelle could be wrong, which had happened before, when she tried to gossip about others. However, he too had noticed the intimacy between the two at Darkwood Manor. If he had deflowered her, as Anthony believed he had, Douglas would marry her if she ended up pregnant. He wouldn't want his heir born out of wedlock.

Anthony knew he had to hurry and get rid of Douglas as soon as possible. He needed to take just a couple of days to make his plans, to decide how to end the life of his cousin. And this time he had to make sure Douglas really died. This time he would do what he should have done the last time—beat the man to death.

"I must say I feel for Wendy, who lives with him, unmarried," Annabelle continued, not noticing her husband's black thoughts. "This will totally ruin her reputation, you know, if it becomes public. I do hope he will marry her as soon as possible, before all the tongues start to wag. I won't say anything about it, as I don't want it to become commonly known that I have a sister who lives such a scandalous life. I hope you too, dear husband, will hold your tongue for me. I don't want such gossip to destroy my chances to advance in society."

Sometimes his wife scared him with her total lack of compassion. Her sister had been forced to work as a companion instead of having a season as was her right. Wendy was now twenty years old and would be put firmly among the wallflowers and spinsters if she did attend any function of the *ton*. For a young woman without dowry and without good family connections, this was indeed a bad start for her social life.

But all Annabelle could think about was how it would affect her own person. He shook his head slowly, knowing Annabelle wouldn't notice, as she always ignored him. She didn't respect his thoughts, or ask his opinion. All Annabelle wanted was to have someone to talk to. Someone who would listen to her every word and agree with everything she said.

He mentally shrugged his wife from his thoughts and concentrated on solving the problem which was of a much more important nature—how to do away with Douglas. He thought of many different solutions and discarded most of them, but when the carriage stopped in front of their friends' house, he had made his decision.

He had to send Douglas into the quarry. Again.

And this time he would make sure his cousin didn't survive.

****

Wendy sat on her bed, looking out the window. She felt more numb than she ever had before. Meeting her sister under these circumstances had felt strange and uncomfortable, a peculiar reaction.

Why did it feel as if she had been abused in the most brutal way?

Annabelle was her sister, and she would have thought any other emotion more believable than to feel as if she had been slaughtered without remorse. It had hurt when she finally, after all these years, understood in what low esteem her sister held her. Wendy wasn't more than a pawn in whatever game her sister played. She was only a shortcut for Annabelle to reach her final goal, which was all about her own happiness and luxurious lifestyle.

The older sister who had taken care of her sibling when their parents were neglecting her was long gone. Instead a cold and calculating woman had taken her place, and she didn't care if Wendy felt used. If Annabelle got her way, she clearly didn't care who had to be walked on to get it.

The adjoining door opened quietly, and Douglas stepped into the bedchamber without knocking. If Wendy hadn't felt so sad, she would have smiled at how carefully he approached her. He was such a dear man, always putting everyone else before himself. He wasn't at all selfish and self-centered like Annabelle. Or her parents. Or Tony.

Even though he had behaved like a beast when she first met him, living alone in his house and on the verge of becoming a ruin, he had always been good to her in an awkward way. He had made her feel important and needed, which was very different from how her own family worked. They always put themselves first, neglecting her until they had use for her.

"Am I disturbing?" he asked softly, and she gave him a teary smile, which made him look even more worried.

"I'm fine," she sniffed. He sat down beside her and put his arm around her, pulling her closer.

His compassion was too much for her, and she threw herself into his arms and wept until the front of his shirt was soaking wet. His warm hands stroked her back carefully until her tears dried and she could handle herself again. When she tried to leave his arms, he tightened his grip, and with a contented sigh she sank back against him, pressing her cheek against his chest so she could feel the beat of his heart.

"I'm fine," she repeated, and he chuckled.

"Are you sure this time?"

She laughed, and hugged him even harder, which made him groan.

"I can't believe you and Annabelle are sisters. You are as different as night and day."

It was obvious he was awed at meeting his former fiancée again, and Wendy couldn't stop the little prick of jealousy, mixed with a large portion of healthy anger. Why was she always compared to her sister? They were two completely different persons, and anyone who didn't know they were sisters would never guess they were related. She didn't know how to respond, so she kept quiet and tried to go back to the wonderful sensation of being held by him.

"I mean," Douglas continued, unaware of the turmoil of feelings his words created, "she is such a beautiful woman, but if you scrape her exterior façade, you only find a bad core. I don't remember her being this selfish and absorbed in her own desires, but I guess ten years is a long time, and I can't expect everyone to stay the same when I haven't. You should have heard how she screamed when we last met, and this time she hardly looked at my scars. It was as if they weren't there at all."

"She has changed since she married Anthony," Wendy murmured, not too pleased with the subject, but aware that refusing to talk about it would only cause questions she didn't want to answer.

"When we were engaged, I was in awe of her beauty and climbed over some pretty large obstacles to be able to marry her."

Wendy's surprise must have been evident, because he chuckled, amused, giving her a peck on her nose before leaning back into the bed, making himself comfortable.

Lord, he was beautiful.

Lying on his back with his hands under his head made his thin white shirt stretch over his muscular torso. His dark hair was too long and framed his tanned face in an utterly romantic way. He looked as she always had pictured a poet did, with wild, uncut hair, a secretive smile, and cloudy eyes filled with a promise of taking her to paradise.

However, the poet in her bed wasn't thinking about her. He was thinking about her sister.

"You are not the only one who has wondered why I, a nobleman, could even think about marrying a lowly gentry miss like your sister. I had many of my equals in society, as well as friends of my late parents, who more than once begged me to reconsider. However, my mind was set, and I persuaded them all, until they all agreed to allow me to marry Annabelle. Little did I know then that they all knew so much better than I did. My godfather even said that a woman like her, who married me only to become someone else, would never stand by me in bad days. I should have listened to him, instead of stubbornly following my heart's wish."

Wendy grabbed the fabric of her skirt, wringing it between her hands to stop herself from hurling something at him. She couldn't believe his smugness. How could he tell her this? What in the world made him think she wanted to know how lowly he thought her sister—and therefore her own low rank in life?

A lowly gentry miss?

How dared he?

"I didn't know our family was so insignificant to you," she said in a rather surly manner, but he was too caught up in his own thoughts to recognize her anger.

"Insignificant is such a hard word," he objected, rather absentmindedly. "She just wasn't meant to be a part of higher society, whereas I am born into it. Such are the rules we live by, and I was wrong to think I could take someone of a much lower class and easily lift her up."

Wendy couldn't stand his condescension any longer and jumped to her feet. When she turned with her hands on her hips and gave him a look of utter disdain, he frowned and sat up without taking his eyes from her.

"How dare you?" she spat at him.

"How dare I what?" he asked, looking as bewildered as he sounded. He clearly had no idea why she was upset, but she was more than willing to enlighten him.

"I'm so sorry you have to live under the same roof as someone of such a lowly class as myself. It must be so hard for you to know that such a worthless person as me sleeps in a bed worth so much more."

"Wendy," he pleaded, "what *are* you talking about? You know I have never thought of you as unworthy."

She froze before him, opening her mouth to lash out on him, but suddenly he realized his big mistake. He had stupidly patronized her more than he needed to. Just thinking about the circumstances she had lived in made him blush with embarrassment, and he didn't know what to say. He tried to remember what he had been talking about, but he had been blathering on and on without thinking about what he said, too caught up in old memories.

"Good Lord, Wendy," he tried, frantically searching for the right words this time. "I was talking about Annabelle, not you. You know how much you mean to everyone in this house. You are nothing like your sister. Nothing."

"You forget that I come from the same family, and from the same *lowly* class," she said, teeth gritted.

"But you must understand—your sister and I had a completely different relationship than you and I do. I was stupid enough to consider marrying her, for goodness' sake."

Staring at him, she opened and closed her mouth for the longest time, until with a snarl she whipped around and marched out of the room. As the door slammed shut, Douglas flew up from the bed, following her downstairs. She clearly didn't want his company, since when he tried to follow her outside she deliberately threw the front door closed behind her, almost knocking him straight in the face. He took a few deep breaths to calm himself down, to remove the anger which boiled inside him due to frustration. Opening the door, he was just in time to see her vanish into the forest, following the old bumpy road.

For once he didn't know what to do. Should he follow her and force her back into his house, or should he leave her alone and pray she would be less agitated later? Hesitating for a little while, he decided to let her cool down, to give her space to collect her thoughts.

She rarely had any time to herself nowadays. If it wasn't him following her around like a lovesick puppy, begging for a moment of her time, there was a servant in need of her opinion. She didn't even have her bedroom to herself, as he threw himself over her as soon as he noticed her disappearing through the door. He kept her up late most nights, making sweet love to her for hours, and while he afterward slept until lunch, she got up early, as all the servants did.

He had more than once told her there was no need for her to rise early with the other servants, as Miss Lila usually stayed in bed all day. But she insisted, and he hadn't thought anything of it. He had of course noticed how tired she was, but he hadn't pondered much about that either.

Re-entering the hall and meeting the indignant eyes of the butler and the footmen, he escaped into his study, where he poured himself a large glass of brandy. He felt ashamed, and he didn't know how to deal with it.

How had he sunk this low?

He was an aristocrat, brought up to act as a knight and to honor all women. He was glad his parents weren't alive to witness his degradation. They would not have liked what he had become.

What was he to do?

He had played with the notion of marrying Wendy, but maybe that wasn't the right thing to do. Maybe she should marry the person her parents had found for her, and be happy with someone who wouldn't think less of her for being born gentry. The only problem with that solution was that any man would expect his maiden bride to be a virgin, and Wendy was anything but.

Being a man himself, he knew any future husband would hold it against her. Perhaps not at first, but someday he probably would. The only one who wouldn't treat her badly for being used was he himself, and the mere thought of marrying her made him all warm inside. It made him think about the time all those years ago when he had thought himself in love and ready to break all rules for a woman.

Maybe he should talk to someone else, someone who would listen and then give him sound advice. Someone who wouldn't hesitate to tell him what a fool he was, if he thought so.

Luckily for him, he knew just the right person for the job.

Chapter Fifteen

Arthur Basset, Duke of Thornbury, stood motionless, staring out through a window in his office, and Douglas held his breath as he awaited the verdict. He had just told his godfather every nasty little detail about what he had done to Wendy and her family, and now he waited, horror-struck at his own audacity, to hear the old man's opinion.

It hadn't felt good to open up as he had, but he knew this was the only way. He needed someone to tell him what to do, and how to do it. After all the wrongs he had done in the past, he needed a sound person to tell him what the right path of life was...marrying Wendy or letting her go.

And Thornbury was the only one he knew who would tell him the truth and then keep the whole mess to himself.

"I met your father while attending Eton, you know, and we stayed close friends until the day he died. When you were born, your father was so filled with love and pride that he beamed brighter than the sun. When he asked me to be your godfather, I was humbled at the gift he bestowed upon me, as I knew how important you were to him. When he died at such a young age, I stood by your side. You were almost twenty, and a man of your own. Even so, I felt I had to be there for you, to monitor your life as a father would. Even though I many times despaired over your obvious lack of good sense, I rested in the belief you were such a good-hearted young man that, whatever mischief you came up with, at least you would never consciously hurt someone else."

Douglas closed his eyes as shame filled his body and soul. The old man's words cut like sharp swords into his heart. His parents would not have been proud of him if they had known what a selfish bastard he had turned into, and that revelation was devastating.

"Then you met the Russell girl," Thornbury continued, still looking out through the window. "I was against it, which I told you more than once. Nevertheless, you were so stubborn in your conviction about her being the one for you, so I gave in and let you have your way. I never understood what you saw in the girl, as I could only see her hunger for higher rank, but I hoped and prayed that I for once was wrong, that there was more to her than met the eye. In the end, she proved me right. She gave it all up for her vanity. You were not her knight in shining armor anymore, and she couldn't stand it. I must admit I was unwillingly impressed at how easily she broke off your engagement without even a back-up plan, and I considered altering my opinion of her, as a more driven fortune hunter would have stayed put."

Douglas nodded slowly, remembering those days before his accident, before everything changed, and he knew Thornbury was right.

He had not listened at all. He had desperately wanted Annabelle, and he hadn't cared about anyone else's opinion, as his mind had been set. Thornbury had tried to talk to him, but he had just brushed the older man's worry aside. Instead he had let Annabelle drag him toward the altar, not once stopping long enough to face what kind of marriage he was heading into.

He had never thought himself a shallow man, but now he knew he had been the worst kind, not thinking about anyone but himself. It was humiliating to think how he had neglected to listen to any of the good advice he had been given by his elders because they cared about him and had cared about his parents.

They were all too aware of what could come of his actions and had tried to enlighten him, but he had refused to listen. Instead, he had complained to his friends and made fun of what he called "the interfering elders."

"I never loved her," he admitted, almost inaudible. "I just liked the way I looked with her on my arm."

Thornbury turned, and the sadness in the old man's eyes almost did Douglas in, but he swallowed hard and forced himself to stay put.

He had to go through with this. Not for his own sake, but for Wendy's. She was such a good person, and she was worth so much more. The question was whether he was worthy of her.

"After your accident you forbade everyone from coming to see you, even me," Thornbury continued. "I sent you more letters than I can remember, and you didn't answer even one of them. When I came to see you, you refused to meet with me, without hearing me out. When my wife became sick, your situation became unimportant to me, just as everything else in my life did. It wasn't until a couple of years later, when she'd finally gone to her rest and you didn't show up for her funeral, that I realized I hadn't talked to you since she became ill. But when you still refused to answer my letters, I gave up."

Douglas winced as the old man's sorrow over his refusal to appear at the duchess's funeral washed over him. He remembered the letter in which Thornbury had told Douglas about his wife's death and begged him to come and stand by his side at the funeral. He had thrown that letter into the fireplace, filled with rage over the patronizing way his godfather was ordering him about without considering how such a visit would effect Douglas.

Not once had he thought about Thornbury, who'd just lost his beloved wife.

"I'm so sorry," he whispered, but the old man didn't answer.

Maybe he had waited too long before coming. Perhaps this relationship was already lost. He had always taken Thornbury for granted, used to him always being there for him, and what had he repaid him with? By being absent in every way for ten years, and neglecting to stand by his side during the worst time in his life.

"When Jarvis told me you had come to see me, I first thought it was a joke. I was convinced it was someone else, making fun of me, but there you were, looking as fit as ever." Thornbury looked Douglas up and down. "Well, maybe not as well as you used to. You could use a valet."

"As good as ever, you say?" Douglas snorted. "Don't you think all my scars have changed my appearance?"

Thornbury frowned, surprised. "What scars?"

Douglas almost snorted again, but managed to stop

himself in time. How could the old man ask him that? His whole face was messed up. "Are you blind?" he sputtered. "What do you mean, 'what scars'?"

Thornbury continued to stare at him, silently, and it wasn't until Douglas was about to give in and repeat his question the older man continued. However, he didn't answer Douglas's question about the scars but proceeded where he had left off.

"I have thought a lot about you, Douglas, over the years. As you never reappeared in London, I couldn't do more than guess that you still resided at Darkwood Manor. When you refused to answer my letters, I decided, out of frustration, to change tactics, and I sent a letter to Quentin instead."

"You did what?"

"What was I supposed to do? Stop thinking about you? I did what every other father, or in my case, godfather, would do. I wrote to your servant instead."

"He has never mentioned exchanging letters with you."

Thornbury looked at Douglas with something that in good light could be called a smile. "I asked him not to. Quentin is a loyal man. He also cares a lot about you, and he wasn't so hard to persuade to keep our correspondence a secret."

Douglas leaned back into the comfortable armchair with an urgent need to sulk. So they had talked behind his back, had they? What kind of ogre did they think he was? He wouldn't have objected. Not too much, anyway.

He hadn't thought he could feel more stupid, but the old man had found a way. The loneliness he'd stubbornly inflicted upon himself seemed more and more illogical and childish. Thinking about it now, he could hardly believe he had kept it up for ten long years. Why had no one told him to stop? Why had everyone kept quiet and let him have his way?

But in his heart, he knew why.

He'd had lots of friends when he was younger, and during the first couple of months after the accident they had all been hovering around him, suffocating him with their tender care. In the end, it had been he who had told them to leave and never return. He wanted to bury himself in self-pity, and that was much easier to do without being surrounded by people wanting nothing more than to cheer you up.

At first, he had received many letters every week, letters that he never replied to. As weeks turned into months and then into a year, the frequency of the letters decreased. After another year, the letters stopped coming completely. He had been ranting to Quentin about his friends' lack of compassion and their disloyalty, naming them the worst of friends. But as he looked back to that dark part of his life it wasn't so difficult to figure out why they gave up on him— because he never wrote back. Not once.

Thornbury sat down, facing him for the first time since he got there. He looked so much older than he had the last time they met, and Douglas felt a string of fear tighten around his heart. His godfather was now an old man, and who knew how much time on earth he had left. Douglas had, with his hermit lifestyle, lost ten wonderful years with the only man who loved him as much as a father could—endlessly.

"Quentin told me about your obsession with your scars, and how it ruled your life. None of us knew how to get through to you, even though poor Quentin tried every way we could think of."

"I'm not obsessed with my scars," Douglas muttered, feeling more and more like the culprit.

Ignoring his contribution to their conversation, Thornbury continued, "I have never seen anyone look as bad as you did after the accident. The skin of your face had been ripped, especially on the right side, and it looked as if you had been attacked by the claws of a lion. However, I sent for the best doctors England can offer, and they did an excellent job with you, and as your skin healed, the scars almost disappeared. Only a few thin lines are visible, and they aren't something easily noticed."

"Have you lost your eyesight completely?" Douglas roared, standing up so fast the heavy armchair tumbled backward. "Can't you see all the hideous marks covering my face? I look like a beast from a fairytale, and to suggest them being minor is a huge insult!"

Thornbury didn't say a word. Instead he sat silent, which infuriated Douglas even more. "I have been to hell and back, and you just brush it off, as if it were nothing!"

To his dismay, tears filled his eyes. Before he could make an even worse fool of himself in front of his godfather, Douglas barged out of the room. Without thinking, he went straight to his favorite place as a child, the old parapet of the Thornbury family castle. He found the hiding spot of his childhood, behind a gruesome statue of a demon, and sat down, hiding his head in his arms.

All the repressed feelings he had kept under guard

for years broke free, and his chest ached as he cried over what he had lost. With deep sobs he faced his anguish over the accident and how it had transformed him.

He didn't know when Thornbury sat down beside him, but when he finally noticed, it didn't feel humiliating, only safe.

"What are your plans about the Russell girl?" Thornbury asked softly, when Douglas had calmed down and regained his composure.

Looking out at the fantastic view that had amazed him since he was a small child, Douglas sighed ruefully. "I don't know."

Thornbury glanced at him without saying anything, but Douglas could sense the confusion and frustration his godfather felt.

"It's the reason why I came here," he continued, "to have you help me sort things out. I seem to have put myself in a corner, and I don't know how to get out without hurting someone somehow."

"Do you love her?"

Douglas took a moment before answering Thornbury's question. Did he love Wendy? The answer to the question came from his heart.

"Yes."

"Forgive me for asking, but are you really sure you do?"

Douglas couldn't stop a crooked smile, and Thornbury smiled back in return. It felt as if loads of weight had fallen from his shoulders. The old man was still there for him, and this time Douglas wouldn't discard him. At least not without listening to him first, he thought with another crooked smile.

"I can understand the reason why you hesitate about my feelings, but trust me when I say I do love her, with all my heart."

"Well," Thornbury admitted, "when you are truly in love, there is no way to mistake your feelings, so I believe you."

Standing up, Douglas offered his hand to the older man to help him up onto his feet. Brushing the moss from their clothes, they walked slowly along the parapet, watching the sun set at the horizon. The landscape showed itself at its most beautiful, and if Douglas hadn't been so tired, he would have enjoyed it immensely.

Too much had happened these last couple of days: the shock of meeting Annabelle again, and finding all the resentment gone; the argument with Wendy, the last straw for him after ten years of self-loathing and emptiness. It had taken him one day, instead of the usual two, to ride to Oldbury Abbey, and, to his relief, find the Duke currently there at his ancestral country home.

He had driven himself to the limit, and now his reserves of strength were emptied. He desperately needed to sleep, and when he stumbled slightly, the old Duke realized this too. Calling for the footmen, which never were far away, he had them help him get Douglas to a guest room. As soon as he lay down in the welcoming bed, Douglas fell asleep.

****

Wendy sat silently in the luxurious carriage, remembering the last time she had shared a vehicle with her parents, and tears filled her eyes. They must have been hiding in the forest, waiting for Douglas to leave the manor. He had been gone for only a couple of minutes when her parents knocked on the door, demanding the servants release their daughter to them.

She had tried to make them understand they were out of line, and at first refused to go with them. It was crazy they could even suggest such a thing, when they'd practically thrown her to Douglas in the first place. But in the end she had to give in. She had no spine nor endurance when it came to her parents, and when her mother threatened to get the local magistrate there, Wendy gave in.

Not for her own sake, but for Douglas's.

He didn't need more problems in his life, and especially not a scandal, which an arrest would create. Just like the last time she'd been hustled off by her parents, she hardly had time to pack a bag before she was tossed into the carriage.

With a cloud of dust behind them, they left Darkwood Manor.

Her parents sat silent, ignoring her now, as they had succeeded with their mission, and she found that a blessing in disguise. She wouldn't have known what to say to them anyway. All her life she had crawled for them, with a desperate hope that someday maybe they would love her just a little. But it had never mattered what she did; she was never worthy of their love.

Her patience, when it came to her parents, had seemed endless, just as her childish wish of being loved. Some good days she had almost been able to imagine that her mother loved her, as Juliet let her comb her hair, or sit on her bed while she readied herself for some assembly.

Now she knew better.

Now that she knew what true love was, she knew whatever it was her mother felt for her, it wasn't love. Juliet Russell was not able to feel emotions toward others. She had only endured her children as long as they could give her something in return. Annabelle, with her astonishing beauty, had made the other mamas of her acquaintance envious. Wendy, who wasn't as beautiful as her older sister and therefore not interesting enough to show off, was more useful as an unpaid maid.

Her father had once let it slip that he was glad he hadn't sired sons, as they would be expected to share for the rest of their lives in the same small income which he had every month. Daughters were much better because once they were married off they didn't cost anything.

She had never thought about it before, but such an attitude said much about what kind of person her father was.

When the carriage turned north, toward Hereford, instead of continuing eastbound to Gloucester, Wendy finally broke the silence.

"We are heading the wrong way."

"No, we are not," her mother answered, without looking away from the passing scenery.

"I thought we were going home."

"Then you thought wrong."

"Where are we going, then?"

"Stop asking all these questions. I have nothing to say to you, and all you give me is a headache," Juliet shrieked at Wendy as her patience ran out.

Frowning at her mother's dismissive profile, Wendy felt a shiver run down her spine. What were her parents up to now? She had heard them tell the servants at Darkwood Manor that they were taking Wendy home.

But if they weren't going to Gloucester, where were they headed?

They didn't know anyone who lived in the counties of northern England. All her parents' friends and relatives lived in the southern part of the country. The only person who had mentioned anyone living in the north was Annabelle, when she visited the day before. She had mentioned it when she'd talked about the man who needed…a wife.

Wendy closed her eyes as the truth hit her, with all its selfishness. "Are you taking me to Yorkshire?" she whispered, as her heart broke into pieces.

Her mother didn't answer her, but Wendy could tell by her rigid posture that it was the truth. Leaning back into the cushions, she took a shaky breath to compose herself again. Tears burned in her eyes, and she swallowed down the sobs that wanted to escape. Somewhere, deep inside, she had hoped they had come for her because they missed her and regretted their actions. She had nursed an impossible wish that they finally had realized how wrongly they'd treated her, and had decided she belonged with them.

Instead, it was all for their own use. They had a new buyer, and now she was being sent away again, for another round sum of money.

"I don't understand what you are so upset about," her father said coldly. "Here we have found a man who wants nothing more than to marry you, and you object?"

"I never thought our own child would treat us this

ungratefully." Juliet sniffed. "After all we have done for you. You really should treat us better."

Wendy met her mother's ice-cold eyes, and something inside her shriveled and died. Maybe it was the last warmth of love she'd felt for them, or the last flickering hope she had held. She didn't know, and more importantly, she didn't care anymore. All she wanted to do was to get out of the carriage and find Douglas, throw herself into his arms, and feel cherished and wanted again.

She wanted to go home.

Not to the little house in Gloucester, but to Darkwood Manor, where her heart was. So what if he never would marry her? She could stay as Miss Lila's companion as long as she lived, and then she could stay on as the housekeeper. Anything would do, as long as she could live near him. And if he married another woman, she would do everything she could for her, to honor her husband. She would love their babies, and, even if she from time to time would fantasize about them being hers, she would never hold it against Douglas or his wife.

She needed him in her life, and if he only wanted her as a servant and an occasional mistress, so what? She didn't care anymore. All she needed in her life was to be close to him, and to be able to feel his warm body against hers…to feel his warm breath caress her hair, and hear his heartbeat against her ear.

"Get some sleep," her mother snapped. "We are traveling a long way today and won't stop for many hours yet."

"Please," Wendy begged, trying for the last time to find a way into her mother's heart, if not to be loved then at least to be heard and acknowledged. "Please don't do this to me. I don't want to leave Darkwood Manor. It's my home now. Please."

Juliet Russell didn't flinch when tears started down Wendy's cheeks. It was of no use. Wendy was caught in her parents' web, and there was nothing she could do about it. She had a sinking feeling that the only possible way out of her predicament would be by marrying the squire they were selling her to.

If she only knew how to contact Douglas—but he had gone so suddenly and only left a note informing her he was going to visit his godfather and wouldn't be back for a few days. He had never mentioned who this godfather was, or where he resided.

Closing her eyes, she sent a prayer, wishing Douglas had returned sooner than expected and was already chasing them. If he wasn't, she knew she would have no way out of this, because he would have no idea where her parents were taking her.

She would be married off, and she would lose Douglas forever.

Chapter Sixteen

At first he didn't know where he was.

The room was grander than all the bedrooms at Darkwood Manor together, and not what he had been used to these past ten years. But something about the decor felt familiar, and when he opened the curtains and looked out over the magnificent gardens below him, he knew exactly where he was.

Oldbury Abbey.

Closing his eyes, he lifted his face toward the sun, which caressed his face with warm summer beams. He couldn't remember how he had gotten to this room, but then he had been completely worn out when he arrived yesterday. The last thing he could remember was sitting with Thornbury on the parapet.

It had been a good talk, and it felt like a millstone had been lifted from his shoulders. He still needed the older man's advice about what to do, and even more importantly—how to do it. But he was in no rush. He and Thornbury had lots of catching up to do, and as Wendy wasn't going anywhere, he could as well visit for a couple of days more. It would be nice to reconnect with his godfather thoroughly, to get to know him again.

When he came downstairs to the breakfast room, Thornbury was already there, reading a newspaper. He didn't look up, but made a gesture toward the chair on the other side of the table.

Sitting down, Douglas accepted the cup of hot tea a servant offered him. He added milk before starting on the plateful of delicious-smelling food placed in front of him. One of the footmen offered him a newspaper, but he declined. He hadn't read about the world surrounding him for a decade, and now wasn't the time to start again.

He just wanted to sit there, silent, enjoying the stillness of the room and, as soon as the older man finished his reading, Thornbury's company. Douglas had just finished his meal when his godfather finally put down the newspaper and took off his glasses.

"Reading about the awfulness in the world makes me feel more and more grateful for the peace and quiet that surround me."

"You are a lucky man indeed," Douglas agreed with a smile, and Thornbury nodded, solemnly.

"Yes, indeed I am. And with you here, talking to me again, my world couldn't be more perfect."

"I'm so sorry…" Douglas started, but Thornbury shook his head.

"No, we're done there. No need to continue with old regrets. Instead I think we should concentrate on the future. I, for one thing, am going to become a great-grandfather any day now."

"That's wonderful news, congratulations. Which of all your grandchildren is the parent-to-be?"

"It's Charlotte." Thornbury laughed. "I don't think Charles ever will find someone to marry, as he is too married to his work here at Oldbury Abbey, overseeing the place."

"I can't believe Charlotte is old enough to be

married, let alone have a child. To me, she is still the child in my memory. I remember her so well, her blonde hair always in a tousled mess, and with bruises all over her arms and legs from climbing up and falling down everywhere."

Thornbury laughed. "Every night Peter used to take her in his lap and count every new bruise and meticulously write the amount in a notebook. I think, if I am not mistaken, the record was thirty-two."

"How is Peter, by the way?"

"He's fine. I think he feels a bit lonely now, as both children have left the house. It would be wonderful if he found a new woman to marry. But unfortunately he insists upon stubbornly playing the role of the grieving widower. A very disturbing situation, as everyone knows how much he loathed his late wife. That was not a blissful marriage."

"Why doesn't he move here, and live with you instead? It would be so much better for both of you to have the company of each other. And besides, he would be closer to Charlotte and the baby too."

"My son is stubborn as a mule, a family trait for sure. He has decided that he needs to live closer to his wife's grave and insists that my brother's old manor suits him just fine. Sooner or later he will have to reside here at Oldbury Abbey because he is, after all, my heir. I just wish he would move here sooner, as it would be so much easier for me to show him everything about the inheritance and the legacy around it before I die."

Sadness at the loneliness of this great man washed through Douglas. Thornbury was living by himself, in this large castle, even though he had quite a large family. One day he wouldn't be around anymore, and his children and grandchildren would regret their absence from him, but then it would be too late. Something he knew all too well himself.

"What do you say…" Thornbury stood up. "Shall we continue this conversation in my office?"

"Indeed," Douglas agreed, and soon after, he was sitting in the same comfortable armchair as yesterday. Thornbury sat down behind his beautiful desk, leaned back, and looked sternly at his godson.

"When is the marriage taking place?"

"As soon as possible."

"Really?" Thornbury chuckled. "Are you so sure of her accepting your hand in marriage?"

"Well," Douglas drawled, "as I don't intend to let her go anywhere, I think it will come down to her choosing between two options. Live with me as my wife, or stay put as my mistress. She's a smart girl. She will do the right thing."

"For your sake, I do hope you're right."

"Will you aid me if she disagrees?"

Thornbury laughed, shaking his gray-haired head. "If she is intelligent enough to decline, I will not force her into anything. I might whisk her away to live with me here, instead. She sounds like the perfect company for an old man like me."

Douglas shook his head, smiling, knowing in his heart that his godfather would adore Wendy after meeting her. For being so young, she was a very serious person and took a vivid interest in everything surrounding her. Considering her willingness to learn, and the Duke's yearning to teach, they would probably be inseparable.

"What are your plans for the wedding?" Thornbury

continued, folding his hands in front of him, while drumming with his thumbs impatiently.

"My only plan is that I want the wedding to take place as soon as possible, before anyone gets the news of her living with me unmarried and more or less without a chaperone."

"You can always head for Scotland. Many marriages have started in Gretna Green."

He hadn't thought about the actual marriage act, he realized. "No, I don't think so. I would rather be married as soon as possible, but a tiring trip to Scotland is not what I would look forward to. I guess I will simply have to get a special license."

"Then you must be the luckiest man in Gloucestershire, as my old friend Charles Manners-Sutton just became the next Archbishop of Canterbury. He currently is visiting his wife's family at Summers Hall for a couple of weeks, and will be visiting me tomorrow. If you can stay until then, you will have your special license with you as you leave for Darkwood Manor."

That was wonderful news indeed, and Douglas immediately accepted the invitation for a prolonged visit. Not only would he be able to spend more time with his godfather, a man he had forsaken for so long, but he would also be granted an easy solution for his problem with Wendy.

****

When Darkwood Manor became visible between the trees, Douglas couldn't hold back a happy smile. Four whole days he had been gone, and now he was desperate to embrace Wendy, before whisking her away to make an honest woman of her. In the pocket of his coat, he had a signed special license, and he could barely contain the happiness bubbling inside.

He had spent the last two days thinking about different ways to ask her to marry him, and every time he thought he had found the perfect way, another idea popped up.

He had enjoyed the days with his godfather. They had used the time well, getting to know each other again after being separated for a decade. The visit had, after its shaky beginning, been filled with intense discussions and laughter.

He had not had time to miss his home and Wendy at all during the days. However, during the long hours of the night, he had dreamt about her, and more than once waked up with her name on his lips. She was in his heart and in his dreams, and now, as he was on his way to make sure she would always be in his life, he couldn't have been happier. Their relationship had begun badly, thanks to his outrageous plan, and he had promised himself he would spend the rest of his life making sure it would end happily.

Somehow he didn't think she would mind.

As he jumped down from his stallion, servants came running from everywhere. Soon he was surrounded by what seemed to be every last servant he had, and their families, and they were all trying to tell him something. In the end he had to shout, "Stop!" and they at once became silent, staring at him with huge, scared eyes. With an uncomfortable feeling in his stomach, he turned to Quentin, who stood beside him, waiting for the commotion to end and his master's full attention.

"They took her."

Frantically, Douglas scanned the surrounding crowd, and it didn't take long time for him to realize the most important person wasn't there.

"Who took her?"

"Her parents. They came, just after you left. Must have been hiding until you had gone far enough. There was no legal way for us to keep her here. They even threatened to get the law officer involved."

"Did they?"

"No. Miss Wendy made sure of it, by agreeing to go with them. I tried to make her change her mind, but you know her. If she gets an idea in her head, she won't let it go. She said she couldn't live with herself if any of us got arrested because of her. So she left, and we couldn't do anything."

Douglas felt something dark rise inside him. Not toward the people surrounding him—they couldn't be blamed for what had happened. What made him furious was Sir Edward Russell and his stone-cold wife. Again and again they had proved to him, and to Wendy, what they really were: bloody, self-centered leeches. Without consideration of the agreement they had made with Douglas, they had kidnapped their own daughter.

"Did they say anything about where they were heading?"

"They said they were bringing Wendy home, but I think that was just a lie to get her to come with them. I had Little Ned follow them, to make sure they went home. He said they had not gone toward Gloucester. Instead, he followed them northbound until he had to turn around because the horse became too tired."

"Thank you," Douglas said, gratefully. "That saves me a day, if I don't have to go by Gloucester."

Leaving the servant to prepare for his departure, he ran up the stairs to his room. He emptied his travel bag on the floor of his bedroom and filled it anew with clean clothes, placed neatly in his chest of drawers days before by Wendy's careful hands. For a short breath of time, he stood still, looking around the cozy bedroom. Everywhere was evidence of Wendy's caring heart—in the flowers on his desk, in the puffed pillows which smelled of sunshine and warm winds, and in the neatness of his bedroom, which used to look like someone had turned it upside down in search of valuables.

He closed his eyes, breathing deeply to calm the seething anger as it started to build again. He was glad he hadn't come home while the Russells were still at Darkwood Manor. He would not have been able to stop himself from going berserk, doing and saying things he would probably have regretted later.

Clenching his teeth, he ran downstairs again and climbed into the waiting carriage. Seconds later, they were speeding through the green darkness of the Forest of Dean, leaving Darkwood Manor in a cloud of dust.

"Where to?" the driver called, and Douglas hesitated for a moment. Even though, thanks to Little Ned, he knew they were heading north, it still meant quite a large area for him to cover. A memory of Annabelle and Tony mentioning a gentleman up north came to him, and suddenly he knew what the Russells were up to.

They were going to sell Wendy to the highest bidder.

Hatred washed through him, filling every last part of his body. Of course. That was their plan. The

Russells would never do anything they couldn't gain from. And now they had that gentleman up north, a man who was desperate enough for a wife to buy one.

That thought led to an idea.

Why not see if he could get Annabelle or Tony to talk? It couldn't be so hard. They were in desperate need of funding, and he had deep pockets. He called out directions to the driver, and in no time at all the carriage halted in front of a house which tried to seem grander than it was.

Chapter Seventeen

Unable to wait for the driver to approach the carriage door, Douglas opened it himself and jumped to the ground. Walking briskly toward the house's front door, he felt his heart beating faster out of pure excitement. He couldn't stop a wicked smile of anticipation. This was a confrontation he really looked forward to.

A young and obviously inexperienced butler welcomed him, bringing him directly to the room in which his cousin spent his time. Without announcing him as a guest, the butler opened the door and let Douglas in.

The small salon looked as if it had been hit by an autumn storm, with clothes and all manner of other things spread everywhere. In front of a soot-smudged fireplace, Tony lay on a worn sofa, eating a selection of sandwiches that looked as if they had come directly from a trash bin. His wife sat in an armchair, writing a letter, clad only in an old, worn dressing gown, her naked feet dirty.

Annabelle's scream when she noticed the uninvited, unannounced man standing in the room was deafening, startling poor Tony, who jumped and tumbled out of the sofa and landed with an "ouf!" on the floor.

Too late, the poor young butler realized what he

had done. Sputtering excuses, he rushed forward to help his master up from the floor, but the embarrassed Tony just brushed away the helping hand and stood up by himself. As he realized it was Douglas standing in the doorway, he froze for a second, and something ugly moving in his bloodshot eyes before he found himself again.

"Cousin? What a surprise to find you here."

Douglas almost laughed at the sight of the ragged Tony, who looked as if he hadn't had a bath in weeks but sounded as if they'd just met in a ballroom and not in his own private salon. Swaying slightly from side to side, Tony bowed his head in what was probably supposed to be an elegant and polite greeting.

Douglas suspected his cousin had started the day with a liquid breakfast, judging from the empty bottles on the floor beneath the sofa. And considering the number of empty bottles, Douglas could only sadly conclude that this had to be a normal occurrence in this household.

Annabelle, who was regaining her composure, clutched her robe over her chest and stepped carefully over to her husband's side, staring at Douglas with the same contempt and disgust she had showed him that horrible day ten years earlier.

"What is wrong with you? How dare you come barging in like this without being announced? I guess you can't expect more from someone who has disguised himself as a hermit for the last decade," she snarled, looking down her nose at him most patronizingly.

"That would be my mistake, madam," the poor butler started, his ears red and his chin trembling, but Annabelle cut him off immediately.

"You! Get out of here, you incompetent fool. I will deal with you later."

With a hesitant glance toward the guest, as if he didn't want to leave another human being alone to face the wrath lurking in Mrs. Scott's blue eyes, the butler disappeared through the doorway. Tony had used the commotion well, grabbing his robe and putting it on, apparently hoping to look more distinguished.

Douglas was getting fed up with the couple's antics, and he quickly decided this was not the time to play games. This was the time to ignore the past in order to gain the future of his heart. After all these years, there was only one thing he wanted, and to his own almost reluctant surprise, he had no need to tramp all over these two pathetic persons anymore. All he wanted was Wendy, but—if he were completely honest with himself—he wouldn't mind doing some real damage to the filthy couple in front of him, if only to get the information he desperately needed.

"Where's Wendy?" he snapped, catching them by surprise. Tony paled visibly, and sank down on the sofa behind him, grabbing one of the bottles to pour himself some liquid strength.

It didn't come as a surprise to Douglas that it was Annabelle who was gifted with the brains in this marriage. Her first natural reaction was fear, but as her mind started to work, he could see how the fear turned into speculation. A vulture will always be a vulture, he thought, as she gave him a small triumphant smile.

"So you want to know where Wendy is?"

He nodded in response, knowing already where this was headed but having nothing to stop it with. He had come here knowing it would cost him. The question was how far she would take it.

"What's it worth to you?" she said, her smile victorious and ugly.

He didn't hesitate. "What is it worth for you?"

"I want you to sign everything over to Tony: the house, the land, and the funds."

"You know I can't do that." Douglas sighed. "It is all entailed and therefore beyond my reach to sign over to anyone."

Annabelle's smile didn't falter, and he could only draw the conclusion that she too was aware of the fact. So what was her game now?

"Asking you to die is too much, I guess?"

An amused snicker reached them from the sofa, and Annabelle lifted her chin triumphantly. Douglas felt ready to throw up. He had known this visit would hurt him, one way or another. But this? He would never have thought they would go this far. Perhaps it's a joke, a little voice said in his head, but he knew there was no fun in this.

With triumphant desperation, they took it as low as they could, and he felt sick knowing he wouldn't come out from this fight without surrendering everything they could grab with their greedy claws.

"What do you want?" Douglas repeated, ignoring the last comment.

"We want everything that is not entailed."

"You must be joking," Douglas growled, trying to sound stronger than he was.

"I never joke about money," Annabelle hissed, her face changing from worn beauty into serpent's malice.

How had he ever found her the most beautiful of women, Douglas wondered, watching her twisted features. Where had she gone, that exquisite young woman who'd had him gawking at her, mesmerized, and following her around like a lovesick puppy? The woman standing before him was still a beauty, although a slightly wrinkled and worn one. She had lost the uncommon fragility which had attracted him ten years ago, and now she was just an ordinary good-looking woman.

"So how much is your precious little Wendy worth to you?" Tony interrupted Douglas's erratic thoughts as he joined his wife, creating a unified front toward the victim of their greed.

"Everything," he admitted, too honest for his own good.

Tony chuckled, amused. "Then hand it all over, Cousin."

"Why would I?"

Annabelle blinked. "Because you just told us you would give us everything for Wendy."

"Not to you," Douglas snorted, making sure to send them his most patronizing glare.

Tony's snicker wasn't as self-assured as before, and Douglas decided to ignore his cousin, who was known to lack a spine. It was Annabelle he needed to defeat, if he could find her weak point. She, of course, wouldn't let him ponder about it as she left her husband's side and strolled to the door. With an overly large gesture, she wordlessly asked him to leave, her blue eyes gleaming with malicious amusement.

Hesitating slightly, Douglas followed her toward the door until he stood towering over her smaller frame. The ugly smile she bestowed upon him showed her rotten soul, and in that moment he knew what he had to do. Or rather what he couldn't do.

Wendy would have to forgive him, but he couldn't give these two anything. There had to be another way to find her. Somehow, somewhere there was a small clue to lead him to the love of his life. His only hope was that this visit hadn't taken too much time, that the Russells hadn't had time to go through with their plans yet.

"You know where to find us, if you change your mind," Annabelle said, with one last triumphant snicker, before closing the door in his face.

For a second he stood still, panic filling every part of his large body.

What had he done?

Had he let his pride destroy the only chance he had to find Wendy? Why didn't he just give the vultures what they wanted so he could be on his way to rescue her?

He lifted his hand to knock on the door, but just as he was about to land his fist on the door's surface, a voice was heard behind him, and his hand stopped still in the middle of the air as he turned his head to the side and met the anxious eyes of the young butler.

"My lord, could I have a minute of your time?"

Lowering his fist to his side, Douglas nodded curtly, and followed the butler downstairs and out onto the small landing outside the front door. The butler reminded him of a small squirrel, bobbing his head in all directions, looking for any danger.

"Is it permissible, my lord, for me to speak freely?"

"Of course."

"I overheard your conversation with my employer's houseguests, and I think I can help you with the whereabouts of the young woman you seek."

Douglas could have hugged the young man. Thank the lord for the nosy butler, with no loyalty toward his master's guests. "I would be most grateful."

The butler's smile was wryly amused, and he lost his anxiety for a second. "No, my lord, I don't need a reward for this information. If telling you what I've heard vexes the couple upstairs, my satisfaction is complete. The Scotts have not been the nicest of guests, misusing my master's kindness, so if I can trouble them in any way, it would be reward enough."

With one last lingering look up at the second floor of the house, the butler lowered his voice slightly. "It was I who opened the door for the Russells when they arrived, and they were in such a rush they didn't think about privacy. Mrs. Scott was not pleased with her parents, who refused to sit in their cold carriage in the dark forest, waiting for you to leave and offer them an opportunity to grab their younger daughter without your interference. Not until Mrs. Scott screamed that it was the Russells' fault that they all were knee-deep in shit did they give in to her demand and head out to their carriage."

Douglas couldn't stop an amused chuckle, the butler's colorful retelling catching him quite by surprise.

"Lady Russell kept complaining about how inconsiderate Mrs. Scott was," the butler continued stoically, his cheeks turning a shade rosier, "forcing her old mother to lurk around Darkwood Manor in an uncomfortable carriage, but the daughter was not impressed. Sir Edward tried to have Mrs. Scott go instead, flattering her for her quick mind and fast tongue. But again, to no avail. Mrs. Scott made it very clear that if the groom-to-might-be had second thoughts, it would be easier for the legal guardians to persuade him than it would be for a mere sister. In the end, it was the Russells who climbed into the shabby carriage, with Mrs. Scott shouting instructions from the outside as they rolled away toward Darkwood Manor."

"The Russells never said where they were heading after the trip to Darkwood Manor?"

The butler shook his head, and Douglas's shoulders slumped. It was all good information, but without a name or a place, completely useless.

"But…" the butler continued, with a little crooked smile, "Mrs. Scott called out to them, wishing them a joyful trip to Yorkshire, and stressed the importance of not missing their stop, just north of Leeds, or they'd find themselves ending up in Scotland."

The endless relief flooding Douglas's mind was almost too much to handle. He thanked the young butler thoroughly, making sure the man understood he should come to him if he ever found himself in need of aid or employment.

With renewed strength, he told the driver to head toward Leeds, and with a last wave to the blushing butler, he sat back in the carriage, his mind full of new hope. He was not that many days behind the threesome, and as his carriage was both better and faster, and his pockets deep enough to change horses at every possible stop, he hoped he wouldn't be too late.

The Russells were in a hurry to get the money for Wendy, but being a man himself, Douglas didn't think the squire would drag his bride to the church as soon as he laid eyes upon her. And besides, as he himself had only just found out, you needed a license to get married, or else you had to go somewhere like Gretna Green to get married fast.

Either way, Douglas could only pray he wouldn't be too late, that Wendy would not be married off before he got there. He could of course kill the poor country squire, but the man was innocent in this game and shouldn't have to pay with his life.

But the mere thought of another man touching Wendy made him nauseous, and he shifted where he sat in the carriage. He wanted his obnoxious wench back, his sweet little sheep who hid the most alluring wolf beneath her innocence, and the sooner the better. All he wanted was to have her in his life again, so that he could make an honest woman of her.

His honest woman.

****

Wendy sat in the salon at Deighton Cross, her hands clasped hard together as they rested on her lap. She welcomed the pain in her fingers, as it was the only thing keeping her from running in embarrassment as far away from her company as she could, screaming at the top of her lungs like a bloody lunatic.

Their host sat silently on the sofa at the other side of the coffee table from Wendy, looking just as embarrassed as she felt. Now and then they would exchange a weak smile while enduring the commotion created by her parents.

"I can't believe you dragged us all the way up here, into the bloody north, without even making sure that the man in question actually wants our daughter," Sir Edward yelled at his wife, too angry to care about the inappropriate audience in the room.

Lady Russell lifted her haughty chin high in the air, her contempt for her red-faced husband quite visible. "His aunt most specifically said that he needed a wife, and what friend would write such words to a loving mother with a daughter to marry off if it weren't true?"

Their host lifted his hand, trying one more time to join the discussion and offer some clarity, but neither Sir Edward nor Juliet Russell acknowledged him. They were in the middle of blaming each other for his refusal to marry Wendy, and they weren't interested in listening to his—as they quite bluntly had called them to his face—weak excuses.

"There is not one person in England claiming even the lowest of intelligence who would believe anything that comes out of that vile woman's mouth. But then you come along, you who should know better, considering all the bloody shit you have been calling Mrs. Bennet over the years, and ignoring your common sense, you let that nitwit serve you her poison. But that is nothing compared to the fact that you believed her!" Sir Edward yelled even louder, his face resembling a sweaty beet.

Nathaniel Wetherby, Marquis of Barkston-Ash, sent Wendy what had to be an umpteenth apologizing smile, his discomfort over the situation clear. Unable to hold back another nauseating wave of embarrassment, Wendy looked down at her lap, concentrating her gaze at her trembling hands and white knuckles. She had tried to make her parents change their mind while still in the carriage, but they hadn't listened. Sir Edward and Lady Russell had stared blindly at the gold on their horizon—and to be honest, what was a mere daughter worth compared to a treasure?

Deighton Cross had been a nice surprise, though.

It was a large, square building, perfectly situated by a man-made lake, surrounded by a flawless formal garden. The place oozed of vast fortune and delightful taste, and Wendy knew as soon as she saw the place that this was not the home of a man desperately searching for any woman who would agree to marry him, and certainly not a scandalous non-virgin. Dread, like none she'd ever felt before, had filled her, and again she had tried to make her parents listen to her, to make them understand this was a visit that couldn't end any way but badly.

But they hadn't listened to her. Enthralled by the wealth laid out in front of their greedy eyes, they had been busy discussing how much more they could ask in return for Wendy's hand in marriage.

The owner and unknowing supposed husband-to-be turned out to be one quite nice-looking man, with windblown blonde hair and beautiful chocolate brown eyes. His soft voice and well-mannered bearing were like balm to Wendy's torn soul, and she could tell that he too recognized the immediate connection between them. Instinctively, she knew this man would have made a perfect husband for her. Their life together would have been light and happy, and she would have loved him dearly for being such a kind and decent man.

But that ship had sailed when her parents dropped her off at Darkwood Manor, throwing her without remorse into Douglas's brooding, angry arms. He too was a good man, but in a completely different way. Where Lord Barkston-Ash was refined and soft-spoken, Douglas was harsh and brutally honest. She didn't know her host very well, as so far they had spent only two awkward hours together, suffering through her horrible parents' indiscriminate ranting the whole time.

Her heart belonged to Douglas, but somewhere deep inside she felt sadness at not being allowed to choose the direction of her life. If both men had been her beaus and courted her, she couldn't for her life say which she would have preferred. Douglas had always been her favorite, ever since her childhood days, but if she was to be completely honest, she might have been put off by his intensity, especially as Lord Barkston-Ash was much easier to warm up to.

"If you hadn't lost everything with your gambling, we wouldn't be in this situation in the first place," Juliet Russell shrieked, grabbing a vase from a small table and hurling it at her husband, only to watch it pass him and, with a loud crash as it hit the stone wall, splinter all over the wooden floor and expensive carpets.

Closing her eyes at the devastation, Wendy wondered what their host thought of them. Arriving at his home uninvited, her parents had demanded that he receive them. At first the couple had been beyond obsequious, flattering their host, his home, and anything about him they could think of.

That was until he, aghast, told them he didn't want to marry Wendy.

"It would be my pleasure if you would join me for a stroll to the gallery," Lord Barkston-Ash now offered gently, interrupting her mortified thoughts, and grateful for his thoughtfulness, she nodded, teary-eyed.

"My parents…" she started, but his gentle smile cut her off.

"The gallery is just on the other side of the door in the corner, and I will leave the door open, so we will be in full view of your parents."

With a hesitant look at her still-brawling parents, Wendy placed her hand lightly on the arm offered to her and followed him into the next room. Lord Barkston-Ash didn't say a word about her parents nor about the reason for their visit. Instead, he told her about the people in the paintings they passed, funny little tidbits that for a moment made her forget about the absurd situation her family was inflicting upon him.

The gallery was one of the loveliest rooms she had ever seen, its walls covered with paintings of Wetherby relatives that looked down at them as they strolled by. As they reached the other end of the room, Lord Barkston-Ash invited her with a polite gesture to sit down on a small sofa that stood there flanked by large French doors overlooking the inviting terrace.

The door to the room in which her parents still shouted at each other was far enough away for their voices to be only a distant mumble. Lord Barkston-Ash and his guest sat in silence, looking out over the grand room, and Wendy knew she had to say something to this kind man, if only to apologize for their intrusion, but she didn't know where to start.

How could she ever explain what this was all about?

She knew the truth sounded like a twisted fairytale, too unreal for anyone to believe. Without realizing it, she sighed deeply, and immediately Lord Barkston-Ash turned his head with an inquiring smile.

"Is something amiss, Miss Russell?" he asked, politely.

"Oh, no, my lord, I was only enjoying the gallery. It is such a lovely and lavish room."

"Please," Lord Barkston-Ash said, his eyes earnest as he took her hand in his. "I know it goes against every rule of society, but Miss Russell, I would be very honored if you would call me Nathan."

"Nathan," Wendy repeated, blushing, and his smile became warmer.

"May I call you Wendolyne?"

She felt her cheeks grow even hotter as his warm gaze caressed her. "Wendy, please. No one calls me Wendolyne. It is such a pompous, stuffy name."

He laughed softly. "In my opinion, it is neither pompous nor stuffy, and I find it quite lovely. I would be honored if I may call you by it."

He was such a dear, dear man, and with a growing sense of panic, Wendy felt herself appreciating him even more. Thank the good Lord they would be on their way as soon as her parents managed to calm down enough to walk themselves out to their waiting carriage. She most definitely did not need another man to claim a piece of her already aching heart.

To hide her bewilderment, she bowed her head slightly. "Well, then I give you my permission to call me by it."

"Thank you, Wendolyne."

"You are welcome…Nathan."

Again they sat silently side by side, but it was such a serene, content silence that Wendy felt herself relaxing. The last few months had been an exhausting time in her life and the undemanding friendliness she was met with here at Deighton Cross eased mental knots she had not been aware existed.

Closing her eyes with a relieved sigh, she leaned her head back until it rested on the upright portion of the sofa, and as exhaustion overtook her, she drifted off to sleep.

Chapter Eighteen

"Wendolyne, meet Bertha. She looks like a giant but is in fact a real sweetie who will never let her temper get the better of her."

Looking up at the large horse standing in front of her, Wendy frowned suspiciously. Nathan chuckled, amused over her apparent distrust, and she frowned at him too, just to make sure he understood what an utterly ridiculous idea this was. She had two good feet. She could most definitely walk.

At the side of Bertha, Nathan offered her his hand. "Come on, Wendolyne, it's only a horse."

"Easy for you to say," Wendy muttered under her breath, as she took his hand, allowing him to help her into the saddle. "You are used to these beasts, but I have only seen them from afar. The closest I ever have been to a horse is when riding in a carriage behind one."

Leaning against Bertha's side, Nathan looked up at her with a warm smile, and her heart fluttered in a way only Douglas had succeeded in eliciting previously. She couldn't believe she was still here, after her horrifying arrival two days earlier. But she was, and so were her parents, even though she'd hardly seen them at all during the last couple of days.

Mary, the giddy maid who had been assigned to be her lady's maid during her stay at Deighton Cross, had told her that the marquis had carried the exhausted Wendy to a guest room, leaving her in the capable hands of his servants. When she waked the next day, she felt more rested than she'd been for a long time. After freshening up, she let Mary help her get dressed in clothing she didn't recognize but was told it belonged to Nathan's sister.

It was such a lovely dress, made of the most exquisite white muslin fabric, with small pink flowers following the modest neckline. She had never had such a delightful dress. All her clothes, even the ones ordered by Douglas, were of darker fabric, and sturdy. Practical. But this dress… It almost made her feel pretty. Almost…

As she'd made her way to the breakfast room, the lovely muslin dress fluttering around her feet, she felt like a new person. The appreciative smile Nathan bestowed upon her when she joined him there told her more than anything that she looked as good as she felt.

They had spent the day together, walking throughout the grand country house. Her parents, who also had been put in a guest room, were not seen anywhere. Instead, an older female relative of Nathan's chaperoned the young couple, staying as far away as she could without breaking protocol.

It had been such a lovely day. Nathan turned out to be a wonderful spinner of tales about the people in the paintings, telling her the most outrageously witty stories about their lives. She hadn't a clue if any of it was true, but she didn't care. Instead she followed him around, listening to his velvet voice as they walked from room to room.

Dinner had not been as nice, as her parents joined

them at the enormous table. They had ceased their earlier shouting, although the constant bickering and disdainful looks between the two of them was just as difficult to countenance. Fortunately, they did not stay late, and as soon as they were out of sight, Nathan ordered his best wine to be delivered to the library.

There he and Wendy had spent the rest of the evening, under the watchful yet tired eyes of his aunt, playing chess while teasing each other gently. She defeated him thoroughly the first time—to his surprise, as he was a well-known chess player of highest rank. With a frown worthy of River Jordan marking his forehead, he begged her to play again, and after an hour of verbose persuasion she let him have his way.

She won again. Of course.

Three games later, she had a hard time hiding her yawns, and he—with an odd mixture of childish poutiness and reverent astonishment—had declared her the champion before sending her, and his already sleeping aunt, off to bed.

When she this second morning had joined him at the breakfast table, he asked her to go with him for a ride on his lands. Not taking no for an answer, he sent her to her room, where Mary had helped her into a beautiful blue riding outfit, which also belonged to his sister.

Ten minutes later, she was now introduced to Bertha in the stable.

Nathan mounted a large black stallion that danced around with wild, rolling eyes. But Nathan obviously was a good horseman, as he skillfully calmed the skittish horse, and soon they rode over the fields surrounding Deighton Cross.

The sun shone brightly, enhancing the vivid blue sky over their heads. It was a perfect day for a ride in the countryside, and to Wendy's relief Bertha was just as sweet as Nathan had promised. It didn't matter what his stallion did; the even-tempered mare didn't blink at any of it.

"You see that ridge over there, Wendy? Standing on top of it, you have the most wonderful view of the moor, and it is a perfect spot to have our luncheon," Nathan said, and he took the lead up the hillside.

When they had reached the top of the ridge, he helped her down, and as subtly as she could, she massaged her aching backside.

When he heard her groan, Nathan smiled mischievously at her. "Feeling a bit sore, are we?"

"Yes, a little." Wendy smiled back as she walked stiffly over to a fallen tree trunk, where she sat down, very carefully.

She hadn't known moors could be this beautiful and peaceful. And large. As far as she could see, heather grew on every soft hill and shallow valley.

Nathan sat down beside her, and quietly she accepted the sandwich he offered her. Looking at his handsome profile, a part of her didn't want this wonderful visit to end, but she knew it had to. In more ways than she would have thought possible, meeting this good man who liked her for what she was had been manna for her lonely soul.

Someone liked her, the unwanted.

The feeling was mutual; she found herself very much in favor of him too. If it hadn't been for that grumbling man who hid in the deepest forest, she might have fallen in love with Nathan. They were so much alike, with the same interests and the same sober view of life.

Douglas never agreed with her on anything. He always had a different opinion, a different view. It was exhausting, always having to argue for her side of things.

But, at the same time, life with Douglas was always a surprise—you never knew what lay around the corner. She had become very much in favor of surprises, too.

"You seem miles away, Wendolyne." Nathan interrupted her thoughts softly, and she mentally sent Douglas back to Gloucestershire.

"Oh, I am sorry. I was merely thinking about how kindly you have opened up your home for us, and I don't know how I ever will be able to repay you."

"I might have a way or two in mind."

"M-my parents have been anything but polite," she stressed with dread, sensing that this conversation was about to take what—for her—would be an unwanted turn. "And yet you opened your door for total strangers, inviting us into your home, letting us stay under your roof. You didn't have to do that, and yet you did."

"Of course I had to." Nathan shrugged. "If you could have seen yourself, how devastated you looked when the three of you arrived. My parents did not raise me to send anyone away in such a condition. Especially not a damsel in distress, whose parents seemed too upset with me to take care of you properly."

A mild way to put it.

"I hope you can forgive my parents for how they behaved when we first arrived. You are not obliged to anything. Just because my mother misunderstood the meaning of her friend's letter does not make you a bad person for turning us away."

"I know," Nathan said slowly, his eyes never leaving the horizon. "But maybe…maybe I no longer find the idea as bad as it first seemed."

She had not expected that. Not this soon, at least. Pain over her situation filled her heart, and she closed her eyes hard. "Please," she whispered. "Please stop. Don't…"

"I can't say I am thrilled that I would have to welcome your parents into my family," Nathan continued, ignoring her anguished input. "But with you as my wife it would be worth it. Definitely."

His warm hands took hold of her cold ones, and as she opened her eyes, she found him kneeling in front of her, his heart clearly visible in his warm gaze.

"Nathan…" Wendy almost groaned, desperately searching for the right words, but her mind was frozen, unable to come up with even one sentence.

"Why not?" he asked, his voice as soft as velvet. "I see no obstacles. Your parents came here with the intention of seeing the two of us wed. Why not oblige them?"

"Please," Wendy repeated, tears falling from her eyelashes to land on his hands that held hers so tightly. "Can't we just leave things where they are? We are friends, aren't we?"

He nodded, solemnly.

"Then, believe me when I tell you that I can't marry you."

His smile felt as warm as the sun. "Perhaps you find me repellent?"

She couldn't hold back a giggle, and immediately

he leaned closer, until their noses almost met. "You know there is something special between the two of us. I have never met anyone who makes me feel so much at ease as you do. I am known to be a cautious man, a man who doesn't let his heart lead his mind. But even though I have only known you for a few days, I know I would die a happy man if you became my wife."

The truth of it was written on his earnest face, and Wendy had no choice. She had to get as far away from him as possible. Before he had an opportunity to react, she ripped her hands from his. In a few seconds' time, she had stood up and rushed over to the waiting Bertha. She succeeded in her first attempt to climb up into the saddle by herself.

"Wendy..."

She looked down at Nathan, who stared at her in confusion. For a moment she hesitated, but in the end her honest heart won. She couldn't lie to this man. She had to tell him the truth, no matter how much it would hurt either one of them. She could not leave him believing her to be a woman she wasn't.

"If you only knew how much I wish I could say yes," she cried. "You make me feel so at peace, something I have never experienced before. I know I would be perfectly happy spending the rest of my life with you, but I can't."

"So say yes." He took a step closer, sensing victory. "I want this, you want this, and furthermore, your parents burn for this. Say yes."

"Promise me you won't tell my parents that I declined you."

"But..."

"Please. Just accept my wish. I promise you,

Nathan, you don't want to marry me."

"But I do."

"If you knew everything there is about me, you wouldn't," Wendy said, and she could tell by his confused face that he didn't know what to think. It wasn't so hard to understand why. She had been anything but direct. She had allowed herself to be lured into a state of fairytale these last couple of days, and now she had to pay the price. If she had cut him off from the beginning, she would not have been in this situation. But he had been so kind, so warm, and her desperate love-yearning soul had not been able to pretend to be otherwise.

"Then enlighten me," he begged softly. "Tell me why the lovely young woman I see, whose kindness and good heart penetrate everything she does, would not make the perfect wife."

Looking down at his face, she memorized his warm chocolate eyes gazing up at her from under the blond hair. She knew he would never look at her this way again, because as soon as she told him the truth, he wouldn't want ever to see her again.

She had never hated her parents as much as she did just then. Their selfish hunt for a lavish lifestyle had made them go against every known rule of etiquette, and, what hurt more, even their own common sense. Their search for wealth had destroyed her every chance for happiness.

"I am not what you think I am," she whispered, and he gave her a contented smile that made her cry even harder, due to its tenderness.

"Wendy," he whispered back, as if he didn't want to destroy the closeness of the situation. "You are such a sweet, loveable young woman, and I promise you there is nothing you could have done that I will find so awful that I will let you go."

She sighed, defeated. There was no way around this; she had to tell him the whole truth, every awful little detail. But how could she, when all her being screamed no?

"You deserve better than me."

He made a noise somewhere between a chuckle and a snort. "You are everything I need."

"Please, let me finish," she begged, and with a sigh he agreed, reluctantly.

With one last strengthening breath taken, she blurted it all out, before she had a chance to change her mind. "I have lived with a man for the last couple of months, without being married to him."

Nathan looked at her blankly, not understanding what she tried to tell him. "Why would this discourage me from wanting to have you as my wife? You have lived with me the last couple of days, without being married to me."

"My parents are with me now."

"Oh," Nathan breathed, finally understanding what she was trying to tell him, and before he had a chance to say anything more, Wendy continued slaughtering the good esteem in which he had held her.

"I was his wife in every way a woman can be, without being married to him. This is the reason why I can't marry you, and the reason why you have to let me go."

His clenched hand, which had held Bertha's reins, fell slowly to his side. Unable to stay put, watching the warmth fade from his face, Wendy forced the horse into action, leaving him alone with her truth. Bertha, the wonderful beast, knew her way home, and soon Wendy rushed through the grand rooms of Deighton Cross in search of her parents. She found them in the breakfast room, spending their time ignoring each other.

"We're leaving," she told them brutally as she marched into the room.

"What…" Her mother started, but Wendy interrupted her harshly.

"I told Nathan about what I am, and now we're leaving."

"You did *what*?" Her father's chair fell over as he stood up, yelling at her, but she didn't care about his anger.

"I am leaving in five minutes, and if you two aren't by the carriage, I will leave without you."

Without waiting for them to respond, she turned and continued upstairs, toward her room. As soon as the door to the guest room closed behind her, she didn't wait for the maid but started to unbutton the beautiful riding gown. Looking down at the lovely blue pile at her feet, she blinked away the tears threatening to fall.

This was not the time to mourn what never would be. She could do that later, when she was somewhere else and not under the roof of the man whose feelings she had just hurt and whose friendship she had just lost.

As she stood dressed only in her thin chemise, the door crashed open and Nathan barged in. He stopped dead when he saw her in front of him in only her undergarments, and something which reminded of pain flashed in his eyes before the seething anger came back.

Wendy took a step back, trying to reach something to hide behind.

"Don't you dare," he practically growled, and she became perfectly still, not knowing how to handle this furious version of Nathan.

"Wendy, what is happening?" Her parents appeared in the doorway behind him, but before they had a chance to enter the room, Nathan kicked the door shut and locked it, leaving them on the outside.

"Nathan," Wendy begged, but he cut her off icily.

"It is Lord Barkston-Ash to you."

Tears dripped down her cheeks, but she managed to stop the sobbing before it started. "My lord," she whispered. "Please, just let me leave."

"Why?" he snarled. "You just told me you were a used woman, and as I see it, you are mine for the taking."

Wendy knew it was only his anger talking. If this had been Douglas, she'd have been terrified of him taking advantage of her, but not Nathan. His kind heart wouldn't let him do something so devastating to her. Or to himself. He just didn't have it in him.

"I told you to let me go. I told you to stop asking me why," she whispered, and he closed his eyes when he heard the sadness in her voice.

"Who is he?" he asked, hoarsely.

"His name is not important."

"Humor me."

His anger was mellowing down, and she grabbed the robe that lay on the bed, hiding her body in it. Nathan hardly noticed, as he sat down heavily on a chair, his face hidden in his hands.

Wendy could hear her parents' voices from the other side of the door, and she kneeled in front of Nathan, leaning her forehead against his soft hair.

"Why wouldn't you just let it be?" she asked, softly. "I told you the truth was only going to hurt you. Please don't think too badly of me. I haven't been allowed much say about the direction of my life, but if I had, I wouldn't be sitting here with you now."

"Tell me his name," Nathan whispered, not acknowledging what she'd just said.

"No," she replied, stubbornly, and fell backward as he stood up.

"I need to know who he is."

"No, you don't. It is for the best. My parents and I will leave as soon as possible, and then you can continue with your life as if we'd never met."

Nathan stared at her, with a strange smile that showed a mix of pain and unbelief, before staggering out the door, ignoring the puffing Sir Edward and the shrieking Juliet as he passed them.

"How could you…" her mother began, but Wendy cut her off again, wagging her finger in front of her mother's gaping mouth.

"Don't you say a word. I am leaving here as soon as I am dressed, and you'd better go and get ready if you don't want to be left behind."

Something in her voice must have cut through her parents' selfishness, because they just looked at her oddly and scurried away to collect the few things they had brought with them.

Ten minutes later, Deighton Cross disappeared behind a bend of the road. Wendy sat silently in a corner of the carriage, staring out through the window, listening to her parents repeatedly tell her exactly how stupid she was, but she didn't acknowledge them.

Her life was a mess, and those two were the sole

reason for her degeneration. Instead of answering them, she slumbered most of the journey, until they reached an inn where they could stay for the night. Without another word, her parents locked her inside a small room, but she was too tired to care. All she wanted to do was to sleep and dream of another life, one filled with love, hope, and fulfillment. All she wanted was to forget how pathetic her own life was, and the gloomy future that awaited her.

****

Douglas arrived at Deighton Cross just as the sun disappeared behind the large house, and he smiled with pleasure even as his stomach growled at him. Too impatient to waste time, he hadn't stopped for something to eat during the day, well aware that his friend Nathan would stuff him full as soon as he reached his destination.

It had been a tiresome couple of days, tracking the threesome. He had thought it would be easy to find them, but he had soon found that it wasn't so unusual for two parents with one or two adult daughters to travel at this time of the year. The Season had come to its end, and now most of the *ton* was heading to their country houses. Every inn he'd passed had been filled with travelers, and it had taken too much time to make sure that none of the companies staying were the one he sought.

In the end, it had been the Russells' unpleasantness which had saved him. No innkeeper forgot a haughty couple that expected to be treated as if they were the King and Queen of England and who then had left in the early morning hours without paying. Few could remember a daughter, but some of them had noticed a quiet maid traveling along.

Douglas's jaw ached from holding in all the anger he felt over the Russells' selfish behavior. It wasn't surprising they let people think Wendy was their maid. Travelers with servants were better treated than those who traveled by themselves. It gave the impression they were nobles who could afford servants and therefore wouldn't have any problem paying for their stay.

"Well, well, well. Look what the cat dragged in."

Douglas turned to look at his friend, who stood in the doorway to the library. Nathan himself looked ragged and disheveled, and, if Douglas wasn't mistaken, more drunk than he'd ever been seen before.

What had happened to him during Douglas's decade of playing the elusive beast of a hermit? Nathan had been one of his most persistent friends, the last one Douglas had chased away all those years ago. In the end, Nathan had also become the friend he had missed most.

Meeting while attending Eton, they had stayed close friends ever since, and only Douglas's accident had come between them.

"I guess I could say the same thing about you." Douglas grinned, and was rewarded with a warm chuckle.

Nathan took a step forward to greet his friend, but as soon as he let go of the doorway, he started to wobble, almost knocking over an expensive vase as he passed it. Douglas rushed forward and led his friend back into the safety of the library. He helped him into the chair Nathan must have spent some time in, judging by the many empty bottles surrounding it.

"S'cuse me," Nathan burped, and Douglas almost

gagged over the smell of it.

His friend was in the worst shape he'd ever seen him in, and he couldn't help to wonder what had caused such a change in him. Nathan had always been a modest drinker, as his father had been a drunk who hadn't cared about who he mistreated when under the spell of the spirits.

Even when young and stupid, Nathan had been careful about not becoming too drunk. He didn't want to misbehave in any way, causing anyone embarrassment, whereas Douglas more than once had thrown himself into the whirl of wine, women, and lovemaking, not thinking twice of the aftermath.

Douglas spent the rest of the evening trying to sober his friend up, and next morning, when they met in the breakfast room, Nathan grinned sheepishly.

"Sorry about that," he said, as Douglas lifted a dark eyebrow questioningly. "I had a bit of a setback, but I feel much better now, thanks to you. It's so good to see you!"

The last part came with a giant hug, which was more the Nathan Douglas had known, the affectionate and compassionate friend.

Douglas grimaced, ashamed. "Sorry about that."

Nathan grinned again, as he sat down at the opposite side of the table, accepting a cup of tea from a footman. "It sure has been a while," he continued, as he spread butter on a hot biscuit. "I think it must be about nine years now, since the last time you threw me out of Darkwood Manor."

Douglas accepted the gentle reprimand, well aware he was being let off easily. When thinking about how brutishly he had behaved toward his loved ones all those years ago, when his heart and body had been broken, he became warm and uncomfortable.

"It is nice to see you again too," Douglas said, softly, and Nathan accepted the vague apology, knowing he wouldn't get more from a proud man like his friend, and instead he let the subject go.

"So what brings you to my part of England?"

"A woman."

"Of course. What else would have a man chase all over the country?"

"And drinking himself into a stupor."

"True," Nathan agreed, and continued with a wicked smile. "I never thought it would come to this—Douglas Scott chasing a female instead of the other way around."

"Me neither. But then I didn't think I would spend ten years hiding like a beast in my castle, either. Life does have a way of surprising a person now and then."

"Do you still have any problems from your accident?"

"No." Douglas shook his head. "Just the scars on my face, which I'll never be rid of."

"Well, then you have been lucky indeed, because I saw the carriage at the bottom of the quarry, and you should have been dead, like your poor driver."

"Lucky?" Douglas grunted, his mouth full of delicious cucumber sandwich. "You wouldn't call yourself lucky if it had been you covered with scars like mine."

"Right," Nathan laughed, but the laughter trailed off when he realized Douglas wasn't joking. "Come on, Douglas, look at yourself. One can hardly see the scars on your face, and if you suffer from having them, then you should rethink the matter and instead consider yourself scarred inside the head, you bloody fool."

It was not that he didn't want to believe it, Douglas thought with a mix of disdain and disbelief as he leaned back in his chair. He had heard it before; Nathan was not the first to dismiss his scars. Both Wendy and Thornbury had, too. Even Quentin had tried to talk to him about it, but he had refused to listen.

Thinking about it, it was only Caroline Peabody who had persisted in telling him how horrible he looked and how repulsive she found him. But now, as he knew her game had been to lure him into marriage, he guessed she probably wasn't the one he should have listened to. Mrs. Peabody's motives were still a bit unclear, but he guessed she had reasons to keep him reluctant to meet others, and especially other women more suited for him.

Like Wendy.

In society's eyes, they were not a match. She had no title, no connections, no overwhelming beauty, and no wealth which would put her higher on the most-wanted list. But to him that didn't matter. Not at all. He had found his match, and as soon as he found her, he would never let her go again.

The only negative thing about Wendy, he thought with a wry smile, was her family. But then again, they didn't have to spend any time with the Russells at all if she preferred not to. Her parents had never treated her with love, only used her, and in his mind she needed to get as far away from them and their bad influence as possible.

If he and Wendy would be blessed with children, he most definitely didn't want them to meet her family.

Not because of their lower class but because of their idiotic behavior, in general, and specifically how they had treated their youngest child.

A really nice round sum would probably do the trick. And to make sure they didn't come pestering Wendy for more, he would force them to sign a letter of confession that he would make public if they did return with an agenda. If it ever became commonly known how they had bartered with their daughter's virtue, the Russell family would be destroyed forever. They would never be accepted into society again, neither by their acquaintances nor by the *ton*.

"Do you want me to fetch you a mirror, old man? So you can see what the rest of us see when we look at you?"

"No," Douglas said with a sheepish grin, much like the one Nathan had bestowed on him earlier.

Nathan, who never had been one to hold a grudge, just bowed his head slightly and then let the subject drop. "So who is this girl you have chased all across England?"

"Someone I used to know before the accident and who has grown up into the most enchanting person."

"You sound like you've met your match."

Douglas nodded, his heart aching for Wendy. Before he did something stupid, like crying in front of his friend, he changed the subject.

"How about you? Your appearance, when I first arrived yesterday, could only have been because of a woman."

This time it was Nathan's turn to look as if in pain, and Douglas's heart went out to him. Loving Wendy must have opened him up to others' feelings, because before he got to know and love her, he'd never used to be sympathetic toward others like this. Another good thing she had brought into his life, he thought tenderly.

"I'm not really in your situation, Douglas, as I have only just met the girl. I can't call myself in love with her, but I do feel such a strong connection to her. It is as if we have been friends of heart and soul forever, and I had every intention of hastening forward with our relationship, with a desperate hope for marriage and happiness until eternity."

"What happened?"

"She denied me, even though it is clear she feels the same way I do."

"So why deny you?" Douglas frowned, not understanding the girl's actions.

"Because of another man."

"Oh."

Poor Nathan. It must be devastating to find the girl of one's dreams and then lose her again. He knew exactly how it felt; he too had lost the woman of his heart. However, in his case it would end well. It had to, because he couldn't see a life in front of him without Wendy in it.

"Not much to say about it, unfortunately. I can't marry her, which we both are aware of, and all due to the other man and his actions. All I have left is an urgent need to drown my sorrows. And, to be honest, one fist that wants to plant itself right on that man's nose."

Nathan did some boxing movements with his hands, and Douglas couldn't help but feel sad about all the years he had thrown away, and all the friends he had lost. Instead of lurking about in his crumbling home, he could have roamed the world with his friend.

"It is sad, though," Nathan continued slowly. "The girl is now in the hands of her horrible parents. The most awful couple I have ever met. It's a wonder she turned out as well as she did, being brought up by them. I guess a good core is indestructible."

Slowly Douglas placed his cup on the table, as he recognized the familiarity of his friend's words. It sounded too close to not be the Russell family Nathan was talking about. A mix of jealousy and fear filled his heart, and he put his hands in his lap to stop himself from leaping over the table and hurling himself onto Nathan.

What had his friend said?

Something about meeting his soul mate, and her not being able to marry him because of another man. A man who had destroyed her chance of marrying Nathan? He took a deep breath, and exhaled slowly in a desperate need to calm his temper.

"May I ask what the girl's name is?" he said between his teeth, and Nathan frowned at him, not understanding the sudden change in his friend.

"Wendolyne Russell," he answered slowly. "Her name is Wendolyne Russell."

Chapter Nineteen

"What are you doing, hiding up here?"

As her parents closed the bedroom door behind them and came toward her, Wendy bit back the frustrated sigh that threatened to escape her. "I am not hiding. I was tired after traveling all day."

Sir Edward didn't bite back his sigh of frustration. "It is your own fault, you know, that we were forced to leave. Had you just held your tongue and stayed silent, we would have been at Deighton Cross now, in perfect, comfortable ease. But no, you just had to spit it all out, forcing the poor man to throw us out."

"But Father…"

"Not one word from you, missy," Sir Edward snarled. "It is your very own selfishness that has put us in this situation, forcing your poor mother and me to suffer on these horrible northern roads. If you just had stayed quiet…"

"It is no use, my dear," Juliet said as she sat down on Wendy's bed, ignoring the loud creaking sound as the bed complained. "The girl is just too selfish to think about how her misconduct impacts her family. If she had cared even the slightest about us, her loving parents, she would have held her tongue, saving both the poor man and us from suffering."

"I had to tell him," Wendy said hoarsely, her voice breaking into pieces.

"Oh, bollocks," Juliet snapped, without compassion. "This is all your fault. You could have chosen to stay quiet and accept that man's proposal, giving us all a golden future, but you didn't. Instead you closed every open door and made sure that he locked them tightly. What lives we could have had if you had not been such a useless daughter."

"Useless," Sir Edward echoed, as he walked over to his wife, his face filled with as much disdain as his wife's.

"I-I'm sorry," Wendy whispered, tears streaming down her face. "But I simply couldn't lie to him. A-and I couldn't marry him. Douglas…"

"Lord Darkwood has nothing to do with this," Juliet interrupted rudely. "He has done too much damage already, whisking you off to that ruin of his in the middle of the forest."

"But, Mother," Wendy said through her tears, "that is not true. It was you and Father who left me there, at Darkwood Manor, remember?"

"If Lord Darkwood hadn't offered us money, we would never have sent you to that godforsaken place."

As she saw her parents staring at her with more contempt than she'd ever thought she'd meet, Wendy knew it was no use. They would never listen to her nor admit their part in what had happened. They called her selfish, but the truth was this was all their doing.

All her life she'd been told she was unworthy and useless, always compared to her sister and never deemed the better, and she had believed them. She had believed every word they had said, finding herself lacking in every way.

Until she arrived at Darkwood Manor and was

forced to grow a spine.

Douglas might seem an uncaring beast, but the truth was he was anything but. Under that rough surface, a wonderful man existed. So what if he might be a bit brutishly honest now and then. Considering all the lies she had grown up with, she actually found his harshness refreshing.

And he trusted her. Without thinking twice about it, he had left her in charge of his house and the people in it, not once considering that she might not have a clue about what to do. Instead he had surmised that she was able, and she had been. To her own surprise, she had grabbed the reins steadily, not once feeling unworthy or useless.

Such trust was endearing.

"You should be grateful that your father is such an efficient man." Juliet interrupted Wendy's melancholic thoughts. "He has found a way for you to make up for your faults. Mr. O'Neil is nothing compared to Lord Barkston-Ash, of course. Few men are. But you can't be picky anymore. You have made sure of that by yourself."

Wendy stared openmouthed at her parents. "Who is Mr. O'Neil?"

"Your savior." Sir Edward lifted his hand and frowned at his nails. "When we arrive in Gloucester, I must have my nails taken care of. I look like a savage."

"M-my savior?" Wendy stuttered, her mind filling with fear. They couldn't have done it again, could they? There had to be another reason for her father finding this Mr. O'Neil to *save* her. There had to be.

But she knew in her heart that there wasn't. They were selling her once again.

The small candle of hope inside her soul, the one she stubbornly had nursed all her life, keeping it barely alive, flickered and then finally died.

"Mr. O'Neil's wife died a few weeks ago giving birth, leaving him to deal with their eleven children. It is a very complicated situation, and he is in desperate need of a woman to care for his family. It is not so easy for a widower to find a woman willing to marry with such haste, and that without any courtship."

"I don't think the eleven children make him more attractive in the eyes of a marriageable woman," Juliet smirked, and Sir Edward chuckled in response to his wife's wit.

"Indeed, my dear. Had he been a better-looking man, perhaps the number of offspring could have been disregarded by a woman of sense. But unfortunately for Mr. O'Neil, his looks leave much to wish for."

Closing her eyes in distress, Wendy finally had had enough. Her parents would never change. It would never matter what she did or what she said—they would never care for her.

"I am not marrying Mr. O'Neil."

"And that's where you are wrong, child." Sir Edward's smile was overbearing and ugly. "Your future husband has already paid me a nice little sum for your hand in marriage, and the deal is sealed. The man has nowhere near the wealth of your former suitor, but considering your situation, we can't be too greedy. You will leave with him as soon as the marriage ceremony is complete."

"There is no license…"

"And yet again you presume wrongly. Mr. O'Neil already has a special license to marry, due to his family's situation. He can marry any woman he wants, whenever he wants to."

Juliet stood up, and the bed squeaked gratefully. "Stop this nonsense, Wendy. This is not your decision to make. Collect your things. Mr. O'Neil is waiting downstairs to take you with him to his estate as soon as the deed is done."

"I am not marrying Mr. O'Neil."

"We have already accepted on your behalf."

She wanted to roll her eyes but forced herself not to. This was not the time to lower herself to their level. She was better than that. Better than them. She was finally done with them, emotionally, and it felt as if a huge weight, one she hadn't been aware she carried, fell from her shoulders.

Briskly, she walked up to the door and opened it. "Get out."

It was funny, really. She had never noticed how much her parents resembled fishes. Their openmouthed astonishment was not attractive, and she found herself holding back a smile.

"You-you…" Sir Edward stuttered, but she ignored him, simply pointing at the open door.

"You have to," Juliet gasped. "We have already accepted your dowry, using part of it to pay that distrustful innkeeper for the rooms."

"That is not my problem anymore," Wendy said with cold satisfaction. "You should have known better than to accept money for something—or someone—that isn't yours to sell."

Sir Edward took an angry step closer to her, his body seething with anger. "I am your legal guardian, and as such it is my prerogative to do whatever I please with you. Mr. O'Neil might not be your choice, but he is mine."

Shrugging indifferently, Wendy ignored her father's anger. "Mr. O'Neil won't find me eligible as a presumptive wife after I have told him the truth. I don't care how many men you try to marry me off to, I will make sure to enlighten them all."

"I am your legal guardian," Sir Edward sputtered as he took another step toward her, his desperation clearly visible, but Wendy didn't flinch.

It was a wonderful feeling to not care anymore—an incredibly satisfying feeling. Now all she had to do was find a way back to Douglas, and nurse the hope that he was still waiting for her.

Juliet, who was a bit cleverer than her husband, put a hand on Sir Edward's arm, effectively stopping him from damaging the situation more. "So be it. You have made your point of view very clear to us, and we cannot do anything but concede. But I tell you this, wench— don't you think that we will continue to take care of you or pay for you, not when you treat us like this. Let's see how far you will get by yourself when we no longer are here to pay your way. You will regret this, I promise you. You will. And when you come crawling back to us, I don't want to ever hear another word about your wishes."

Dragging her gaping husband behind her, Juliet disappeared out through the doorway, her head held high. With a strange mix of sadness and relief, Wendy closed the door behind her parents as they walked out of her life, leaving her stranded in an inn in the middle of nowhere.

It was odd, but she didn't care about being

abandoned by her parents and left without the means even to pay for the room she was staying in. She would have to deal with that problem eventually, but first she needed time to come up with a plan. If her suspicions were correct, she was carrying Douglas's baby under her heart, and if so, she had no choice but to force him to marry her.

Oh, she would so much prefer that he asked her to marry him out of love, but this was not the time to stay sentimentally stubborn. She had the baby's future to think about now, and if that meant marrying an unwilling Douglas, so be it. Even if Douglas wouldn't love her as much as she needed for him to do, she knew, without doubt, that he would love their child beyond all reason.

A knock on the door brought her back from her shattered thoughts, and for a second she considered not opening it, in case it was the innkeeper wanting money, or her parents who had come up with a way to force her to bend to their will. But when another knock was heard, she opened the door, bracing herself for the verbal attack she was expecting.

There in the shadowy hallway stood Douglas, a worried frown marring his forehead. With a squeal, she threw herself into his waiting arms, hiding her face against his broad chest as his trembling hands pressed her even harder to him. Lightly, as if she didn't weigh more than a feather, he lifted her up into his arms, carrying her over the threshold and closing the door behind him with his foot.

As he sat down on the bed, with her safely on his lap, she opened her eyes and looked up at him, ravishing his beautiful face with her eyes, until he lifted his head and met her gaze. Without thinking, she lifted her hand and placed it against his cheek, watching him lean closer to it.

"Promise me one thing," he whispered, his eyes glistening. "Never, ever, leave me again. Ever."

She blinked away the tears clouding her eyes, her answer visible in her face, in her smile, and in her eyes. With a moan, he pressed his lips against hers, kissing her deeply until they both were breathless. Unable to stay still, now as she had him so close again, she started to unbutton his shirt, and with a chuckle he helped her. His trousers and her dress followed the shirt to the floor, and soon she lay there in the creaking bed, his roaming hands creating waves of ecstasy.

The fulfillment was like none she ever had experienced before, and by his astonished, painful growl when he came deep inside her, she could tell he felt the same. Afterward, he lay down beside her, playing tenderly with a strand of her hair, which had escaped her now ruined coiffure.

Wendy couldn't stop a happy sigh filled with contentment, and Douglas gave her his slow, wicked smile. He leaned forward and nibbled lightly on the tip of her ear, and she knew she was where she belonged.

She was home.

The only lasting obstacle, the last thing she had to do before oblivion, was to persuade him to marry her. She had a sinking feeling it would be like banging her head against a brick wall, but she had no choice. Not anymore. She was not fighting for her own future anymore. She was fighting for her child's.

"I have missed you so much," she breathed, and he smiled softly, placing small kisses on the strand of hair.

"I have missed you sorely too," Douglas whispered as his lips left her hair and continued with placing lingering kisses on her breast. "If you ever leave me like this again, I will lock you inside the bedroom and never let you go."

"As long as you lock yourself in there with me." She laughed, and he laughed too, an open, hearty laughter that made her all teary-eyed again.

His hand left her breast and caressed her belly softly before continuing to the other breast, and she lost her breath for a moment. His unknowing touch of his child made her heart ache with sheer happiness. Should she tell him now that she suspected she was carrying his heir? She knew informing him about the child would make it easier for her to persuade him into marriage, but a part of her didn't want that. The little unwanted girl in her needed him to marry her out of love, and not because he had to.

Absentmindedly, he grabbed the strand of hair again, his gaze miles away. "It was hell coming home and finding you long gone. At first I didn't know where to start. I only knew about your sister mentioning some old farmer up north."

"So how did you find me?"

"Quite by chance, my dear. Quite by chance."

She lifted her head and looked down at him where he lay beside her. His naked skin reminded her of polished bronze, and when she put her hand on his torso, she could feel the heat of him. She looked up and met his beautiful eyes, drowning in their sparkling blue warmth, and out of nowhere a small shiver of fear moved through her mind.

Something had changed.

Douglas had never looked at her with such unshielded warmth before. Sometimes, if she was lucky, he would give her an unguarded smile after they'd made love, but never this much and most definitely not this openly.

It was as if he was showering her with his love.

A normal woman would have felt loved and cherished, but she was not a normal woman. She was a woman used to being met with arrogant disdain and a constant frown. Being the strange woman that she was, she felt almost betrayed instead of cherished.

Her Douglas was supposed to frown toward her, while his hands made her feel all warm and soft. He was supposed to glare at her, not stare at her softly. He was not supposed to make her feel cherished.

Douglas didn't notice her distress. Instead he gently stroked the back of her arm, where it rested across his chest. "Quentin told me it was your parents who took you, and at first I didn't know what to do. I had been away for four long days, and for all I knew, you could have left the country by then, and I would have lost you forever. When I calmed down, I remembered that your sister was staying nearby, so I found out where and went there."

"Did Annabelle help you?" Wendy asked, astonished.

"No," Douglas said with a dry laughter. "Neither your sister or my cousin helped me. Instead they tried to blackmail me out of everything. If I gave them everything, my wealth, my house, and my life, they would give up your whereabouts."

"But you didn't?"

"I couldn't. I'm sorry, Wendy, but I simply

couldn't give away what my ancestors left me so lightly, not even for you."

He looked like a sad little puppy, begging her for forgiveness. She just smiled warmly and gave him a peck on the nose. "Who helped you, then?"

"The butler. He didn't like them very much, and told me everything he had overheard when your parents were visiting on their way to Darkwood Manor to get you. And as soon as I had the direction, it wasn't so hard to find you."

"Really?" Wendy frowned. "With every inn filled to the limit, I would have guessed that tracking one small family amid all the travelers should be almost impossible."

"Not if you are traveling with *your* parents. Innkeepers tend to remember customers who sneak away without paying for the rooms."

"Oh, no," Wendy groaned, ashamed at the thought of all the honest men her parents without remorse had fooled.

"No harm has been done," Douglas said softly, placing a light kiss on her forehead. "I paid all the debts I heard of. I must admit it pained me that helping you meant helping your parents too, especially considering how much money they've already had me pay them."

"Douglas…" Wendy started, but he held a finger against her lips, silencing her effectively.

"You don't have to say anything. It was my choice."

She nodded, grateful tears filling her eyes.

"I lost you again after I passed Leeds. It was as if you had vanished and were nowhere to be found. My first thought was to knock on every door until I found someone who had seen you, but that would have taken too much time. So instead, I decided to visit an old friend of mine, thinking maybe he would know who this local farmer in need of a wife was, and thus make my search much easier. To my great surprise, I found out that he knew all too well about your whereabouts, because you had stayed with him for a couple of days."

"What?" Wendy cried out in delighted surprise. "Nathan is a friend of yours?"

"Known him since Eton."

"Well, how about that." Wendy laughed. "Oh, how I wish I could have told my parents about this. It would have vexed them vastly to know how the far-off husband they found for me is a friend of yours. Oh, this is hilarious!"

"Nathan?"

Wendy's giddy laughter died, as she met Douglas's cold eyes. What had happened? One second they had been laughing and kissing in bed, and now he was staring at her as if he wanted to kill her.

"Why do you call him Nathan?" Douglas said between his teeth, and that all-telling frown was back on his forehead.

"Because he asked me to."

"What more did he ask you to?"

"Nothing," Wendy sighed, as she recognized the jealousy oozing from him.

"So he never asked you to marry him, then?"

"Why, yes, but…" Wendy sputtered.

"Why didn't you accept? Marrying a marquis would have been one heck of a feather in the hat for you, considering your social status."

"Now you are being rude."

"So what," he snorted, unable to stop his jealousy. "You never cared about me being rude before you met Nathan."

Wendy sank back deeper into the pillows. How would she ever be able to have a normal discussion with him if he was going to jump all over her as soon as she opened her mouth? Oh, how she wished she had spunk enough to talk back to him, to put him in his place. But even though she knew he was a kind man who never would hurt her, she still couldn't muster enough courage.

With one last surly look, Douglas turned his back to her, ignoring her pitiful state. Silently she lay down beside him, closing her eyes in an attempt to stop the tears from overflowing.

It was impossible to do anything right, when it came to Douglas. So what if Nathan had asked her to marry him. She had denied him, hadn't she? She was Douglas's woman, body and soul, whatever it meant to him.

She would always keep a little memory of Nathan tucked away in a little chamber of her heart, but that didn't change her feelings for Douglas. How could the stupid man even think she would welcome him to her bed if she had feelings for Nathan?

Although...maybe Douglas too realized Nathan was the much better choice for her, that their characters were the same kind. She and Douglas were complete opposites, not having the same opinion or reaction to anything. The truth was that if she had met them in a ballroom, she would probably have picked Nathan over Douglas, as his kindness soothed her nerves much better than Douglas's volcanic temperament.

"There's no need for you to worry about Nathan," she said, finally breaking the thick silence of the chamber. "As you must already know, I turned his marriage offer away. I told him that I belonged to you, and even though he got upset over the admission, he admitted that my refusal was the correct answer to his question."

She waited for the longest time for him to answer, and just as she gave up on him, he sighed deeply before turning to face her. "Why did you tell him about us, and our…arrangement? Why not simply decline his marriage offer and leave things alone? You upset my friend with your honesty, and he was so angry with me that he threw me out of his house."

"Why?" Wendy echoed. "Because he is a good man and deserves to know the truth, even though it's most uncomfortable to me personally. And besides everything, I didn't know that he was your friend. Please remember it was my parents who brought me to Deighton Cross, not I who went there on my own."

"Still." Douglas yawned as he shifted into his favorite sleeping position. "You shouldn't tell strangers about us. It is not anyone's business. What you and I have together should stay between us."

She lay awake a long time after he fell asleep, pondering the options she had. What did she want out of life? If she was perfectly honest with herself, she had to admit that all she really wanted was to be Douglas's wife, happily ever after.

But what if that weren't an option?

No one would open their arms and home for a pregnant unwed woman. The only real option she had was to stay put under his roof, to make sure the child would have a good place to call home.

And if she stayed at Darkwood Manor, the child would at least be able to see his father, even though only from afar. She couldn't see the image of Douglas playing and cuddling with an illegitimate child.

She closed her eyes in an attempt to fall asleep, but she failed miserably. There were simply too many questions in need of an answer, and the most important one was: How would she ever be able to convince him to marry her because it was the right thing to do?

He didn't want a wife, and he had never asked for an heir. Instead he had made it perfectly clear for her, during the months she had stayed with him, that he wasn't going to marry anyone, especially not her.

When she finally drifted to sleep, she dreamt about babies.

****

Anthony Scott walked slowly down the streets of Mansfield, unaware of the people who had to jump out of his way so he wouldn't crash into them.

Their angry voices followed him but disappeared into the haze that had taken over his brain; all he could think about was what a friend had just told him— Douglas had gotten himself a special license.

His cousin, who had lived all alone in his forest hideout for a decade, had waked from his sleep and was about to tear down the walls of his self-inflicted refuge. And the worst thing was that the bride-to-be was no one else but his own sister-in-law, whom he had helped send to Darkwood Manor in the first place.

Remembering how Douglas had looked at Wendy, he guessed it wouldn't be too long until little feet pattered over the ancient floors of Darkwood Manor.

The Scott family fortune, of which he had dreamt for years, was becoming unreachable.

He should have taken care of Douglas as soon as he'd heard that his cat-like cousin had survived the crash. But, after his failed attempt to suffocate Douglas, he had momentarily given up the idea of killing him. Instead, he had felt oddly sorry for the man who had been hurt so badly, his face covered with scars which deformed his former handsomeness into beastly horridness. Convinced that Douglas would die soon anyway, he had left his cousin alone, but to his surprise Douglas had survived.

For the last decade he hadn't cared much about his cousin and his wasted, hermit life, as his own life had been good for a while, and he had been happy in a very unfamiliar way. So sure that he soon would inherit his cousin's estate, he had concentrated on his own life instead, not realizing how fast time passed.

His happiness had not lasted that long, though. Annabelle had not been what he had thought her, but there were many servant girls who were more than willing to spread their legs for him, so his wife's frigidity didn't mean too much. She still looked good on his arm, and he could still bathe in other men's jealousy.

But as most good things in his life, it had to end, and, as always, it had to do with money. He had been playing a lot with some lowly scumbags lately, and they seemed to be more eager about collecting their winnings than his friends were. He had given them everything he had, but they still wanted more, and in the end, they had made him go to his wife and beg her to help him, but in vain, as Annabelle refused to sell her jewelry.

Instead she had sent a letter to her parents, asking them for help. The only thing was that Sir Edward had also been gambling too much lately, and it was a dead end. When Douglas had contacted Sir Edward about his debts and paid thousands of dollars for Wendy to become his aunt's companion, they all had been ecstatic. All his previous fear disappeared, and instead he had thrown himself into a merry dance of lush women, cheap wine, and extensive gambling, not thinking about how much he lost.

He had ended up in the same situation as he'd been in a few months before. He had lost all the money and was in such deep debt to the same lowly thugs that his life was hanging on a very frail thread.

The situation was, in his mind, more than unfair. Why was he always the one who had no easy way out of a problem? Annabelle had been furious with him when he told her about his losses, and he'd had a really hard time persuading her to write to her parents and ask them for a bigger share of Douglas's money.

The answer they got was devastating, as Sir Edward had lost the rest of the gigantic sum and was now in deep distress himself.

As always, when buried in problems, Anthony tried to find the easy way out. The mere thought of Darkwood and the immense wealth almost within his reach made it an easy choice. He had to kill Douglas. And he had to succeed this time.

But how?

Douglas was not an easy prey, not like the last time, when he had been young and innocent when it came to the dark side of life. Now it was different. Now

Douglas was suspicious of everyone and everything.

Perhaps he should kill Wendy first?

Before she came into his life, Douglas had been an elusive hermit, hiding from life. No one would suspect anything if his life became in disarray again after losing the woman he had loved.

The woman who had saved him.

And a lonely, secluded Douglas was easier to reach. Easier to fool. No one would think twice if he killed himself out of grief.

Again, Anthony didn't notice the sour faces surrounding him as he stopped, an ugly smile growing on his flushed face. Now he knew what to do.

He was going to kill Wendy.

Chapter Twenty

Wendy slept most of the way home to Darkwood Manor, resting safely in Douglas's arms. As soon as they arrived at the country house, the servants whisked their mistress away to fill her stomach with Mrs. Robbins' wonderful food, and from there to soaking her in a much-needed bath.

When Douglas later came into her bedroom, she was already fast asleep, too tired to wait for him to join her. He stood silent for a moment, watching her sleep, his chest aching with love for this delightful woman. What if she'd never come to Darkwood Manor? How gruesome and lonely his life would still have been.

With one last lingering look at her angelic face, he quietly left her and went to his study to write a note, asking the Coleford minister to come and wed him and Wendy by the special license his godfather had helped him obtain. Just the thought of being able to call her his wife made him warm all over. The only thing that still worried him was how she would react.

He knew nothing about her feelings for him.

Wendolyne Russell was a hard woman to read sometimes, as she was too used to hiding her true feelings from her parents. He knew she had tender feelings for him; the way she responded to him in bed told him as much. It would be much easier if he knew that she cared for him, that she loved him as much as he loved her. Then he wouldn't feel this nervous about her answer.

She was far too intelligent to say no, considering their situation, and before her trip to Yorkshire, he wouldn't have been this distressed over her answer. But now she had met Nathan, and it was easy to see she had found him very likeable, even though she had declined his marriage proposal.

Nathan had shown her that she had options, that Douglas was not the only man in the world who would like to marry her. So why would she choose the beast in the woods when there were men out there who were so much nicer?

Five days later, Douglas still hadn't been able to ask Wendy to marry him, and he was starting to fret about it. He wanted nothing more than to grab her capable hands in his and ask her to be his wife, but he found himself being quite the coward when it came to matters of the heart. Declaring his love to someone was something he'd never done before, and he wanted to do it with utmost delicacy.

He wanted Wendy to cry out of joy over the gift he would bestow upon her. And then she should tell him about her feelings for him as soon as possible, and preferably of the warmer kind.

"May I order new curtains for the small dining room?"

Wendy's soft voice interrupted his fantasies, and he looked at her across the breakfast table. Why on earth was she asking him about curtains? She was a woman and should be able to handle it by herself.

"You don't have to ask me about buying curtains. Go ahead and purchase whatever you think is needed."

"I can't just use your money without your permission."

"Of course you can," he muttered, and she looked at him with unreadable eyes.

"If you say so, my lord."

"Douglas," he growled, and started to pull his biscuit into small pieces out of frustration over his own curtness.

Why couldn't he just blurt it out? Why was it so hard to tell her that he loved her and wanted to marry her?

"Douglas," she echoed, still without emotion.

"Yes?" he asked, already forgetting he'd asked her to call him by his given name.

When she raised her eyebrows at him in a silent question over his odd behavior, he frowned at her at first, before remembering. He felt his face becoming warm, and by the small smile she was trying to hide, he could tell Wendy had noticed him blushing too.

"So, Douglas, can I?"

"Can you what?"

She was starting to become frustrated with him, and this time it was he who tried to hide a smile. He loved the way she wrinkled her forehead when she got upset with him. It made her look absolutely enchanting.

"Order new curtains," she said slowly, over-pronouncing every word as if he were a dimwit.

"Why?"

She growled at him, and he gave her his most wicked grin in response.

"What is wrong with you?" she finally yelled, too frustrated with him to care about the two footmen who were trying hard not to laugh out loud.

"I am fine, thank you."

This time she growled at him with so much disdain that the footmen lost their smiles and scurried out of the room, mumbling something or other as they closed the door behind them. Douglas leaned back in his chair and gave her a lazy grin, daring her to continue.

She too leaned back, and it was clear she was trying to calm her trashed nerves and keep from making a complete fool of herself.

"So you want to change the curtains, do you?"

"Yes, I do."

"All right."

"Really?"

"Really."

Her smile was bright and grateful as she put her napkin on her plate, ready to leave him and go make plans for the small dining room. "Thank you. You will not regret this."

"Before you go, I need you to do something for me." Douglas's words interrupted her dash from the room.

"Oh?" she said slowly, hesitating by the door.

"I want you to come here and kiss me."

"Oh," she breathed, and he enjoyed the blush which covered her lovely cheeks. He really did prefer her blushing rather than staring at him emotionlessly.

"Come," he said, holding his hand out invitingly.

Looking nervously at the door, she hesitated slightly, so he stood up, stepped over to the door, and locked it before going to her and hauling her close to him. He heard her swallow as he leaned down until their noses almost touched. She blushed even more fiercely as he let his lips touch hers lightly.

"You never kiss me outside the bedroom anymore," she squealed, just as he started to nibble on her lower lip.

"I do now," he murmured before deepening the kiss until they both were breathless.

A knock on the door announced someone wanting access to the room, but he didn't care. All he wanted was to continue with the kissing until he couldn't tell where he ended and she started. Wendy's small moans made him tremble with need, and for a moment he played with the thought of making room on the table to fulfill the throbbing need which had his body screaming for satisfaction.

Unfortunately, the knocking at the door was starting to sound more and more as if someone was trying to break through it, and Douglas halted the kiss with a disappointed sigh. With a tender peck on Wendy's nose, he stood up and went to the door to open it.

He had just time enough to move aside when his godfather came barging into the room. With a small bow in greeting toward the big-eyed Wendy, Thornbury pointed at the door. "Close it."

Douglas did as he was told, not understanding why Thornbury was there, and, furthermore, why he would be angrier than he had ever seen him before.

"This has to end," Thornbury snapped. "You have to marry the girl now, or I promise you I will drag you down the aisle myself."

Wendy's pretty face lost its enchanting blush as she turned white with shock and embarrassment. Douglas gave her an encouraging smile, but he had a sinking feeling that it failed miserably.

What was the old man's game?

Thornbury knew Douglas had left Oldbury Abbey with the sole mission of marrying her. The only reason they weren't married yet was because of her parents and their little trip to Yorkshire. And his cowardice regarding his proposal.

"You know what we talked about when I visited you the other week," Douglas hissed, trying to keep the truth hidden from Wendy. He still wanted her to know that he wanted to marry her, and not because he was forced by Thornbury.

But the old man must have lost his famous sixth sense, because he continued without acknowledging Douglas's input. "You promised me that you would marry the girl as soon as possible. But instead of cheerful news, I hear that you two still reside here unwed."

"Aunt Lila…"

"Is as good a chaperone as my dog," Thornbury snorted. "I know exactly how dimwitted your so-called chaperone is, and I don't think anyone believes that she does a good job of saving the virtue of your lovely girl."

"Something came between…"

"I don't care!" Thornbury snapped. "You promised me to make an honest woman of the poor girl, and now I am here to make it happen."

"W-what?" Douglas stuttered, not believing his ears. Why was Thornbury acting like a raving mad lunatic? "I don't understand why you are this upset. I told you of my intention to marry Wendy, but while I was visiting you, her parents came and took her away from me. It took me quite some time to find her, all the way up in Yorkshire, and get her back here."

"When did you come back?"

"Five days ago."

Thornbury breathed deeply through his nose, as if he were trying to calm his bad temper, giving Douglas time to send Wendy an apologizing look. Not that she noticed, though. She was staring in awe at the old man who now was pacing to and fro in front of her.

Douglas could have cried. This was exactly what he had tried to avoid. All his plans to make Wendy understand that he asked her to marry him because he wanted to were now wasted by Thornbury's demands.

"Yesterday I had a visitor," Thornbury said between his teeth. "A very old and dear friend of mine, who told me about the rumors starting to circle about you. Rumors saying that you live here alone with an unwed girl. The last thing my friend heard, before leaving London, was how a couple of your old friends talked about coming here to see for themselves. As quickly as I could I raced here, only stopping long enough to drag the poor vicar with me, to make sure you use that special license you got when you visited me last."

Damn, Douglas thought, and this time he didn't dare to cast a glance at Wendy, as he really didn't want to see what she looked like now. What did she think about all of this? Did she get that his plan had been to marry her, or had she missed that information completely?

"Manners," Thornbury shouted, and immediately the door opened and a flustered vicar came rushing into the dining room. "Wed them."

Two minutes later they were married. After that

brief ceremony, Thornbury ignored the newlyweds, instead ushering the nervous vicar out of the room and closing the door behind them.

Douglas looked down at Wendy, who stood beside him, staring in confusion at the now closed door. Smiling softly, he couldn't help but feel very satisfied with having his problem solved in the best of ways. She was his wife, and now he had the rest of his life to show her how much he adored her.

"Can you promise me one thing," he whispered, and she looked up at him with a dazed look in her eyes.

"Y-yes?"

"Promise to never ask me about curtains again. Ever."

A small, shivering smile broke across her face, washing away the confusion, and tears filled her eyes. Leaning down, he kissed away every last teardrop running down her peachy cheeks. Then, with his arms embracing her, he let his chin rest on the top of her head.

"You know," he said slowly against her soft hair, "all in all this was clearly the best thing to happen."

"Really?" she whispered, leaning back so she could look him in the eyes.

He gave her his most wicked grin before continuing. "Yes, indeed. Now I can bed you whenever and wherever I want to, and no one can tell me not to."

"Douglas," Wendy hissed, but he could see that she wasn't too upset with him. If he wasn't too wrong, she also seemed to find this something to look forward to.

"How about giving your new husband a kiss?" he coerced, and she blushed but gave him a fast peck on the lips. He shook his head, disappointed, before grabbing her chin in his hand and giving her a long, hot kiss that made them both breathless.

"I'm so sorry," she whispered, when she found her voice again. "I know you never wanted to marry me, and now you have been forced to it."

"Oh, I can't say I mind too much," he murmured, as he nibbled lightly on her ear. "As my godfather said, I had already gotten the license, so I was not as unwilling as you think."

She sighed with delight, and he chuckled in response. She was a true treasure indeed. Her immediate and honest response to his touch was extremely satisfying. She was just as honest in most things she did. The only thing which vexed him a little was her unreadable face when she chose not to show him her true feelings. But he had all the time in the world to make her realize that he wanted to know what she felt, good or bad. They were now husband and wife, and should not be keeping anything from each other.

"No more secrets," he whispered into her hair, and when he felt her tense, something cold grabbed hold of his heart.

So she had secrets, did she?

Leaning back, he looked down at her face, which was as emotionless as ever, and he got his answer. She was definitely hiding something from him.

"You know you can tell me anything?" he asked, and she nodded, still not showing any emotions. "Or to be completely honest...don't think you can hide something from me. You should tell me everything, and you can start now by telling me what it is you're hiding."

"No."

Oh, the little tease wanted to stay secretive? Well, he wouldn't allow it, which was exactly what he told her, which only rendered him a cheeky grin. "I will tell you, in time," she begged. "Please understand my need to keep this to myself for a while. It is not because I don't want you to know, it is just that I need to understand the truth myself first."

Unfortunately for her, he wasn't the understanding sort of man, he was not known for considering the feelings of others, and he wasn't about to start right now. She hid something, and he wasn't going to stop until she told what it was. He knew he was acting idiotic, but he was too afraid of losing her to let her have her way. He knew how secrets could destroy confidence, and knowing what issues he had with trust, he needed to be able to trust her completely.

"No, you will tell me now."

"Douglas, can this please wait for a while, until I know for certain?"

"Know what for certain?"

"What I don't want to tell you," she said, impatiently, rolling her eyes at him. "It is my secret, and for now mine alone."

"I won't have it."

"Really?" she snorted, and he gave her his most disgruntled look.

"Yes, really. As my wife, it is your obligation to tell me everything."

"Is it? Oh, I didn't know that." Now she was clearly laughing at him, and he had to smile back, as her smugness was quite catching. He had to give her a little kiss, and then he had to kiss her again just because the first kiss felt so good. When she returned both kisses with enough heat to make his toes curl, he just had to kiss her a third and fourth time.

When their lips finally broke apart, they stood there staring at each other with passion in their eyes as they tried to catch their breath. Her chest heaved under the thick fabric of her dress, and his fingers ached to unbutton the practical thing, so he could take her full breasts in his hands and make love to them with his hands and his tongue.

"Lock the door," he growled, and she blushed even more fiercely. But as she immediately went to the door to fulfill his wish, he could only surmise that she was just as eager to drown in the sensational passion they created together as he was.

Unfortunately, Thornbury opened the door just as Wendy grabbed the doorknob, and he gave her a fatherly grin as he stepped out of her way. "Here you go, my dear. Don't let me be in your way if you were leaving."

Wendy turned and gave a frustrated look at Douglas, and all he could do was shrug, knowing all too well that he couldn't dismiss his godfather.

"I'll be in the garden," she said pointedly, and Douglas nodded curtly, accepting the information for later.

As soon as he got rid of his godfather, he would go after her, and then she would be where she should be—in his arms.

When they were alone, Thornbury turned and gave him a winning smile. Without a word, Douglas went to his godfather and put his arm around him.

"Thank you," he whispered.

Chapter Twenty-One

Walking through the glorious gardens of Darkwood Manor, Wendy tried to grasp what had happened in the past hour. She was now Douglas's wife, or at least she thought so. It all had happened so fast. But then again, the Duke was not a man to dally, so it must be true. She was the real mistress of this estate. Even though she had been treated as the lady of the house before, it had all been a lie.

But not anymore. Now she was Wendolyne Scott, Countess of Darkwood. Absentmindedly, she let her hand touch the bushes as she passed, her clouded mind trying to bring some order into her consideration of the last days' happenings. She was so intent on her thoughts that she almost missed seeing Anthony, who stood in the gate to one of the more deserted gardens.

"Tony?" Wendy said with a welcoming smile that didn't show how unsure he made her feel. She had never really liked her sister's choice of husband, as she thought of him as a lying, selfish bastard. He had always preferred to gamble away everything he and Annabelle owned instead of leaving the money for more important things like food, clothing, and a home where rats didn't thrive.

"Wendy, I didn't see you there," Anthony said with a smile meant to be reassuring but only frightened her, as it didn't reach the dead coldness of his watery eyes.

"What are you doing here?"

"I thought I was welcome to visit my family's ancestral home."

"Of course you are, and so is Annabelle. But what are you doing out here in the garden, all alone? You should have announced your arrival, so that I could have tea and sandwiches prepared."

"You want me to announce my whereabouts to you?"

"It would be very kind of you, if you did. When I'm wandering in the garden, I tend to think I'm alone."

"Like we are right now." He grabbed her arm with his large, sweaty hand, and before she had a chance to react, he dragged her into the neglected part of the garden behind him. Silently, she struggled to get her arm loose, but in vain. Anthony's hand held her tightly, and she whimpered at the pain he caused her.

"Am I hurting you, little sister?" Anthony smirked, not hiding how much he enjoyed inflicting pain on her. His nails dug deeper into the soft skin of her arm, and she started to feel nauseous. "Tell me that you like it, and I might let you go."

She could tell he was enjoying this too much, and in a strange jump of thoughts, she felt sad for Annabelle, who had to live with this man. Did he hurt her as well? The thought of her sister having to endure this brutish man on a daily basis made Wendy's heart ache.

"Tell me you like it!" Anthony yelled, his face turning red and blotchy.

"Never," Wendy whimpered, with the last ounce of strength she could muster.

Anthony's free hand seared through the air and

landed hard on her cheek, sending her tumbling backward. The arm he still held was jerked back, forcing her into an unnatural position, and Wendy screamed in pain.

"Yes," Anthony breathed heavily. "Scream for me. Show me that I hurt you. Show me your pain." He leaned forward and grabbed her hair with his other hand, forcing her face up so he could cover her mouth with his. Wendy pressed her lips together against the probing wet tongue that licked all over the lower part of her face.

Her unwillingness and show of defiance clearly aroused him more, and he let go of her arm and instead pushed her down onto the ground. Wendy had never felt anything so disgusting as the wet kisses he gave her, and she tried to move her head to get away from them. But his hand in her hair held her head in place, and all she could do was close her eyes and mouth as wave after wave of nausea rolled over her.

"How does it feel to be with a real man?" Anthony whispered into her ear, and he pressed his groin against hers, showing her his arousal.

"No!" she screamed, but he only chuckled, taking the opportunity her reply offered him to thrust his tongue deep into her mouth, ravishing it.

As both her arms now were loose, she fought back as much as she could, kicking and scratching every part of him she could reach. When her knee hit the junction of his legs, he howled and threw himself backward. With all the strength she could muster, she hit him as hard as she could in the chest and got enough room to slip out from underneath him.

The punch he gave her in return sent her flying into

the trunk of a tree head first.

"You little bitch," he growled, before he hit her again over the head with his knuckles. She could feel warm blood pulsating down her cheek, and she knew she was hurt worse than she'd ever been before.

"Tony, please," she begged, but in vain.

"If you only knew how much I will enjoy killing you," he snapped. "At first I felt some remorse, as you have never been anything but nice to me. But now I know I will find utter delight in taking your life. And if I'm lucky, your husband will die right beside you."

Wendy stared through the blood at him, not understanding what he was talking about. Killing her? Killing Douglas?

"Why?"

"Why do you think? How dumb are you?" Anthony gave her a patronizing look, and she felt as stupid as he said she was.

"I-I don't understand," she stuttered.

"This time I will succeed," Anthony mumbled, not listening to her. "*This time* he will die. All his nine lives must be gone by now, and he will finally die, leaving to me what is supposed to be mine."

"W-what?"

Anthony laughed hysterically, with a crazy look in his eyes, and she knew he had lost his mind. This was not a sane man standing in front of her. This was an insane man, lost from this world.

"Do you want to hear something funny?" He giggled, and continued without waiting for her to reply. "I actually thought it was safe to send you here. Not even in my wildest dreams would I have guessed he would fall in love with someone as homely as you, my little mouse. But the bastard did, and that has made it so much easier for me to choose the right path."

Wendy could only stare at him as his words started to make sense to her. The accident which had turned Douglas into the wounded man he was today had not been an accident.

"How did you do it?" Wendy whispered, knowing that she needed to hear the truth for Douglas's sake. He needed to know his cousin wanted him dead.

"If you knew how easy it is to frighten horses at night... Jump in front of them, and they bolt away, unstoppable. All the way down to the sharp rocks at the bottom of the quarry. Unfortunately, my intelligent plan did not work out as I had planned. My awful cousin survived. He must have a lucky bone, indeed. The doctors called it a miracle, but I knew it was my punishment for wanting too much too soon. But I was convinced he didn't have much time left in this world, so I left him alone, and I went after his former fiancée. Annabelle, the most beautiful woman in the world, agreed to marry me, and for several years things were good. Douglas was no problem to me then, as he had withdrawn from everything and everyone. And the more he made himself alone, turning himself into a hermit, the better I was satisfied. But then I made two mistakes. I gambled too much, and I let your parents send you here. If I had known what an impact your arrival would have on my cousin's life, I would never have agreed to sending you here in the first place."

"Anthony, please," Wendy begged, trying to reach through the insanity which ruled his mind, but he interrupted her, sounding like a whining three-year-old child.

"Why did you have to make him happy? Life was wonderful when he was sad, lonely, and pathetic. Now when he is happy, I must be sad. But I don't want to be sad. I want to be happy too."

"You can be happy," she tried. "You have a wonderful wife, and you two can have an amazing life…"

"Rubbish," he interrupted her, and an ugly sneer changed his face into a horrid mask. "There will never be an amazing life as long as I don't have what Douglas has. He doesn't need the money, the title, or the standing. He doesn't care about any of it, but I do. I want the life I'm worth, and not this half-life, always wondering where I'll get the money I need. And I will have the life I deserve when Douglas is dead."

"But killing Douglas is not the answer," she cried, but too late. He had already stopped listening to her. He grabbed her arm again and dragged her with him through the gate at the back of the gardens. She had no choice but to follow him through the forest.

She didn't know how long they walked, or where they were heading, as her head throbbed painfully. Every now and then she had to stop and throw up, while Anthony pulled her arm, demanding that she hurry up. It was as though she were taking a walk through purgatory, and when they finally stopped at the highest point of the quarry, she felt relief as she stumbled down to the ground close to the edge.

Dusk settled around them, and soon they were surrounded by darkness. She lay still on the ground, not caring what her brother-in-law was doing as he moved around her, muttering this and that. Not even when he grabbed her arm again, lifting her up, had she strength enough to fight him, as the searing pain in her head had her vomiting again. He placed her in some sort of cage, and she lay down on the small floor, letting herself fade away.

It wasn't until she heard Douglas's beautiful voice, calling her name frantically, that she reacted. She tried to sit up, but Anthony immediately was there, pushing her down again. She opened her mouth to scream, but he pressed a dirty rag into her mouth, and the smell and taste of it made her nauseous again.

As Douglas's voice came closer, Anthony pushed the cage to the edge of the quarry, until the only thing stopping it from falling down was a rope tied to a nearby tree trunk. Wendy stared into the darkness, desperately trying to see the man of her heart, but the night took away every shape. When Douglas's voice was heard again, it was much closer, and this time she could also hear the voices of other men calling her name.

Flickering lights could be seen deep in the forest, slowly making progress, coming closer to where she and Anthony were. When Douglas walked out from the forest and saw them in the light from his lamp, he stopped dead. His gaze flew from Anthony's sneering face to her own scared eyes behind bars made of wood. All the color drained from his face until he was as pale as a ghost in the flickering light from his lamp. She looked at the men behind her husband, recognizing the servants from the manor, together with Thornbury.

"Tony," Douglas said in a broken voice, "please let her go."

Anthony laughed hysterically, revealing to everyone how insane he was, and Douglas closed his eyes for a second. Wendy felt the pain in her head getting worse, and something warm started to run down her cheek again, and she knew she needed medical attention soon. But then again, maybe she wouldn't. Not if Anthony had his way.

"Give me what is mine, and I might let her live."

"I don't have anything of yours." Douglas frowned.

"Yes, you do," Anthony screamed, shaking the rope attached to the cage, and almost sending Wendy over the edge into the quarry then and there.

"I'll give you anything," Douglas begged, and took a step closer with his hand out, as if he tried to save her from afar.

"Don't come any closer," Anthony said. "Not until you have given me what I want."

Wendy met Douglas's desperate eyes, and she tried to put all the love she felt for him in her own, to encourage him. But he was too distraught at seeing how close she was to dying at the hand of his cousin to notice her silent message.

"Anything," Douglas whispered, and Anthony howled with laughter again.

"Then tell all your men to go away."

Douglas didn't turn around, he just made a dismissive wave with his hand, and soon the three of them were alone. "Please, let her go, and I will do anything you want."

"Anything?"

Douglas nodded, with tears in his eyes.

Anthony laughed again, but this time it sounded evil instead of insane. "Jump," he chuckled, pointing at the quarry. Douglas frowned at him, still not understanding what it was his cousin wanted from him.

"I don't want to have to ask you again, cousin. Jump into the quarry, and I might let her go."

"You want me to kill myself?" Douglas breathed, finally understanding.

"Yes," Anthony replied, cheerfully. "Then I will have everything I want, and this little one might live to see the daylight."

He shook the rope again, and this time the cage went over the edge. Wendy closed her eyes, waiting for the crash which would end her life, as she tried to hold on to the bars of the cage even with her hands tied behind her. But the rope stopped the fall just below the ridge at the quarry's brink.

The cage squeaked and chirred, but held, and Wendy couldn't stop herself from throwing up again. The cage slowly moved from side to side, where it dangled over the sharp rocks at the bottom of the quarry, but she didn't care anymore. She knew she was only seconds away from dying, and she was tired of being afraid.

Her mind started to race, as she now had only one mission—to save Douglas. She didn't want him to die. She loved him too much to sit here and do nothing. She could hear voices, but the edge of the quarry took away the words.

Frantically, she looked around, trying to see through the darkness, but it was no use. She knew she had to figure something out from where she was. Her hands were bound tightly, but wasn't there the slightest give of the rope when she moved her hands? She shifted her hands.

Yes, there was a small error in the way Anthony had tied the knot, and she was loose in seconds. She ripped the rag out of her mouth, taking a few deep breaths. Her first reaction was to call out Douglas's name, but she shut her mouth, as she realized that surprise was her best advantage. Examining the cage with her hands, she found the part where the small door was.

She looked upward, where she could see the light from the lamps shining over the edge of the quarry, and tried to see how high it was. If she stood up on top of the cage, she would probably be able to look over the edge, and she might be able to climb up again. But climbing out from the cage seemed reckless, and she shivered when she thought about the sharpness of the rocks below her.

Thank goodness she couldn't see them in the darkness; seeing them, she might have lost all her spunk. She took a few deep breaths before slowly climbing out of the cage and heaving herself up onto it, while the cage slowly rocked from side to side. Grabbing the rope firmly, she sat still, waiting for the cage to stop rocking so she could stand up.

Looking over the edge, she could see Anthony standing in front of her, his back toward her. Douglas stood farther away, and when he saw her peeping head, his eyes grew wider, and a single tear fell down his cheek. Anthony didn't notice his cousin's reaction, as he was telling how thrilling it had been the last time he and Douglas had been here together.

With the smallest movement of his finger, Douglas made a sign to her, but Wendy understood. He wanted her out of the way, and so she heaved herself up onto the grass, silently sending a thank-you to her parents, who had made her carry all sorts of things in the course of her household chores for them. Those duties had developed muscles that now took her up onto safe ground, although she felt she wouldn't be able to walk away, as her head throbbed too much. Instead she crawled as silently as she could to the side, where she hid behind a pile of rocks gracing the edge of the quarry.

"It is so unfair," Anthony whined. "I am your senior by a couple of years and should be the one who inherits the title. Just because my father happened to be the younger brother, that doesn't mean I wouldn't make a good earl."

"You know the laws of inheritance," Douglas said coldly, and Anthony laughed nastily.

"Still...I am the better man, and now I want you to do as you have been told. Die."

"How can you even think that you will be able to succeed with this? Didn't you see all those men who stood here with me? They all saw what you had done with Wendy, and not one of them will believe that I happened to fall when trying to save her."

"Yes, they will. By then I will have enough money to buy whatever truth I want."

"You can't buy Thornbury."

Anthony snorted. "Thornbury is an old man, and he might have an accident, too. These are dangerous woods, you know."

"You can't kill everyone."

"Oh, come on, Douglas, you know what power money has. I will offer them money, and if they happen to refuse, I will make sure they know how easily their loved ones can die if they don't fulfill my wishes."

It was no use trying to talk Anthony out of his

plans. His insanity had blown its mellow cover, and now there was no turning back for him. Wendy saw, from her hideout, how Douglas straightened his back before taking one step closer to Anthony. His cousin laughed nervously, extracting a large knife from a hidden pocket in his coat.

"Don't you try anything. This little sweetheart is sharp enough to slice through the rope at first touch, and then you can say goodbye to your pretty wife."

Douglas took another step closer, and this time Anthony didn't laugh. Too afraid to meet his cousin's eyes directly, Anthony looked at anything but Douglas, who immediately grabbed the opportunity and took another step forward, but this time Anthony didn't hesitate. Instead he stood up and gave Douglas an ugly smile before he let the knife cut through the air—and through the rope.

The rope flew over the edge, disappearing into darkness. In a moment, a loud crashing sound was heard from far down in the quarry. Anthony shouted in excitement, unable to restrain all his glorious feelings of triumph, but as Douglas stood still and didn't say a word, he soon grew quiet and started to look unsure.

"Why aren't you screaming? I just killed your wife."

"No, you didn't," Wendy answered, and came forward from behind the rock, so she became visible in the dim light.

"No," Anthony wailed, and took a step toward her. "You are dead. I killed you!" He raised the knife and lurched forward to complete the task he thought he had finished.

A shot echoed among the cliffs, and Anthony

stopped in midstride, his hand on his chest. Looking down, he watched blood flowing between his fingers. With his last breaths, he staggered backward and disappeared into the darkness of the quarry.

Wendy threw herself to the edge in an attempt to catch him, but too late. Anthony fell screaming into the darkness, and then it became quiet.

"Wendy," Douglas cried out, hoarsely, and she turned toward his beloved face. Behind him, she saw Thornbury, a smoking gun in his hand, and she gave him a wobbly, grateful smile. He bowed his noble head slightly before giving the gun to a servant who had come up beside him.

Wendy looked at Douglas again, and to her amazement she found his face wet from the tears streaming down. She held out her hands to him, unable to stand up, and he grabbed them with his shaking ones. With a growl, he put his arms around her waist, dragging her to his chest in a hug which told her all about the relief he felt at her still being alive.

She closed her eyes, as the pain in her head was becoming unbearable, and the last thing she heard, before everything went black, was Douglas's crying voice whispering her name.

Epilogue

Wendy hid behind the billowing curtain, scanning the laughing crowd gathered on the green lawn. She searched for her husband, needing desperately to talk to Douglas in private.

Without realizing it, she bit her lower lip as her eyes flew from one dark masculine head to another until she found the right one in the middle of the almost one hundred members of the *ton* who were chatting away on the emerald carpet, present for the annual summer picnic at Darkwood Manor.

Wendy left her hideout and walked slowly down the limestone steps to the lawn, where she made her way through the noisy crowd until she reached the small group which contained her husband.

Douglas was laughing politely at something the Duke of Thornbury had said. While waiting for him to notice her, Wendy stole a glance at the beautiful young woman who stood beside him, listening to whatever he and Thornbury were talking about. As always, something fabulous moved inside her when she looked upon her daughter.

Georgiana Scott was the spitting image of her father, with the same dark hair and sparkling blue eyes. If it hadn't been for the lush lips, which were just the same as Wendy's, she would have been a female duplicate of Douglas.

Georgiana sent her mother a secretive smile, and Wendy took hold of her hand, savoring the feeling of the warm hand in hers. It was hard to believe their oldest child had turned eighteen already; it felt as though she had been born just the other day.

She guessed this was how all mothers felt when their children grew up, and all she could do was appreciate every small moment they had together as much as she could. Soon all three of her children would have left their childhood behind, and then it would be only she and Douglas again.

A glance at her husband caught him watching her. She nodded pointedly toward the house, and he nodded back to her. Ten minutes later they stood alone in the dark library, and Wendy immediately threw herself into her husband's waiting arms. The kiss was just as hot and exciting as the first one they had shared all those years ago, and it left them both breathless.

"What is it, my dear?" Douglas asked when he regained his composure.

"I need money."

Douglas looked at her with an arched eyebrow before he sighed deeply. "Why do you ask me about money? You are the one who keeps the ledgers around here."

She gave him a secretive smile, which she could tell made him curious. Douglas had never liked it when she kept something from him, and he immediately started to frown. "You don't want to know," she said, trying to sound as if it was nothing, well aware that it would only make him more curious.

"No, really, I do."

"You told me once to never speak with you about it

again, and so I just wonder if it is all right with you if I use a rather large sum of money on something."

"Have you been gambling?"

She laughed at his joke. "Just say yes, my love."

He let go of her and walked over to the desk. "I always agree with you about everything, so you know I will say yes. But I really would like to know what it is I am agreeing about."

"No, you don't."

This time he actually growled toward her, and she couldn't help the giggle bubbling up inside of her. "All right, then," she gave in, and went up to him, pressing her body against his in a warm hug, before she bent back so she could look deeply into his blue eyes.

"Can I buy new curtains?"

A word about the author...

Jennifer Wenn is a mother of kids and a writer of romance, as well as an addict of coffee.

www.jenniferwenn.com